"Do you have the note?"

"Yes, it's in my purse. Hold on." She dug through the purse. "Here."

The detective compared it to the writing on the back of the business card. "I will get the lab to analyze it, but it looks like the victim's writing. What did she say when you met with her?"

"I didn't. I mean, I went to the back of the student union building after class and waited, but she never showed."

"She wasn't one of your students? You're certain?"

"I can check my roster." She opened the laptop and drummed her fingers on the coffee table waiting for it to load. She scrolled through her two classes. "Nope. No Isabel Hernandez." She scrolled through previous class lists. "Not a former student either."

"Don't you find it strange? Someone you never met before died with your card in her pocket. And now you tell me you received a note. If you know something you aren't sharing…"

"I told you I've never met her and I have no idea why she had my information."

"Well then, here's my card. If you think of anything, any possible connection to this girl, call us immediately."

"I will." She resented the detective's tone. *Does he think I had something to do with this? I won't be blamed for another death—not in this lifetime.*

Goodnight, Murder

by

Diane Weiner

This is a work of fiction. Names, characters, places, and incidents are either the product of the author's imagination or are used fictitiously, and any resemblance to actual persons living or dead, business establishments, events, or locales, is entirely coincidental.

Goodnight, Murder

Cover Art by *Jennifer Greeff*

The Wild Rose Press, Inc.
PO Box 708
Adams Basin, NY 14410-0708
Visit us at www.thewildrosepress.com

Publishing History
First Edition, 2023
Trade Paperback ISBN 978-1-5092-5126-1
Digital ISBN 978-1-5092-5127-8

Published in the United States of America

Dedication

This book is dedicated to Robert Weiner, the world's most supportive husband.

Prologue

His hair smelled of baby shampoo. Jenna tucked the little tow-haired boy under her left arm, hugging him close to minimize the trembling. Jenna hadn't chosen to go into teaching for the adrenaline rush, yet here she was, listening hard for the sound of footsteps or the click of a trigger. Jenna wanted to scream. She wanted to flee. Instead, she whispered the comforting words of Margaret Wise Brown into her student's ear. *"In the great green room there was a telephone and a red balloon."*

"Snug as a bug in a rug?" whispered the tow-haired boy.

"Shh. That's right. Safe and sound."

Under Jenna's right arm, hard plastic barrettes made indentations like shells against wet sand. The girl with the head full of miniature corn rows wasn't convinced. Jenna felt the girl's warm breaths and cradled her tighter. She fought to keep her own heart from breaking through her chest.

"My legs hurt. I'm tired of playing the quiet game." The little girl squirmed. Jenna tightened her grip.

"It's going to be okay. *There were three little bears sitting on chairs.* Let's see who wins."

Jenna had corralled most of her students into the closet, but there wasn't enough room for all. She'd

1

pulled a vinyl media cart cover over herself and the two who hadn't fit. They sat small in the dark corner. Waiting.

The media center door smashed. She squeezed the children into a tight ball under the tarp, praying they'd stay silent. Glass shattered. Shelves crashed. Shots broke her world to pieces.

Chapter 1

The brick campus came into view as Dr. Jenna Blake rounded the curve on the mountain road. Monk Haven was the newest of New York's state universities, in existence for less than a decade. Jenna parked in front of the education building. A few weeks into the second semester, she was thankful to be working again after the school shooting and her husband's death this past year. She clicked a leash on her therapy dog, Bijou.

"Hey, wait up." Jenna's best friend, Hayley, followed behind her. "Did you sleep well?"

"Just fine." Her achy lower back didn't agree. The lumpy guest room mattress had been taking its toll, but she couldn't bring herself to sleep in the master bedroom.

"Are you getting used to being back in the house yet?"

"Do I have a choice? No one's knocking down my door to buy my place in the condition it's in." She jiggled her key into the lock.

Hayley followed her. "Did I tell you how much I love your bouncy new haircut? And how the highlights bring out your eyes?"

"Every day since the semester began." Jenna, growing tired of people trying too hard, forced a smile.

Hayley said, "Want to get lunch after my class?"

"Sure."

Hayley glanced at her watch. "Speaking of class, I'd better run. See you in a few."

"Bye, Hayley." Jenna flicked on the gooseneck lamp and saw it. Her heart skipped a beat. A handwritten envelope. *Who was in my office while I was gone?*

Jenna sat her things down and tore it open.

Meet me after class today behind the student union building. It's urgent. A matter of life and death.

Life and death? Who'd use those words after what she'd been through? After class? Could be one of her students, but with the semester just starting, she barely knew any of them.

Her teaching assistant, Kyle, popped in. He was older than the typical grad student, but still a few years younger than Jenna.

"Ms. Blake?" He glanced at the newly framed diploma behind her desk. "I mean Dr. Blake." "New sweater? Bright colors look good on you."

Like Hayley, he was trying a little too hard. However, he wasn't wrong. Her black sweaters and pants had been washed so many times they'd turned gray, and she could barely zipper her old size twelve jeans these days thanks to all the stress eating she'd been doing.

"How's the dissertation going? I have to approve your topic by the end of the semester."

"It will get done. Scout's honor." He tossed his coffee cup into the trash.

"If I've told you once, I've told you a thousand times…"

"I know, I know." Kyle took the cup out and put it in the recycling bin. "Better?"

"Much. Hey, did you notice anyone coming or going out of my office this morning?"

"No, why?"

"Someone left me an anonymous note. As far as I know, you and I are the only ones with keys to this office."

"Wasn't me. Who writes notes these days, anyway? Anyone I know would send a text. Unless…"

"Unless what?"

He crept around to the back of her chair and leaned on it with both arms. "Unless the custodians are luring you into an intervention. Your fanaticism over recycling verges on addiction."

"Very funny." She looked at her watch. "Let's head over to class. You can set up the projector while I arrange the center materials."

"I'll meet you over there, Dr. Jen. I forgot something in my car."

"Okay." If it wasn't just Kyle being Kyle, she'd have been offended long ago at being addressed as *Dr. Jen, Ms. Blake*, or more often, *Prof.* "Pick up the copies on your way."

With his long legs and slight build, he glided out the door.

When she got to the classroom, the students were already waiting. The class was small—a dozen juniors taking the teaching methods course. The number of education majors had dwindled steadily over the past few years and knowing she couldn't ever set foot inside her old elementary school classroom, Jenna thanked her lucky stars for this college job—even if she'd had to play the pity card to get it.

She scanned the class. "Where's Brooke?"

"I saw her this morning. She said she was coming," said one of the girls.

Jenna gave instructions, and while walking around the class, she overheard bits of whispered conversations.

"I hope she doesn't quit this time. I had to drop this class last semester."

"Who can blame her after what her loser of a husband did? How embarrassing."

Jenna no longer fell to pieces when hearing hurtful comments about Giles. She glanced at the door. Where was Kyle? If he didn't show up soon, it'd be too late to do the presentation. Kyle added a touch of humor to the department and Jenna appreciated it, but sometimes his airy attitude and lack of punctuality got on her nerves. Minutes later, he sauntered through the door. Snow flurries clung like dandruff to his dark curls. He brushed dead leaves off his jacket onto the floor.

"Speak of the devil."

"Sorry, *Dr.* Blake. I got caught up in something. Here are the copies."

"Shake the snow off your boots and help me while they finish creating their experiments." *Millennials. No sense of responsibility.*

Jenna barely paid attention while Kyle did his presentation. That anonymous note was deep in her thoughts. Jenna felt dizzy. If she opted to go to the student union and meet the anonymous note writer, who or what would she find? *I'm not going. I'll bet it's a prank. Life and death?* She reconsidered. *What if this person truly needs my help?*

As the students left, she was still contemplating her decision. *A matter of life and death.* Curiosity got the better of her. "Let's go, Bijou."

Built in the quad design, the fastest route to the destination was across the open area, but fighting a rare form of agoraphobia, she chose to hug the buildings instead. When she had reached the end of the education building, the ground swayed like a lopsided merry-go-round under her feet. She braced herself against the brick wall and closed her eyes. *I can do this.*

Jenna took a deep breath, opened her eyes, and inched along until she approached the brick student union building abutting the woods. Passing through the student union, she exited out the back door where metal tables sat empty on the patio as they did all winter in dreary upstate New York. Because she had taken the longer route, she'd arrived a few minutes later than expected.

Shivering, she pulled the knitted scarf tighter around her neck. *Guess this wasn't as urgent as the note writer said. Perhaps she changed her mind or maybe I was right, and it was a prank.* She glanced to the left, then to the right, squinting as she strained to see down the path. *I was an idiot for coming here.* Nonetheless, she waited another fifteen minutes before turning back.

Returning to the education building, sirens screamed in the distance, setting her nerves on fire. She hugged the walls and scooted back to where Hayley waited.

"I'm starving," said Hayley. "I was afraid you'd forgotten."

A patrol car whizzed by. "I didn't forget. Sirens? What's with the police?"

Kyle scooted out the front door of the building.

"Oh, my God. Did you hear? They found a body."

"Did your boyfriend, the spy, tell you that?" said Hayley. "The one who said Russia stole our curriculum off the server?"

"Never mind if you don't want to hear it."

"A body? Where?" Jenna shivered.

"In the woods," said Kyle.

Hayley said, "Sure they did."

Jenna said, "Wait. I heard sirens on my way back from the student union. And the patrol car whizzed by us earlier."

Hayley's blond ponytail shook with her head. "I'll bet someone saw a pile of garbage or a backpack and assumed it was a dead body. Maybe even an animal carcass. It *is* hunting season."

"You're probably right. Come to think of it—remember when they broke ground to construct the middle school wing at Elmwood and found a skeleton?"

Kyle said, "A real skeleton?"

"Turned out to be a deer skeleton, but not before the entire school was yapping about hauntings and serial killers. Keep us posted, Kyle. See you later."

Jenna unlocked the car with two quick chirps and brushed snow dust off the windshield with one mitten. The heated leather seats barely warmed her bottom before she spotted the green and white canopy of The Monk Haven Café just off the campus grounds. Had the weather been warmer, they may have opted to walk.

The aroma of breakfast—bacon, pancakes, coffee—still filled the air as Jenna and Bijou followed Hayley inside the airy café for lunch.

"I'm glad we could find a table at this hour," said Hayley.

"Do you think the police really found a body?"

"I doubt it. You know Kyle and his flair for the dramatic."

A young waitress filled their water glasses and offered them menus. Hayley brushed the menu away.

"I know what I want. The grilled chicken sandwich and waffle fries, please."

Jenna ordered tomato soup. When the server left, Hayley leaned over the booth and whispered, "Are you feeling okay? You look tired."

She was tired all right. Sick and tired of the same question over and over again. Sick and tired of feeling like the world was watching to see if she was going to fall apart like she did last semester. She reminded herself that Hayley was a loyal friend—one of the few friends who hadn't dropped out of sight after Giles. She tried to temper her annoyance.

"I'm fine."

"You know I'm here for you."

I'm here for you. Bull. She isn't here when I wake up with my chest pounding in the middle of the night after having a nightmare. She doesn't re-live the sound of shots approaching from down the hall or the sound of sobbing children. She'd already switched jobs and was nestled safely in her ivy tower by the time it happened. And her husband is still alive.

Jenna resisted rolling her eyes. "I know. You're a good friend." She took a spoonful of soup. "If I don't make it work, I'll be living in my car eating wild berries. If I can afford my car payments, that is."

Hayley shook her head. "Hate to break it to you, but…never mind."

"What? You may as well say it."

"I don't think you'll find berries for another couple of months."

Caught off guard by the humor, Jenna cracked a smile, releasing the tension she'd been accruing.

The waitress turned up the already too loud TV mounted on the wall. TVs in restaurants was one of Jenna's pet peeves. However, this time, the screen caught her attention.

The news camera panned the campus in the back of the student union building. Police tape marked off the entrance to the woods.

"*Breaking new*s. *A body was found in the woods just behind the student union building. Police haven't released the name of the victim. Stay tuned for details as they unfold.*"

Jenna felt the blood drain from her face.

"Oh no. Kyle was right? I hope it wasn't one of our students," said Hayley. "Jenna, what's wrong? You look like you saw a ghost."

Chapter 2

The campus was buzzing when they returned. Several news vans, police cruisers, and an ambulance lined the road while clusters of onlookers huddled in the cold. Kyle, long legs flying like a gazelle, immediately ran up to them. "See, they found a body. Someone *was* murdered."

Hayley said, "Who said anything about murder? Could have been a heart attack, or an accidental shooting, what with hunting season and all. Kyle, your imagination works overtime."

Kyle swiped his index finger across his pointy chin. "Perhaps a suicide." His face turned bright red. "I'm so sorry, Dr. Blake."

Jenna said, "Stop walking on eggshells around me. Do they know who it is?"

"Is it a student?" asked Hayley.

"Have you heard any details?" *Does this have anything to do with the person I was supposed to meet this morning?*

"Nothing yet. The whole area is blocked off."

Hayley said, "They haven't canceled classes, have they?"

"Not that I heard," said Kyle. He snuggled his head against Bijou, and then pulled back. "This dog stinks. He needs a bath."

"We'll talk later."

Back in the office, Jenna's mind wandered away from work. Her fingers shook while typing. The thought of a dead body made Jenna feel sick. She corralled her breathing in an effort to avoid a panic attack while wondering if the dead person was the one who wrote the cryptic note left on her computer.

With the semester just beginning, she hadn't yet gotten behind on grading and opted to 'put herself first' as her therapist had suggested. "Come on, Bijou. Let's go home." She nuzzled her face in his fur. "Kyle's right. You do stink."

In the car, Jenna turned on the radio, the music helping the tightness in her shoulders loosen. *I'm sure it was an accident.* Traffic was non-existent on the country road leading home. At one time, this area was teeming with farms and apple orchards. Many of the old homes still had barns on the property. The gravel crunched beneath the tires while pulling into the driveway in front of the garage rather than inside because the garage door opener had never worked. They'd gotten a price reduction on the house because of it.

Leaving the heated car, the dog shivered, so she tucked him under the jacket. Once inside, Jenna cranked up the heat in the igloo she called home. Sitting on the sofa in the middle of the living room, the wind whipped through the walls and the door whistled where the weather stripping had pulled off.

Giles, an HDTV addict, insisted on buying this monster right before the wedding. Jenna laughed out loud at the memory of him trying to break down the wall between the dining room and kitchen for 'a fresh, open look'. He'd be proud to know she was determined to finish the job and had already hacked away a few inches with the sledgehammer he'd left in the middle of the dining room on his last day here. At first, she cried whenever she heard his name. Later, anger became the emotion of choice. Recently, she was able to hear her husband's name without crying—or wanting to kill him again. Progress.

She made herself a cup of tea, then snuggled under the afghan on the sofa with Bijou for a nap. Sometime later, she woke to the evening news and a barking dog. Someone was banging on the door. "Coming."

A man held his badge up to the peephole. "Ms. Blake? I'm Detective Russo. I'm working the Isabel Hernandez homicide. May I come in?"

She unlatched the door. Detective Russo was muscular with thick, dark hair and a Brooklyn-Italian accent. She put his age at around fifty, maybe a decade older than she was.

"Who is Isabel Hernandez?"

"The victim was found just off campus this afternoon."

"You mean the body in the woods? It was murder?"

"Correct. I have a few questions."

"Come in." She felt completely puzzled as to why he'd be questioning her about a murder case. Maybe not completely puzzled. The thought this victim was the person she was set to meet had been nagging her all afternoon. "I don't know how I can help you."

"Did you know the victim?"

"Me? No. I just resumed teaching a couple of weeks ago. I don't have any students named Isabel."

The detective pulled a business card from his

pocket. "We found this on the body. That's you, isn't it?"

"Yes, that's my business card. I just got them in the mail a few days ago."

"This is your home address scribbled on the back. And your phone number, correct? Did you write this? Have you given away many cards?"

She grabbed her reading glasses. "Yes, it's my address and phone number. No, I didn't write it, nor have I given away any cards yet. I have no idea who this girl is. Do you have a photo?"

The detective opened his iPad. "Her fiancé sent this to us."

Jenna stared at a beautiful young woman in a party gown, with huge brown eyes. "I've never seen her before."

"Are you sure?"

"I'm sure." She considered whether to mention her concern. "Wait. I don't know her, but I received a strange note when I went to work today. It said to meet behind the student union building after my class. Isn't that near where the body was found? It was..."

"It was what?"

"The note said it was a matter of life and death." Her heart sank.

"Do you have the note?"

"Yes, it's in my purse. Hold on." She dug through the purse. "Here."

The detective compared it to the writing on the back of the business card. "I will get the lab to analyze it, but it looks like the victim's writing. What did she say when you met with her?"

"I didn't. I mean, I went to the back of the student

union building after class and waited, but she never showed."

"She wasn't one of your students? You're certain?"

"I can check my roster." She opened the laptop and drummed her fingers on the coffee table waiting for it to load. She scrolled through her two classes. "Nope. No Isabel Hernandez." She scrolled through previous class lists. "Not a former student either."

"Don't you find it strange? Someone you never met before died with your card in her pocket. And now you tell me you received a note. If you know something you aren't sharing…"

"I told you I've never met her and I have no idea why she had my information."

"Well then, here's my card. If you think of anything, any possible connection to this girl, call us immediately."

"I will." She resented the detective's tone. *Does he think I had something to do with this? I won't be blamed for another death—not in this lifetime.*

The microwave buzzed and Jenna ate her soggy lasagna entrée, right from the plastic container. *I've got to get my act together and make real meals again. Besides, all this plastic is terrible for the environment.* When Giles was alive, he did most of the cooking, and they almost always ate dinner together. During the past few months living with her parents, her mother's home cooking had spoiled her.

She poured dog food into Bijou's bowl, thinking it looked more appetizing than her frozen lasagna. The calendar on the fridge caught her eye. *Grief support group 7 p.m.* She'd circled the date in red. *It's cold out, and I'm tired. But if I sit home all night, I'll just ruminate about the detective's insinuation and drive myself crazy trying to figure out why the victim reached out to me.*

She ate half her dinner, then tossed the remainder in the trash and tore open a sleeve of Oreos from the pantry. She changed into fleece-lined leggings and a long, green cable-knit sweater. After the beauty make-over and two-hundred-dollar haircut her mother had treated her to, Jenna's hair fell beautifully into place with a stroke of the brush.

"Bijou, let's go." He sat next to her on the heated passenger seat for the short ride to the local hospital.

The grief group met in a conference room. When she walked in, half a dozen people were seated on chrome chairs around a long table. She recognized the regulars—a couple who'd lost their daughter to cancer, a widow like herself but older, a student whose mother died from ALS. She'd only been attending since moving back from her parents' house, but the intimacy of grieving together made these people feel like old friends.

A man with a five o'clock shadow and wearing a ski jacket sat down next to her. He smelled like fresh cut Christmas trees. He reached out his hand.

"Max Colby."

"Jenna Blake." Bijou barked. "And my bodyguard, Bijou."

Max allowed Bijou to sniff his hand, then wriggled out of his jacket, or tried to.

"Let me help." She grabbed the sleeve. "Here you go."

"Thanks. Did I miss much? I've been out of town on business this past month."

"I've only been coming for a few weeks. Looks like we're starting."

The group leader, a mental health nurse, welcomed Max back, then opened the group up for sharing. The widow talked about finally packing her husband's closet and donating to Good Will. The couple who'd lost their daughter held hands.

Max spoke. "I'm trying to let go of this anger but until the bastard who killed my daughter is behind bars, I don't think I can."

The leader said, "We've talked about this. It may never happen. A hit-and-run driver and no witnesses? You can't let it consume your life. You'll have to compartmentalize the anger and move on. Wouldn't your daughter have wanted you to be happy?"

He shook his head. "I can't let it go."

The young student said, "Working out at the gym has helped me."

Jenna watched Max's fists ball up and sensed he was trying hard not to explode. She could hear him breathing like a dragon but was impressed by how he managed to calm himself before responding.

He leaned back in the chair. "Thank you for the suggestion." Bijou licked his hand.

"Jenna, how has it been at work this week?" asked the moderator.

"I've been managing. Even today."

"What happened today?"

"I don't really want to talk about it."

The female half of the couple said, "Have you been able to go into the bedroom where…"

"Not yet. I make it halfway up the stairs and the room starts spinning. The bed in the guest room is killing my back and I've got clothes in the closet I can't even remember." *Though I doubt they fit anymore.* Food had become her drug of choice.

After the meeting, a mumbling Max caught up to Jenna. "Try going to the gym. Compartmentalize your anger. Idiots."

Jenna laughed. "If you knew how many times people have suggested taking walks or going for runs…"

"Or chamomile tea, my personal favorite. They don't get it. Especially the one who lost his mother."

"He's just a kid. Give him credit for trying. I mean, if it works for him, great."

"I need a cup of coffee. Want to join me?"

"I'd prefer chamomile tea. Just kidding. Sure. The Monk Haven Café is down the block."

"Yeah. Are you too cold to walk? What about him?" He pointed to Bijou.

"He's wearing his sweater. He'll be okay."

"I'm not sure they allow pets."

"He's a therapy dog. I have a doctor's note."

"A therapy dog? Like those dogs who get to ride free in the plane cabin because they are medically necessary?"

Jenna glared at him and he averted her eyes. "Um, I'm sorry. You were serious. Does he help you?"

"Definitely. I was afraid to leave my apartment after the shooting. I'd have died of starvation if Bijou hadn't come along."

"You can order groceries online."

"Not the point."

"Shooting? Is that how your husband died?"

That's rather blunt of him. And he's awfully nosy.

"Indirectly."

They entered the cafe and were greeted by a case full of Greek pastries and baklava, as they made their way into a booth.

"You said you'd only been going to meetings for a few weeks. Did you just move here?" asked Max.

"No. I moved here about ten years ago when I started teaching. I was...helping out my parents these past couple of months." She didn't want to get into how she fell apart after Giles' death.

"So you're a teacher? Where?"

"Elmwood Charter. Until the shooting."

"Elmwood Charter...you mean *that* shooting? The one that made the national news?"

"That'd be the one."

"Oh my God, it must have been awful."

For the thousandth time, she heard the shooter in her mind. Heard him break the glass and storm through the media center door while she hid, terrified, with her class. "I'm sure you saw images on the news."

"Didn't everyone? I mean, it was tragic, but the media milked stories out of it for months. Hell, I still occasionally see things in the paper—father of Elmwood shooting victim fights for gun laws, or there's a new scholarship named for one of the victims."

"Wow. Are you kidding me? Do you know what it meant to live through that? I couldn't get out of bed, let alone leave the house for months."

Max squirmed, trapped in the booth—forced to look her in the eye. "I'm sorry. It must have been horrific. How did you cope?"

"That's when I got Bijou. I'd always been more of a cat person, but this little guy saved me—so to speak."

"Do you still teach there?"

"I tried to go back but couldn't. My friend Hayley got me in at Monk Haven U."

"So you were able to stay in town."

"Yes, until…well. Let's talk about something more interesting than my life. Here comes the server. Are we just getting coffee, or splurging on the baklava? Did I tell you I'm a sugerholic?"

"So am I," said Max. "Of course, we're getting baklava."

When they were the only ones left in the place and the server asked if they wanted refills for the umpteenth time, the lateness of the hour sunk in. Bijou had long since fallen asleep. On the way back to their cars, Jenna thought she heard footsteps. Her hands trembled. She was afraid to look over her shoulder. When she did, the sidewalk was deserted.

"What's wrong?"

"Did you hear someone behind us?" Bijou's ears popped out like wings on a bi-plane.

Max turned around and scanned the street. "No, I don't see anyone. You okay?"

"I need a minute." She felt the ground move and clutched onto Max's arm. *Breathe in, breathe out.*

"You're so jumpy. Too much coffee?"

"I wish that's all it was."

He wrapped an arm around her, and her heart rate fell back into rhythm. "Better now?"

"Yes, thanks." She pulled away, beginning to calm down when Bijou let out a bark. She jumped. "Is someone there?"

Max looked up and down the dark street lined with bony trees. "No." He ruffled Bijou's furry head, then held his chin and looked him in the eye. "What kind of guard dog are you, anyway?" He squeezed Jenna close like a weighted security blanket and she felt calmer. "Just us. Come on. The cars are right around the corner. Will you be okay to drive home?"

"Yes. Thanks for the coffee and chat." *He must think I'm a total basket case.*

"I enjoyed it. See you at next week's meeting?"

"I'll be there."

"Here's my card, in case you want to reach me sooner."

"Your card? Give me your phone." In a bolder than her usual move, she took it and entered her contact info. "There. Now you can reach me, too."

Bijou fell asleep in the passenger seat. Jenna replayed the evening with Max. She'd enjoyed talking with him, except for when he acted like an asshole talking about people milking stories out of the shooting. Aside from that, they seemed to click. Hayley would do anything for her, and she loved her to pieces. Her parents were always there to catch her when she fell. But Max knew what it felt like to lose someone you love. She felt his intensity when he spoke at the meeting.

When she pulled into the dark driveway, her neck hair tingled. The kitchen light should be on—she always left it on when going out at night. She tip-toed up the sidewalk, looking for footprints or some sign of an intruder. Bijou wasn't barking. If someone were near, he'd warn her. Heart racing, she tugged on the front door. *Locked. Just as I left it.* Still, something wasn't right.

She clicked on the living room lamp, then crept

into the kitchen. Leaving the carpet for tile, glass crunched beneath her boots. Hand quivering, she flipped the light switch, illuminating the kitchen. *Oh, my God. What happened here?* Bijou ran to her side. The kitchen window looked like a shattered spider web. Hands still trembling, Jenna pulled out two cards—the one from Max, and the card the detective had given her. *Should I call Max? No, Max might make me feel better, but it's the police I need now.* Heart thumping, Jenna checked to make sure the kitchen door leading outside and the one leading to the garage were both locked before she sat at the table and waited.

The detective was there in a flash.

"I'll bet a rock or branch had hit it from that strong gust earlier this evening."

"It's been windy before and the glass didn't shatter," she said, shaking her head.

"Is anything missing?"

"I don't think so."

"Did you check?"

She wandered through the dining room to the living room, wondering how anyone could have stolen something through the hole in the glass, but she followed the detective's instruction. "Nothing's missing."

"Did you see an unfamiliar car in the neighborhood on your way home?"

"No."

He checked the kitchen door. "It's locked. So is the window."

"I know. I never leave without locking the doors."

"I didn't see tire tracks in the driveway, other than yours. Though with gravel it's hard to tell. It's a small hole. I'll help you tape it up if you've got some cardboard lying around. In the morning, call your insurance company and I'll send over a copy of the police report."

"Tape it with cardboard? Really?"

Detective Russo picked up a piece of wood from the pile of debris next to the half-demolished kitchen wall. "Ah, a nail. This will do. Have you got a hammer?"

She picked up the sledgehammer lying on the floor. "How about this?"

He chuckled. "Too big. You got a regular hammer?"

Jenna foraged through the junk drawer. Scissor, string, tape…"Here you go."

Jenna noticed his muscular hands, then his forearms—olive skin under a forest of coarse dark Italian hair. The heart tattoo on his wrist seemed out of place. While she swept up the glass, he patched the hole as if he were used to working with his hands. He reminded her of a younger version of her father.

"Good as new."

"Thank you." She scooped up Bijou.

"Funny, being out here twice in one day. I wonder if whoever killed Isabel Hernandez is after you, too?"

"Seriously?" That's all she needed to hear.

"Just seems like a coincidence, that's all. You sure you hadn't met? Maybe you had something in common, like a gym or church?"

"I don't belong to a gym, and don't go regularly to church."

"Hmmm. She may have been trying to warn you before she was killed."

"Warn me of what? I don't see a connection." *Though now I'm worried there is one.*

"If you think of anything, anywhere you may have met or a friend you had in common…"

"If I do, I'll call. Will you keep me informed since I may be at risk, too?"

"To the extent I can. Have a good night."

After he left, Jenna checked all the windows and doors downstairs, reassuring herself they were locked. Halfway up the staircase, the banister vibrated under her hand. *Not tonight.* Nauseated, Jenna retreated downstairs into the guest room. *Where could I have possibly met Isabel Hernandez? The photo didn't look at all familiar. The grocery store, the grief group, walks through the neighborhood… She looks older than any of my recent students.* Tossing and turning, her head buzzing with possibilities, it wasn't easy to fall asleep.

Chapter 3

In the morning, Jenna wriggled the sweater through Bijou's paws and snapped the leash onto his harness. The cold air numbed her cheeks before she reached the end of the driveway. *I'll have to order a heavier sweater or a coat for Bijou.* The houses sat on large lots—close to an acre, according to the real estate agent. Giles had insisted on a large backyard, envisioning children playing on a wooden swing set and splashing in a plastic wading pool. Children they never got to share. If only she hadn't lost the baby the night of the shooting, she'd still have a piece of Giles with her. If only…

Thankfully, pine trees and a guard rail shielded the sidewalk. Open areas presented a challenge ever since the shooting. The neighbor boy, eleven or twelve Jenna guessed, hustled to the end of his driveway and caught the school bus in the nick of time.

I've seen him playing catch with his father. Maybe he threw his baseball and accidentally broke my window. A gust of wind blew snow off the branches over her head. *Baseball? At night? In the middle of winter?* There had to be a better explanation.

She scanned each house and the few cars she passed, looking for—she didn't know what. Further down the road, she passed a neighbor walking his Beagle.

"Hey, Jenna. I'm glad to see you back. We've been meaning to stop by and say hello. The first Christmas is tough."

"Let's say it's good to be home. Thanks for keeping an eye on the house while I was gone."

"Happy to help. Has your mother recuperated?"

"Yes, thanks. She's getting stronger every day." She said a silent prayer God wouldn't take revenge on her for lying about why she'd fled town last fall.

"You'll have to come by for dinner one night."

"Absolutely. I'll bring dessert. By the way, when you were out walking the dog last night, did you happen to see anyone on our street who looked like they didn't belong?" She ruffled the Beagle's short hair. She couldn't remember the dog's name.

"No, why?"

"Someone or something broke my kitchen window last night. It could have been an accident, but that's weird, right? Windows don't spontaneously spring holes in them."

"No, they don't. I'll keep an extra eye out. What else have I got to do all day other than putter around the house?"

"I can think of lots of things—crossword puzzles, Netflix…"

"It's not as good as it sounds. Especially living on a fixed income. Mabel's got a never-ending to-do list for me—replace the cabinet handle, sand the door so it doesn't stick… Cheaper than hiring a handyman, I suppose."

She pushed down her glove, exposing her watch. "Speaking of income, I'd better get to work. Say hello to Mabel for me."

"Will do. Bye, Bijou."

She stopped home long enough to change into work clothes and pack a lunch. With hardly any traffic to speak of in her small town, the commute to campus took just over ten minutes when the weather cooperated.

Once at the school, she was surprised to find Hayley's office door closed. She knocked. "Hey, are you in there?"

"Come on in, Jenna." Hayley struggled to adjust her skirt. "Close the door."

"What's wrong? Are you sick?"

"I need help. Can I trust you to keep something just between us?"

"Do you even have to ask?"

Jenna's eyes opened wide when Hayley pulled out a hypodermic needle and an alcohol wipe. "How are you at giving shots?"

"Wait a minute. Are you using drugs?" Although she knew better, the words tumbled out unfiltered.

"Of course not. Oliver and I are trying to have a baby. I'll turn thirty-eight next month and time is ticking."

"I had no idea." She'd been so absorbed in her own problems she hadn't noticed her friend was unhappy. "How is it you never mentioned this before?"

"I didn't want to bother you after all you were going through."

"How long have you guys been trying?"

"Over a year. How naïve. I thought as soon as I got off the pill it would happen."

"It takes a while for your body to get back in sync."

"It's been more than a while. We did the temperature charts and even tried artificial insemination. Time's running out. Now we're using the big guns."

Jenna shuddered at the word *guns*. "Fertility drugs?"

"Yeah. Can you help give me this shot? Oliver is out of town on business, again. I tried calling his cell this morning just to hear his voice but he didn't pick up."

"Um, a shot?" She glanced at the needle. "I guess. I don't want to hurt you."

"You won't. I've been poked and prodded so much, I'm numb to it." She handed Jenna the needle. "Besides, it's my wallet that's really hurting these days. We're running through our savings like there's no tomorrow. I hope it'll all be worth it."

"I'm sure it will." She winced as she pierced Hayley's skin. "Can you help me figure out where I might have met the girl they found dead in the woods?"

"Who is she? They haven't released her name."

"Isabel Hernandez. A detective came by my house. She had my business card on her when she died. And the handwriting matches the handwriting on the note left on my computer."

"Wow. She's the one who left you the note? Now she's dead? Creepy."

"Tell me about it. They found her body right near where we were supposed to meet."

"Was she a student, or ex-student?"

"No. I checked. Besides, from the picture, she looks closer to our age than to a student's."

A knock on the door and a "Hey, can't I come in?"

announced Kyle's presence.

"Just a minute," said Hayley.

Jenna threw away the needle. Hayley straightened her skirt.

"Since when is your door locked?" Kyle handed them each an insulated cardboard cup.

"Coffee? Thanks, Kyle," said Hayley.

"Not just coffee. It's a peppermint latte from the new coffee shop down the road. And they were giving out dog treats." He took a treat from his pocket and Bijou licked it out of his hand.

Jenna blew across the lid opening to cool the coffee. "We were talking about what happened yesterday. The students are going to be scared to walk the campus."

"Worse yet, the new breed of helicopter parents will start yanking them out," said Hayley. "Our enrollment in this department has been sliding steadily downward."

And if enrollment slips, it's last hired, first fired. I'll be up shit's creek. Jenna sipped her latte. "Kyle, do you know anything about the dead girl? Her name was Isabel Hernandez."

"No, but I can find out in a heartbeat," said Kyle. "What do you need to know?" He pulled out his phone.

"The police detective came to my house last night. He found my business card on the victim. And the handwriting on the note I found on my computer looks like it matches hers."

"Seriously? I don't recognize the name and I know all the Ed majors. Who do you know on campus who isn't an education major? Why did she have your card?"

"Exactly. Why would this girl try to contact me? I don't think she was a student."

"And it had to be something big if it got her killed before she talked to you," said Kyle. "Maybe she was trying to warn you about something, or she needed your help."

"My help specifically? Unless she was looking for someone to chair a graduate student committee, I don't see how I could have helped her. I don't know how she managed to put the note in my locked office."

"Don't look at me," Kyle said. "I don't share your office key with anyone."

"Could someone have borrowed it without you knowing? You have a million friends on this campus," Hayley said.

"I swear these keys haven't been anywhere but in my pocket." He patted both jean pockets before finding them in his jacket.

"Knock, knock." Delores, a masculine-looking woman with a smoker's voice, pushed open the slightly ajar office door. "Jenna, where were you this morning?"

"What are you talking about?"

"We had a meeting with the associate dean. She asked where you were. Looked rather ticked, if you ask me."

"I never got any notice about a meeting."

"Sure you did. Your name was on the email. A shame with the tenure position up for grabs and all. Maybe you weren't feeling up to it." She tossed an empty donut bag in the trash.

"Worry about yourself. What did I miss?"

"Ask her yourself. Tata." She strutted out, chin in the air.

Jenna picked the bag out of the trash and tossed it into the recycling bin. "Did you know about a meeting?"

Hayley shook her head. "Jenna, she's toying with you. You know she resents you. She thinks you were hired because of your connections, which you were thanks to me, and she was counting on that tenured position. You're the competition."

"She's just jealous. You're younger, prettier, and way more fashionable," added Kyle. "No competition. She might as well pack her bags and get out of Dodge."

"Thanks, Kyle. Hey, I'd better get moving. Thanks for the coff—I mean thanks for the latte." She emphasized the word latte using her best aristocratic accent. She remembered Max joking about drinking tea last night and smiled.

Detective Russo was waiting outside her office door. "Good morning, Ms. Blake. If you don't mind, I have a few more questions."

"It's Dr. Blake." She unlocked the office. "Come in."

"Did the window hold up?"

"Yes, for now. I'll get a repairman over this afternoon to replace it."

"There's got to be a connection between you and the murder victim. Have you given it some thought?"

"I've racked my brain trying to find one, but I can't. Like I said, I'd never met her before."

"We recovered her car. The GPS showed directions to your house. It was the last place she'd driven."

"Impossible."

"Show me where you found the note."

She pointed to the computer. "It was propped up

here."

"Do you always lock your office?"

"Yes, of course."

"Who else has a key?"

"Only my TA. And the cleaning crew, of course."

"How well do you know your TA? What's her name?"

"His name is Kyle. Kyle Porter."

"Is there any chance he wrote that note?"

"No way. Besides, it's not his handwriting."

"Perhaps a third party wrote the address and gave her the card. Perhaps he knew the victim."

"Although he appears to know almost everyone, he didn't know her. We were just talking and he's as puzzled as we are."

"No one came to your house in the past few days? You never saw a white Nissan drive by?"

"I don't spend the day staring out my window, but nothing sticks out."

His dark eyes squinted skepticism. "She obviously wanted to talk to you before she was murdered. Are you sure you don't know why?"

"No. And I resent the implication that I know more than I'm saying."

"I'll speak with Kyle Porter and the cleaning crew. Then I'll swing by your neighborhood and see if any of the neighbors saw a white Nissan hanging around."

"A retired couple live two houses down. Check with them." She'd already asked her neighbor this morning, but let the detective hear it from the horse's mouth.

"I'll check it out."

She gathered her things once he left. *I never*

noticed a white Nissan driving through the neighborhood. I'm sure of it. It's not like I live on a main street. The only cars that pass by most days are driven by my neighbors. She got to her class just before it was scheduled to begin, which was unusual. Anyone who knew her would describe her as punctual. Hayley teased that she was *uber punctual*—five or ten minutes early to most anything.

Once inside the class, she glanced at the seats, mentally taking attendance. *Brooke is missing again.* A debilitating flu hit hard this winter and other than death, illness was the only excuse Jenna would buy for missing two classes in a row right at the start of the semester.

A student whose name Jenna couldn't remember said, "Dr. Blake, did you hear anything else about the murdered girl? Walking home from the library last night, I thought I heard something, so I ducked inside a building and called my roommate to come walk me back to the dorm."

Jenna said, "The police are keeping an eye on the area."

Sadie stood up. "My parents said if they don't have someone in jail by the weekend, they're making me come back home." *She sounds like a ten-year-old. I know I was more mature when I was a college junior.*

"What if it's a serial killer?" said another girl.

Be patient. Don't tell them they watch too much TV. What do they know about serial killers, anyway? Use your reassuring voice.

"It's scary, I know," said Jenna. "As far as I know, there has never been a murder or even a violent attack on this campus. If you walk in groups, avoid going out at night unnecessarily, and stay along the main paths, you'll be fine. Chances are this was a one-off."

One of the students pulled a keychain from her purse. "I have Mace. I keep my keys in my hand whenever I'm out alone at night."

She was losing patience. "You know, when you become a teacher, there will be times when your students are scared and will need reassurance. It's a different world from even when you all were students. Active shooter drills, practice lockdowns—it's scary, especially for the little ones."

They don't know the half of it. She wasn't talking about a drill. She felt the bite marks on her palm where she'd clamped her hand over little Janelle's mouth to silence her. Thank God her students remained safe.

"How do you keep a bunch of kids quiet for more than a minute?" said another.

Jenna said, "You have to stay calm and focused. They pick up on your vibes." She was mentally back in that media center. *Good night cow jumping over the moon. Shh. Don't cry, Ryan. I've got you.*

"Dr. Blake?"

"Sorry, what did you ask?"

"Are we going to present the lesson plans we made?"

"Sure. Who wants to start?"

Chapter 4

Five o'clock and it might as well be midnight. She loathed winter. If she could unload the money pit of a house Giles left her with, maybe she'd move somewhere warmer and cheerier. A fresh start. She wished. Even if the house was sold, college teaching jobs weren't easy to come by. She turned on the headlights and headed home.

The hair on her neck tingled, and it wasn't because the heat hadn't kicked on. She caught a glance of a dark sedan in the rearview mirror. Her heart pounded. *Who's following me? Maybe I should turn around and let him follow me into the police station.*

When she looked again, the car had vanished. She took a deep breath, her hands aching from the death grip on the steering wheel.

"Bijou, am I losing it? Do you think we're being followed?"

He answered with a quick bark.

"There, it's behind us again." A plain, black sedan. Nothing outstanding. She couldn't read a plate number or determine the make or model. Was it the same car that followed her earlier? In a flash, it turned down a side street. *Just someone on their way home from work. If I don't relax, I'll never get to see forty.*

Pulling into the driveway, Jenna parked in front of the garage, relieved to see the kitchen light on. The automatic door opener was broken when they bought the house and Giles kept promising to fix it—two years of broken promises, though he'd insisted on keeping the remote in the car as if he'd get to it soon. Anger sprinted through her already adrenaline-hyped blood. She and Giles had both survived the shooting. They'd both felt the grief and loss. Why didn't he do the work and piece his life back together as she had?

Once inside, she turned up the heat and foraged through the freezer. A bean burrito, or mac and cheese—again? She opted for the burrito and stuck it in the microwave. After changing into sweats, her feet continued to feel cold. A pair of fleecy socks waited in her bedroom drawer upstairs. *This is ridiculous. No more nonsense.* She started up the stairs.

Giles ruined my life. I was on the road to recovery and he set me back a year. I can't avoid the bedroom! If Hayley hadn't come by after the funeral and gathered a bunch of her things to put in the guest room, she'd have needed a whole new wardrobe. Three-quarters of the way to the top she froze, her emotions changing like Oklahoma weather. The four-poster bed they'd shared, the awful note sitting on the pillow...the sheriff standing at her door...picking out readings for the memorial service. Tears streamed down her cheeks. Sorrow jabbed at her heart like an invisible needle.

By the time she backed down to the first floor, sorrow had again morphed into anger. She ran into the kitchen, grabbed the sledgehammer, and attacked the eyesore of a wall. *This is for leaving me with bills to pay on a teacher's salary.* She lifted it again. *Here's to leaving me stuck with this eyesore of a house that I can't afford to renovate.*

Lifting it for a third whack, Bijou barked from the living room alerting her to a knock at the front door. She tossed the sledgehammer down and wiped her eyes with the bottom of her sweatshirt.

"Coming."

She squinted into the peephole. *How does he know where I live?*

She opened the door, and he took a step back. "Jenna?"

"Max? What are you doing here?"

"Jenna? This is your house? May I come in? I'm as surprised to see you as you are to see me. This is business."

"Business?"

"You know the girl who was murdered on campus? Isabel Hernandez?"

"Don't tell me. You're another detective assigned to the case."

"Not exactly. I'm a private investigator hired by the girl's fiancé."

"You didn't tell me you were a private investigator."

"You didn't ask. I wasn't trying to hide it."

"You were hired by the victim's fiancé, and you came to me?"

"Only because he thinks you were the last one to see her."

"Like I told the cops, I never met her. I have no idea why she left a note and wanted to meet with me."

"Or why her GPS was set for this house?"

"Right. Come in."

He took off his jacket. "It's freezing in here."

"This place costs a fortune to heat. The insulation

is non-existent. Can I get you coffee or something?"

"Was that the microwave?"

"Yeah. Dinner is ready."

"I didn't mean to interrupt your meal."

"If you can call it that. I'll be right back."

While she was in the kitchen, another knock sounded. "Max, can you see who it is?" She rarely had unexpected visitors and tonight there were two. While she searched for potholders, she heard yelling coming from the living room. The dog barked. Was that the detective's voice?

"You're no longer on the force. Stop meddling in police business."

"If you did your job, the victim's fiancé wouldn't need to hire a private investigator. You've instilled zero confidence in your ability to find Isabel's killer. Been there, experienced that."

"Confidence? Does he know you got thrown off the force?"

Jenna barged in. "What's going on here? You sound like two little boys arguing over a toy car."

"Sorry. We have history," Max said.

"Obviously. Detective Russo? What are you doing here?"

"I swung through the neighborhood asking about Isabel's white Nissan."

"And did anyone see her car in our neighborhood?"

"No."

"I told you she was never here."

"Just because no one saw it doesn't mean it didn't happen. Witnesses are notoriously unreliable as it is, let alone busy parents or myopic retirees."

"So you came by to let me know I was right.

Thanks for dropping by."

"Not so fast. About the key. You said only you and your TA had copies, right?"

"Right."

"We looked at the security footage from outside the building. We caught your TA talking to Isabel Hernandez the morning you discovered the note."

"Impossible. He said he never met her before."

"He lied. And he has a key to your office."

"You think Kyle let Isabel into my office?"

"They obviously knew each other and he has a key. Why did he lie about knowing the victim?"

Jenna's stomach twisted into a knot. Was she wrong about Kyle? No one else had a key. She didn't want to show the detective any doubts. There had to be an explanation.

"Kyle embellishes stuff all the time. He doesn't out-and-out lie. He's creative—exaggerates sometimes. If he had seen Isabel, believe me, he'd have made a big deal out of it. And he knows better than to let anyone in my office. Did you hear what they were saying to each other?"

"No. A visual only."

Max said, "Why don't you go ask this Kyle about it instead of interrupting Jenna's dinner?"

"Jenna? You're already on a first-name basis with a suspect in the death of your client's daughter." He huffed. "Professional all the way."

"A suspect?" Jenna opened the front door. "If there's nothing else, Detective…"

"I'm going, but don't leave town. I'll likely have more questions." He pulled the door closed behind him and Jenna turned the lock, adding the chain across the top.

"He can't tell you not to leave town, you know. It's illegal."

"I'm not going anywhere. Is it true what he said? You were thrown off the force?"

"It was right after my daughter's hit and run. The police were dragging their feet looking for the driver. I started staying late and using police resources to do my own investigation. When they caught on, I was canned."

"I'm sorry."

"I got my PI license and, frankly, it's been more interesting than being on the force ever was. Don't let Detective Russo push you around. He's a bully."

"I can handle him."

"Your dinner must be freezing cold by now. How about we order a pizza, my treat?"

"You're on."

Chapter 5

The next day, Jenna worked on lesson plans while her mind drifted back to sharing the pizza with Max the previous night. He chewed with his mouth open. And he always had to have the last word. But he made her laugh—something she hadn't done in a long time. Being around Max was like padding around the house in her fluffy old slippers—comfortable, secure, and a good fit. *I just met him. What am I doing? For all I know, he's a serial killer.*

She replayed her conversation with the detective. The nerve he had implying—stating in fact—she was a murder suspect. Did he know what she'd been through these past few years? The last thing she wanted was a connection to anyone's death. She'd had enough. And as far as Kyle? So what if he had a key? She knew him well enough to trust him. Besides, what possible motive did he have?

Screw it. I'll text Kyle and tell him to make this week's lesson plans. She had to admit having an assistant to pick up the slack was one of the many perks of teaching college over elementary school.

Bijou jumped up next to her and she nuzzled her nose against his fur. "You do stink, boy. Let's run to the groomers and see if we can get you spiffed up." She parked down the street from Puppy Paradise. Walking down the sidewalk hugging the buildings, she found herself continually glancing over her shoulder and listening for footsteps. *I've got to relax and hang onto my equilibrium. No one is here.* When she got to the groomer, she saw a reflection as she opened the glass door. The reflection of a car whizzing past. The reflection of a black sedan.

****

Thursday morning, Jenna spotted the associate dean down the hall as she approached her office. She gazed at the ground and upped her pace, hoping the dean wouldn't notice her as she heard the tapping of the stilettos clicking toward her. Dean Williams. Business suit, hair in a neat bun, librarian glasses—and her signature stilettos. The whole department had laughs speculating about what she did after hours. Too late to avoid her. Soon they were nose to nose.

"Dean Williams, I'm so sorry I missed the meeting the other morning."

"Meeting? What meeting?"

"The one you called Monday morning."

"I never called a meeting. In fact, I was out of town and didn't come to campus until later in the afternoon." She took off the glasses, softened her voice, and whispered, "Is everything okay?"

Jenna's face burned from the inside out. "Yes, fine. I must have been mistaken."

The dean pushed the glasses back on with her index finger and checked her watch. "Right now, I *do* have a meeting to attend." Once again, she broke into a concerned whisper. "Stay well."

"You too." She heard the sound of the heels clicking away. *Stay well.* She hated being treated like a child. Unless they were coughing or puking, would the dean use the words *stay well* to any other professor? *Fricking condescending.*

She stormed away, fantasizing about throwing Delores into a den of hungry tigers. She stomped down the hall to Delores's office, formally known as the supply closet, and pounded on the door.

A gritty voice said, "Come in."

The office smelled like bleach, a reminder of its former function. "Delores, thanks for making me seem like a fool."

"What are you talking about?"

"There never was a meeting Monday morning. I just ran into the dean."

"A meeting? What meeting?"

"The meeting with the dean you told me I missed."

Delores got up, walked around the makeshift desk, and put the back of her palm on Jenna's forehead as if checking for a fever. Jenna swatted it away. "Get your filthy hand off me."

"Do you feel okay? I know it's stressful being back at work. We haven't had a meeting since the start of the semester. The dean's been out of town. Maybe you need more rest."

Jenna looked her right in the eyes. "Don't think you're going to play me like this. Just because you can't get a full-time position on your own merit, don't screw around with me or you'll regret it."

"Is that a threat? HR doesn't take kindly to threats."

"I don't have time for this. Move out of my way." It took much restraint not to push her fat head into the desk. She slammed the door behind her on the way out. *Breathe. Chair, desk, door. Chair, desk, door.* By the time she reached the end of the hall, the therapist's techniques had done absolutely nothing. She stopped at Hayley's office to vent before going to her own.

"Jenna, you look like you're about to rip someone's head off."

"Yeah, Delores's. The meeting she told me I missed? I ran into the dean. There never was a meeting in the first place. I felt like a fool."

"I told you as much. She's a piece of work. Old, ugly, and she can't teach her way out of a bucket."

"I can't let her get under my skin."

"But you are. Put it in perspective. She's a jealous you know what."

Jenna leaned on the edge of Haley's desk. "You're right. And she looks like a Sumo wrestler."

"You know what they say. You can't put lipstick on a pig."

"Not with that stinky breath. Who could get near enough?"

Hayley laughed. "That's what I'm talking about."

"You know we sound like we're in middle school, right?" Jenna slid into the leather office chair. "How's the fertility treatment going?"

"Oliver came home yesterday. I hate he's out of town so often."

"What's with all the traveling?"

"The company has started sending him all over the country to recruit clients. His boss tells him earning trust is his superpower." She took a vial and needle from her desk drawer. "Speaking of fertility, do you mind?"

"Hand it over." Jenna winced as she pierced Hayley's skin.

Hayley jumped. "Ouch!"

"I'm sorry."

Hayley smiled. "I'm kidding. You're way better at this than Oliver. I've got a bruise the size of a quarter from yesterday's shot, but he's so afraid of hurting me, I can't say anything."

"It must be hard on him, too."

"I guess. I secretly wonder if he likes all the traveling he's doing. He gets away from me."

"Don't be ridiculous. That's your hormones talking. Think positive."

"I'm trying. Hopefully, there are tons of eggs waiting to be fertilized." She patted her stomach. "I go for an ultrasound tomorrow."

Jenna mirrored her motion. She could still feel the relentless cramps and the sensation of warm blood trickling down her legs the night after the shooting. Her insides felt hollow thinking about it. When it happened, she hadn't even had the chance to tell Giles she was pregnant yet. He drove her to the emergency room, concerned, and angry. She hadn't been sure if he was angry about losing the baby, or about her not having told him.

"Jenna, you okay?" asked Hayley.

"Yes. Stop asking me if I'm okay."

"Hey, don't bite my head off. I'm the one who's supposed to be moody right now."

"I'm sorry. I know you mean well."

"You seem to have a handle on it. I'll shut up."

"I haven't come in here crying or having a panic attack since I came back. And that's with being roped into this whole murder investigation." She imagined violin music floating through the air.

Then, Kyle sauntered in like a brass band wielding lattes. "Thought you could use these. I had them add a shot of expresso to mine."

Hayley grabbed one. "I'll bite. Why do you need expresso, Kyle?"

"He must have been up all night looking for a dissertation topic," said Jenna.

"Or his new boyfriend kept him up," said Hayley.

Kyle clicked his tongue and shook his head. Jenna stifled a giggle.

"What are you smiling about?"

"You look like a GIF. You know, the one where the guy from the office shakes his head over and over while waving his finger back and forth?"

"Steve Carell?" Kyle clutched his heart, latte in hand. "How dare you! He's old enough to be my father."

"Not the point. Doesn't he look like a GIF, Hayley?"

Kyle clicked his tongue and shook his head once again.

Hayley walked around Kyle, pretending to inspect him. "Absolutely."

"Do you want me to tell you or not?"

In unison, they responded, "Go on."

Kyle leaned in closer. "This police detective stopped me in the parking lot. He says he's working the Isabel Hernandez homicide. At this point, I'm completely confused as to why he's talking to me. I didn't know the victim. I never met her—or so I thought."

"You mean you *did* know her?" said Jenna. She didn't let on about the detective's visit last night and the security footage.

"I didn't say that. Apparently, I had *met* her. The morning of the murder. Police have CCTV footage showing me talking to her outside this building. He made it sound like I was a suspect. I was about to invite him to frisk me, but I've been working on my social filter." He sprinkled a bit of expresso on his fingers and let Bijou lick it off.

"Good thing or you might be sitting in a jail cell," said Hayley.

"What were you talking about?" asked Jenna. She swatted his hand away from Bijou. "Caffeine isn't good for dogs."

"But he likes peppermint. Right, buddy?" He set his drink down and scratched Bijou behind the ears. "The girl asked me for directions to the student union. I swear, I had no idea who she was until the hunky detective pointed it out."

"That might have been right after she left the note on my computer."

"It was early—before you arrived."

"You didn't let her into my office, did you?"

Kyle folded his arms and gave her a look. "Of course not. Prof, you know me better than that."

"Yes, I do. You're nothing if not loyal. I'd better get to my office. I'll see you in class."

Hayley said, "Wait a minute. That's the same shirt you were wearing yesterday. You never repeat an outfit in the same week. You were with your new boyfriend. Spill it."

"We want details," said Jenna.

"Ross is...he's like...he's...what's the word I'm looking for?"

Hayley chimed in, "Tolerant? I mean, if he's willing to put up with you…"

Kyle folded his arms and huffed. "Okay, if you don't want to hear about him, fine."

Jenna said, "You know Hayley can't resist giving you a hard time. Deep down she loves you. Right, Hayley?"

Hayley rolled her eyes. "Yes. Tell us more."

"I think he's the one."

"Haven't you only been going out a few weeks?" said Jenna.

"Yeah, but Ross is different. I feel like I've known him my whole life. Like maybe we knew each other in a former life or something."

Hayley rolled her eyes again. "You can't be serious. It's far too soon to know if he's *the one.*"

Jenna said, "Not necessarily. I knew I wanted to marry Giles after our second date. I get what he's saying."

He gave Jenna a high five. "You get it. I might just ask you to be a bridesmaid."

"What about me?" said Hayley."

"On my timeline, you'll be way too pregnant to fit in a frilly dress. But perhaps you can do a reading for us."

He gave Bijou another lick of his latte. "Hey, girl. Lose the silly bow from the groomer. It makes him look like a fag."

Jenna shook her head, wiped the froth from her dog's nose, and grabbed the harness. "Go work on finding a topic!"

When she got to her office, she fumbled with her keys. Despite the respite with her coworkers, her hands had been trembling on and off since talking to the detective last night. *Got it.*

She pushed the door open and flicked on the lights. *What the hell?* A prickly cactus stared at her from her desk. *That bitch.* In her hurry to toss it, she cut her finger on a prickly spine before smashing it into the trash can. *How did she get in here?* She kicked the trash can, nearly knocking it over. *Wait. She used my office while I was on leave last semester.* Sucking her hurt finger, she ran down the hall to the cubicles near the mail room. Mona, the department secretary, simultaneously typed and listened to voice mail at her desk. Multitasking at its best, thought Jenna. Mona looked up when she realized Jenna was calling her name.

"Hi, Jenna. You startled me." The secretary scratched Bijou behind the ears. "Can I get a doggie kiss? Ooh, you smell good."

"Mona, I have an important question to ask."

"Shoot." She flushed the color of cherry blossom. "I'm sorry for using that word. I meant, ask me anything."

"Mona, it's okay. Really."

"Sorry. I mean, you look well. I didn't mean to be insensitive."

"You couldn't be insensitive if you tried."

"What can I do for you?"

"Last fall when I went out on leave, Delores took my keys, right?"

"She must have. There's only one set made for each door, other than the master, of course. Security reasons." She flushed again.

"And she had to have returned them, right?"

"Yes. I can grab the log if you'd like. It's here somewhere." She searched through the filing cabinet. "Voila."

Jenna looked at the dates. Sure enough, Delores had signed out her keys last fall and returned them at the end of the semester. "She could have made a copy, right?"

"There's a strict policy against that."

"Yes, you're right." *Like I think for a minute Delores wouldn't make a copy.* "Thanks. How's the grandbaby?"

"Light of my life. See." She picked up the photo on her desk.

"He's handsome. He has your smile."

"You think so? I think he looks like my husband." She winced. "I'm…"

"Don't apologize. I'd better run or I'll be late for my class." Did she think she hadn't heard the word *husband* since it happened?

Not in the mood to teach, she let Kyle take the lead. Since he hadn't yet nailed down a topic for his dissertation as of this morning, he had to earn his stipend somehow. She scanned the room. No Brooke. It was early enough to drop classes without penalty, and she assumed that's what happened. Millennials. As soon as they faced a challenge, bingo, they bailed.

Kyle gave the class directions. "Now go into your groups and reflect on how you'd use this material in a lesson." Chairs screeched against the wooden floor. Conversations chattered like little flocks of birds echoing through the room while Kyle circulated. Jenna figured he'd be an inspiring professor one day if he could get a grip on his time management skills.

One of the students came up to her.

"Dr. Blake, I'm worried about Brooke. She isn't answering her phone and her roommate hasn't seen her in days."

Jenna flipped over her phone on the desk, hoping the student didn't notice she'd been shoe shopping online while they were working. "She may have dropped the class."

"No, I'm sure she didn't. They closed down this section last fall, and she couldn't get a replacement to fit her schedule. She needs this class to graduate."

"Did you talk to the resident assistant? Or her roommate?"

"The RA won't know anything, and her roommate is a bitch. Sorry. I shouldn't use that kind of language in front of you. I'm just worried."

"Nothing I haven't heard before. Go on."

"She hasn't been on social media either—not since Sunday."

Can you call her parents and see if anything's wrong? Her father's got a heart problem."

"Why don't you call?"

"I don't have her parents' phone number. I thought you'd have access to her records."

Jenna didn't feel this was her responsibility, but then again, if something happened and she hadn't made the call, she'd probably be sued and definitely fired. "Okay. I'll give her parents a call."

Jenna opened her laptop and searched for Brooke's information. Her dorm was across the courtyard. Of course it was. Maybe she should drop by and talk to the RA before alarming the girl's parents. She hit the 'buy now' button on a pair of Easy Spirit ankle boots and stuck her phone back in her bag while Kyle wrapped up the class.

After the students left, she gathered her things and wandered outside. Looking across the open courtyard was like viewing the ocean from a ship's balcony during a storm. The buildings swayed like windshield wipers in front of her eyes. She scooped up her life jacket—Bijou. She teetered, grabbing the brick wall for support. *Tree, bush, sidewalk. One, two, three.*

I can't do this. She ducked back inside. She could take the easy way out and skip the visit, or exit from the other end of the building and shelter herself by groping along the buildings around the perimeter. It would take twice as long, but if she opted to continue, it was her only choice.

The air stung her cheeks, and she tightened her scarf. She hugged the buildings like in the movies when the potential jumper changes his mind and inches back toward the open window. *The RA or the roommate better be there after this.*

She entered the building, which smelled like rotten leftovers. The cinder block walls had been painted white but were scuffed and in need of repainting. *Rundown, just like my house. But I'm sure mine doesn't smell this bad.*

She made her way to the second floor and knocked on the resident assistant's door. A young woman wearing sweats and a long sleeve crop top opened the door with an attitude.

"Yeah?" Bijou barked, tail wagging. The RA bent down, her face softening. "Cute dog. Can I pet her?"

"It's a him, and go ahead. My name is Dr. Blake. I'm a professor in the education department. One of my students has been missing from class for several days and I want to check on her."

"Which one?"

"Brooke Adams."

"Yeah. Her room's down the hall."

"Have you seen her the past few days?"

"No. As a matter of fact, she didn't come to our floor meeting last night. You can knock on the door. Her roommate is there. I saw her carrying laundry down about half an hour ago. It's room 203."

"Thanks." Jenna made her way down the hall and knocked. Over the loud music, she had to knock a second time before a girl, also wearing sweats, opened the door.

"You shouldn't open the door without asking who it is," said Jenna. *Don't parents teach these kids anything these days?*

"Okay, Boomer." She closed the door and chirped, "Who's there?"

The little snot. Why am I doing this again? "Professor Blake." She emphasized professor. "I'm looking for Brooke Adams."

The door opened a second time. "She isn't here. Hasn't been for a few days." She scratched Bijou under the chin. "What a pretty girl. What's her name?"

"Bijou. It's a him. Do you know where I can find Brooke?"

"No. She left her laptop and her favorite leather booties. I'm surprised she hasn't been back."

"Does she have a boyfriend she might be staying with? Or do you think she went home?" She knew she sounded incredibly nosy.

"What am I, a psychic? No boyfriend at the

moment, and her car is in the parking lot, so she didn't go home. Should I start worrying?"

Start worrying? Her roommate's been gone for three days and she didn't bother telling the RA or campus police? "Where's home for her?"

"Millford. A couple of hours away."

"When's the last time you saw her?"

"Monday night, I think. I left for the library. When I got back, she wasn't here, and then I went to class in the morning."

"She didn't come home at all that night?"

"Hard to say. I fell asleep with my music on and she has early classes."

"Was her bed slept in?"

The roommate pointed to a rumpled bunk. "It always looks like that. Who can tell?"

"Do you happen to have her parents' number?"

"Why would I have her parents' phone number? Did something happen to her?"

"Hope not."

"That girl who got killed on campus. Did they catch who did it?"

"Not yet."

"You don't think he got Brooke, do you? You don't think there's a serial killer on the loose?"

She wasn't sure if the roommate was being sincere or sarcastic. "Let's hope not. Thanks for your time. And next time, ask who it is before opening the door." *Millennials.* On her way out, she picked up an empty can of Red Bull and threw it into the recycling bin.

Jenna returned to her office and called Brooke's parents, praying Brooke had gotten a bout of homesickness and caught a bus home. *Sure. Her car's sitting in the dorm lot and she took a bus.* One ring, two rings…

"Hello."

"Hello, is this Brooke's mother? I'm Dr. Blake, one of your daughter's professors."

"I'm her mother. Is something wrong? Is she having academic issues?"

"Nothing like that." *This isn't elementary school. We don't call the parents if the child is failing.* "When's the last time you saw or talked to your daughter?"

"Sunday night. We call her every Sunday night after dinner. Why?"

"She hasn't shown up to class and her friends are worried. Her roommate hasn't seen her since Monday."

"Oh, my God. A girl was killed on campus—we saw it on the news. Did they catch him? Do you think he has Brooke?"

"Don't panic. There haven't been any reports of foul play since. I don't mean to frighten you, but perhaps we should report her missing."

"Perhaps? My husband and I will jump in the car and be there in a few hours."

"I'll contact the police in the meantime. Try not to worry." She knew those words were hollow. Of course they will worry. If her child went missing, she'd be hysterical. She called Detective Russo and explained the situation.

"You said her parents are on the way? And they haven't heard from her?"

"Not since Sunday. And the roommate said she last saw her on Monday. Her car is in the parking lot and she left her purse in the dorm room."

"How old is this girl? Over eighteen? Over twenty-one?"

"She's a senior. I'd say she's twenty-one."

"Then she isn't a minor. Did anyone see her being abducted?"

"Don't you think if someone did they'd have called you?"

He ignored the comment. "Any history of mental illness? Talk of suicide?"

Cringing at the word suicide had become a knee-jerk reaction. "No!"

"She's not a minor and there's no evidence of foul play. My guess is she needed some space."

"You won't start a search for her?"

"You can fill out a missing person report, but it won't go anywhere unless we find evidence a crime has been committed. I'm just being honest. You can notify campus police to be on the lookout."

"I'll be right over." After she hung up, she tossed the paper with the parents' number in the trash can. Vincenzo never emptied the trash until the evening; so where was the cactus and broken pot she'd thrown in there this morning?

Chapter 6

Jenna drummed her fingers on the dingy plastic armrest while waiting outside Detective Russo's door at the police station. The fluorescent light above flickered, deciding whether or not it had any life left in it. Gray walls, the smell of slightly damp file folders, and a stained carpet contributed to the depressive atmosphere. *One girl I never met but wanted to meet me is dead; another, one of my students, is missing.* Bijou licked her face.

She poured a cup of coffee, which tasted like sewer sludge. Not even in the same ballpark as Kyle's lattes. Though the pulsing light made it difficult, she scrolled through her phone and scanned social media while she waited. Social media! Maybe they should put out something about Brooke.

Detective Russo opened his door. "Busy day. Come on in. Let's fill in the details and we'll file it." He gulped coffee from a Thermos. *Kudos to him for bringing his own.*

File it. Sure. Under a stack of papers since he doesn't believe she's missing. She took the clipboard. "Have you gotten any leads on Isabel's killer?"

"If I did, I couldn't discuss it."

"Do you think the two cases are related?"

"What two cases? So far, we have one crime to solve. A twenty-one-year-old going away for a couple of days isn't a crime. Didn't I make myself clear over the phone?"

"Can't you at least post something on social media?"

His lips twisted like taffy. "Brilliant."

Sarcastic son of a... "I was trying to help."

"Be patient and we'll follow the protocol *if* she turns out to be missing."

"Then I'll trust you know what you're doing." *We'll start making fliers, talk to her other friends, organize a search...*

"Speaking of trust, I'd advise you to stay clear of Max Colby. He isn't who he claims to be. If you get any further info, bring it to my attention, not his."

Advise me to stay away? "I'll take it under advisement. He's working for Isabel Hernandez's fiancé. I couldn't tell him much of anything."

"The fiancé is wasting his money. We've been working day and night on the homicide case. Colby's just getting in the way. Not what you'd call a team player. He used to be a cop, you know."

"He told me all about it."

"Then he told you he was fired?"

"He did."

"What story did he give you?"

"Story? His daughter was killed crossing the street and he's been obsessed with finding the driver. Since his own department didn't deem it a priority, he took things into his own hands. He got fired for tapping department resources for his personal use."

"That's what he told you?"

"Yes."

"Did he tell you he went postal and assaulted

another officer right here in the station? Did he tell you he put the officer in the hospital? And he trashed computers, pulled phones out of the sockets, and smashed a window with a chair?"

"I don't believe you."

"Believe what you want. I tried to warn you."

"Yeah, right."

"Excuse me?" He pushed back from his desk and glared at her. "I have work to do. You know the way out, right?"

"Yes. Not pursuing Brooke Adams's disappearance is a heck of a lot of work. I hope you're putting a little more effort into finding Isabel's killer." She shut the door harder than intended and it felt satisfying. *Smug son of a ... Good thing Isabel's fiancé didn't rely solely on him. It was a smart move hiring Max to investigate.*

When she got back in the car, she saw her mother had called. She used the ride home to call her back.

"Mom? Is everything okay?"

"Everything's fine here. We saw on the news that there was a murder at your school and we were worried."

"A body was found in the woods behind the student union building. Technically, it wasn't even on campus."

"Did you know her? Was she a Monk Haven student?"

"No. Never heard of her."

"If there's a killer on campus—"

"It was probably a domestic issue. Most violent crimes are committed by people the victim knows. Don't worry."

"Why don't you come home for the weekend?"

"It's not exactly around the corner. I appreciate the offer, but I have tons of work to do for school. And I'd like to clean up some of the debris from Giles' half-finished renovation projects."

"Are you sure?"

"Yes, but I love you for asking. I'm doing well. Don't worry."

"Did your friends notice your new haircut?"

"And my new wardrobe. Thanks again for the spa day and shopping spree."

"I enjoyed it. We'll do it again."

"I'll hold you to that."

"Do you need money? Are you able to pay your bills?"

She didn't want to admit she was barely making ends meet. "Yes, Mom."

"You can call us any time you need anything."

"I know. Say hi to Dad for me. I love you."

"Love you, too."

Although living with her parents the past few months had made her feel like a helpless child much of the time, she knew she wouldn't have survived without their support—emotional as well as financial. Paying the bills while on leave from her job was impossible. It was tough enough now without Giles' paycheck to supplement what she earned as a professor. If she couldn't sell the house in the near future, she'd have to find a second job or take in a renter. She refused to keep taking money from her parents. *Ugh.*

When she arrived home, a package was waiting on the front stoop.

"Come on, Bijou. Let's go in and open this. I'll bet it's the heavier doggie coat I ordered."

She sat on the sofa and tore open the box. None of that delicate unboxing that was all over YouTube these days. It wasn't the dog coat. It was a sealed baggie. She opened it and pulled out a gold locket. *No velvet box? Had Giles ordered it and it was just now getting here?* He loved making her happy and ordering a locket for her was something he'd do—would have done. How could she stay mad at him? It looked expensive. She opened the locket. *He must have a receipt somewhere in his things. Where did he stash it?* She tried to convince herself the receipt would be for insurance purposes, but in reality, she was just plain curious. She searched for a return address or some sort of tracking number but found none. It had come through the postal service and would be impossible to trace.

Maybe he ordered it from work and the receipt was mixed up in there? Giles' colleague cleared out his school office after his death and shoved photos, ribbons, and band memorabilia into a big box, which she'd left sitting untouched in the garage. She hadn't yet summoned the strength to go through it. If Hayley hadn't convinced her she may one day want the memories, she'd have told the school to dump everything.

An empty locket. Wasn't the point of wearing a locket to carry a loved one's picture close to your heart? *I'll bet he planned to put his picture inside before giving it to me.* She glanced at her watch and picked up her phone. Elmwood Charter would still be open.

"Elmwood Charter. How may I direct your call?"

"Lisa? It's me, Jenna Blake."

"Jenna? I didn't recognize your voice at first. How are you? Sorry I was out of town for Giles' funeral. I meant to call."

"It was more of a memorial service since the body..." She wiped tears from her eyes, glad Lisa couldn't see her fighting off an emotional meltdown.

"The school added his name to the memorial wall. He wouldn't have done what he did if he hadn't gone through what he had. Only a handful of teachers returned to work after the shooting. Your husband had courage."

Courage? He was a coward. "He didn't want to let the students down. He wanted to help them through the tragedy." If he'd not gone back so soon, or if he'd found another position like she did, he might be alive today. Instead, he opted for an easy fix.

"The new building is finished. Not a trace of the old band building. The school's planning a ribbon-cutting ceremony. I'm sure you'll get an invitation in the mail. I'm sorry I didn't reach out to you after the funeral."

"It's okay. All the funerals and hospital visits the school went through? It was overwhelming. A few of the faculty and band parents came, and of course, the new principal—the one who replaced," —she swallowed the knot in her throat— "Principal Kaminsky, may he rest in peace. I've prayed every night that the shooter would be caught and yet he's still out there."

"You called here. Is there something I can help you with?"

She'd almost forgotten. "I received a package today without a return address and wondered if the school sent it to me."

"What sort of package?"

"It was a gold locket. I thought it may have been left behind in Giles' office after I cleared out his things."

"A locket?"

"He may have had it sent to the school so I wouldn't find it. It looks expensive."

"I'm in charge of the mail here, and I didn't send anything official from the school. And no one's said anything about finding a lost necklace."

"Okay. Thanks."

She wondered if there was a clue in the box in the garage or the bedroom. Giles kept records of everything in the file cabinet by the bed. She started up the steps, holding Bijou. Her chest tightened. *Sofa, rug, step*...She clutched Bijou, took a deep breath, and climbed up one more step before the room started spinning. *Step, banister, bedroom door*...She repeated the mantra as she retreated down the stairs to the safety of the living room. Hugging Bijou closer to her, she curled into a fetal position under the afghan and fell asleep.

She'd have remained asleep if not for the loud knock on the front door. She scooted to the door and shouted, "Who is it?"

"Are you Jenna Blake?"

"Who are you?"

"I am, I was, Isabel Hernandez's fiancé. Santiago Salas. The doorbell doesn't work. May I come in?"

Max had mentioned the fiancé was his client. She unhitched the chain and unlocked the door. "What can I do for you?"

"I need your help."

"Come in. I'm so sorry for your loss. Have a seat."

She couldn't imagine what help she'd be. Detective Russo and Max were both investigating, and they were professionals.

"I'm all she had left, you know. Isabel's mother lived in Guatemala. Never recuperated after her younger daughter's death a few years ago."

"I'm so sorry." He looked as fragile as she'd felt after Giles died. She wanted to hug him but stopped herself.

"I worked up the courage to go by Isabel's apartment today. I found your name and address on a pad in the kitchen. I hope you can shed some light."

"I never met Isabel. I'd received a note. I showed it to the police and they are fairly certain it's Isabel's handwriting. She wanted to meet with me—said it was a matter of life and death."

He leaned forward, eyes full of anticipation. "What'd she tell you?"

"Nothing. I waited and she never showed up."

"She didn't show up? You're telling me she made an appointment to meet you and then blew it off?"

"Later that day, someone found her body. Do *you* have any idea why she wanted to talk to me?"

"No. She'd been agitated lately. I knew something was bothering her, but she wouldn't open up about it."

"If Isabel was scared or found something important, why not report it to the police? Why reach out to me?"

Santiago looked down at the floor. "She had a visa to be in this country, but it had expired. With her mother gone, she couldn't face going back home."

"She was afraid of being deported?"

"Yes."

"How did she support herself?"

"She worked as a freelance translator from home. Translated contracts, letters, documents…"

"Did you go through her things? Maybe there are clues as to her concerns."

"I was going to, but when I found your address, I thought I'd start here."

"Did you tell the police she was a translator?"

"No. I don't want to alert them she was working with an expired visa."

"It could be important." *Any detective worth his salt would uncover her illegal status in a New York minute.*

Santiago looked at the floor, then at her. "Besides, when the detective questioned me after they found Isabel, I got the idea I was a suspect. I don't feel he'd be helpful."

"I gotcha. I felt the same when he questioned me."

"Can I call you if I find anything after I look through her things?"

"Of course."

She locked the door after him. "Come on, Bijou. Let's get dinner."

Chapter 7

In the morning, her back in spasms from the guest bed, Jenna tried to go upstairs once again. *One step at a time. One foot in front of the other.* She got a step further than yesterday and paused. Her heart felt as though it had received a direct shot of caffeine into the aorta. *I can do this. Breathe.* She knew what was coming. Her pounding heart signaled the onset of a panic attack. Fight or flight? She took a few slow breaths and tried to fight it. Her throat tightened.

Jenna grabbed the banister. Unable to pick up her foot and continue, she had no choice. She counted to ten. When her pulse slowed, she turned around and fled down the steps.

She couldn't suppress the gut feeling that Giles hadn't ordered the locket for her. More than once over the course of their marriage, she had suspected Giles was having an affair, but always managed to talk herself out of it. Until she caught him in the act. Hurt, embarrassed— she never told a soul. Not even Hayley. At this point, it shouldn't matter, but if she could find a receipt showing Giles purchased the locket around her birthday or anniversary she'd feel a little less foolish.

She couldn't make it upstairs, but the box from his office was in the garage, just through the kitchen door. *Maybe after work.* "Bijou? Let's go."

The charcoal sky threatened bad weather. It felt

extra cold, but she was thankful for the heated seats in the new Honda her parents bought for her. Too bad the sofa in her living room didn't have the same technology. The commute was blissfully shorter than her commute to Elmwood Charter had been.

She ran into Hayley in the parking lot. "What's wrong? Have you been crying?" Normally, Hayley would be the one asking that question.

"I went for the ultrasound yesterday and didn't have a single viable egg. All those hormones for nothing, not to mention the price tag."

She wrapped an arm around her friend. "You can try again. Don't give up."

"I would quit, but the fee includes three trials, so one down and two to go. After that, it's over. We won't have a family."

"You do have a family. You have Oliver."

"I'm sorry, I shouldn't have said that."

"It's okay. There are other options."

"Don't say adoption. I'm sick of hearing how there are tons of babies out there waiting for homes. The wait for a healthy baby is long and if you aren't rich, it's longer."

"What about adopting through foster care?"

"It's hard enough raising a baby, let alone one who comes with baggage." She stopped and turned to Jenna. "Oh, my God, that sounded awful."

"You're disappointed, I get it." A car pulled into the space next to Jenna's. "I'd better tell them they'll be towed without a parking permit, let alone it's a handicapped spot." She got to the car as the driver got out.

"Sir, you need a permit…"

A woman got out of the passenger side. "We need to find Professor Blake." She spoke rapidly in a high-pitched voice. "Our daughter is missing."

Now the pieces fell into place—Brooke's parents. "Come inside, it's freezing."

Hayley said, "I'll catch you later."

Once inside, she cleared a stack of papers off the small loveseat she'd inherited from the previous professor. "Can I get you coffee or water?"

"No, thanks," said Brooke's father.

"How can I help?"

He spoke for both of them. "We were just at the local police station."

The mother said, "The detective treated our daughter's disappearance like another item on his to-do list. He hasn't started searching for her because there's no evidence of foul play."

"And she's legally an adult," said her father. "I know my daughter. She wouldn't disappear without telling us where she was going."

"Detective Russo? Was that who you spoke to?"

"That was him."

"He's all business, not an ounce of empathy. I suppose it's an asset for a detective."

Mr. Adams put his arm around his wife. "We don't need him to be warm and fuzzy. We need to know he's doing everything he can to find our daughter. Can you tell us anything more?"

"No, I'm sorry. The semester just begun, so I barely got an opportunity to know your daughter. Brooke's friends were worried because she'd missed a few classes. The RA and her roommate haven't seen Brooke since Monday."

"Why don't they search the area? What about police dogs? We're losing valuable time."

"Mrs. Adams, I don't know what their plan is. They have their protocols."

Mr. Adams said, "How about we organize a search party?"

"I've seen them do that on TV," said his wife.

"You should ask the university for permission. And we'll need a little time to organize. The weather is supposed to deteriorate this afternoon. They're predicting six inches of snow."

"Then we'd better get busy," said Mrs. Adams. "I'll make flyers in the meantime, and we'll post them around campus."

"I can round up people to help with the flyers and the search when I'm finished here. You should talk to her friend, Sadie. She's the one who brought her disappearance to my attention."

"We've met Sadie. They live in the same dorm. We'll talk to her." Mr. Adams led his wife out of the office.

Maybe I should hook them up with Max. She sat at her computer and began going through emails. The dean walked in.

"Dr. Blake, where is your attendance report? It was due yesterday and I need it in order to meet my own deadlines."

"I wasn't aware you'd requested a report."

"Really? I sent out an email over a week ago and flagged it as important."

"I apologize." *How did I miss that?* "I'll have it for you within the hour. Do you want it in an Excel document?"

"I'll resend the form along with my original message."

"Thank you, and I apologize."

"Everything going okay? Classes going well?"

You mean if I'm going to fall apart and quit? Not a chance. "Everything's great. I'm enjoying my students and they're soaking up info like thirsty sponges." *Hunky-dory.* She faked a smile.

"Good to hear. I'll be expecting that report."

When she could no longer hear the sound of heels clicking on the tile floor, she opened the spam and trash files on her email and scanned through them. *There it is! Deleted. How did I manage to delete it, especially with that red exclamation mark in front of it? Or did Delores sneak in here again?* She had to focus on completing the report, but afterward, she'd talk to someone about changing the lock on her office door. She chastised herself for not doing it earlier.

She gathered her records and was in the middle of completing the report when Detective Russo came in. He hadn't knocked, and she jumped when she saw him standing in front of her desk.

"Can I help you, detective?"

"That student who's gone missing, Brooke Adams, I wonder if you happened to see her at the student union building when you went to meet Isabel Hernandez on Monday?"

"Brooke? The girl I came to *you* about? The one whose parents asked you for help and you brushed them off? Now you want to know if I saw her at the student union?"

"That's what I asked."

She shook her head. "I don't remember seeing her.

In fact, she'd missed my class earlier." *To be truthful, I barely remember what she looks like. She only came to a handful of classes.*

"She swiped her university card to pay for a coffee at the student union building close to the time you were supposed to meet Isabel Hernandez."

"I didn't see her, but I wasn't looking for her. There were plenty of people there. She could have lent the card to a friend."

"No, the cashier remembered her. Said she often came by for a coffee on her way to class."

"I was behind the student union building, not inside. She might have been there—I didn't notice."

"It's quite a coincidence, right? You're supposed to meet Isabel Hernandez and she turns up dead. Then one of your students, one who has gone missing, crossed your path at around the same time."

"I don't like your tone. I had nothing to do with Isabel's death or Brooke's disappearance. Besides, I thought you didn't believe Brooke was missing."

"One of your colleagues told me you took medical leave last semester because you experienced blackouts."

"Which colleague?" *Like I have to ask.* She'd bet her bottom dollar Delores gave him that information. "I was under stress, but I never had a blackout. I'd recently lost my husband."

"Perhaps returning to work triggered your previous issues."

She wanted to slug him. "You're harassing me and I'm about to go to your supervisor."

"Harassing you? I had a few questions. Don't you want us to catch Isabel's killer and find Brooke

Adams?"

"Of course I do."

"Then stop acting so thin-skinned when I ask for information. Unless you have something to hide…"

Rage welled like a volcano inside, but she fought to keep it from erupting. "If you have any more legitimate questions, you're free to ask, but if you're done, I have work to do. So do you. Brooke's parents weren't happy with your response to their missing daughter."

"Get back to work. You do your job and I'll do mine." He pulled the door shut behind him, probably a little harder than he intended. And probably feeling satisfied.

Now he believes she's missing? He must have found something pointing to foul play. Is it just the fact she swiped her card at the student union around the time Isabel was in those woods?

Jenna sat down at her computer and finished the attendance report. She couldn't believe she'd accidentally sent the original request to trash. Was she slipping? *No, I feel clear-minded—I've been on my game since returning to work. Did Delores sneak in and sabotage me once again?* She looked at the empty trash can where she knew she'd thrown the cactus. Kyle came in.

"Hey, Prof. I heard rumors about a search party for Brooke tonight."

"Seriously, Kyle? I just spoke to her parents."

"The university said after classes ended today would be a good time. They expect a lot of students will leave for the long weekend, and they don't want to cause more alarm than necessary."

How did he know all this already? Maybe he should be a detective. "I think searching in the dark will make things more difficult. They're predicting several inches of snow tonight."

"Imagine if Brooke is out in those woods somewhere. She's been without food and water for a few days and with the temperature dropping, it's urgent."

If she's been outside in this weather since Monday, chances are great she won't be alive. We're past urgent. "What makes you think she's out in the woods?" Kyle was a magnet for information, both real and gossip. Sometimes it was hard to unravel which strands were the truth.

"Her friends say she was taking a photography class and had to make a photo collage of wildlife. The morning she disappeared was clear and beautiful, not the January norm. What if she took advantage of the weather to do her assignment?"

"The detective said she swiped her card at the student union building and the woods are right behind it…" She wished Kyle was right about Brooke being alive but doubted it. "Did she take her camera with her?"

"Hmm, a good question." He placed his index finger on his chin.

"Speaking of searching, are you planning on searching for a dissertation topic this weekend?"

"I'll find one before the deadline. You know I'm good for it."

"You're my first doctoral candidate. If you screw this up, you'll make me look bad. Someone needs to light a fire under you."

"Exactly." Kyle winked. "Ross and I will be at the search party. We have weekend plans but I'll set aside some time to think about topics. I promise."

"So things are going well with Ross, I take it."

"Yeah. I feel like I've known him forever. And he's good for me. Keeps me on a schedule, urges me to stick to a budget. And I'm good for him too."

"I'm sure you make him laugh."

"Yeah, he can be such a little old man sometimes. I bring him out of his shell, he says. And he can cook."

"You should have led with that. Can I borrow him?"

"I'm going to help Brooke's parents copy flyers. I ran into them outside. See you tonight."

Jenna simply shook her head. She wished she could be as stress-free as Kyle. As his mentor, it was frustrating.

Hayley walked in. "Did you hear about the search party?"

"Yeah. Boy, word gets around fast."

"Oliver and I will be there. Do you want us to pick you up?"

"I'll let you know. I'm hoping Max will come along." She hoped Max might be available, not only because his skills would prove helpful, but because she'd enjoy his company. She snapped her laptop shut. "Report is done. I'm going home."

"See you tonight."

On her way out, Jenna tried calling Brooke's parents. *Come on, pick up.* She wanted to verify Brooke was taking the photography class. Was this an ongoing interest? Did she have a camera? The call went to voicemail. Bijou pulled ahead of her.

"Hold on to your horses, Bijou. I'm trying to call Max." Voicemail as well. She sent him a text. *Strike three. Maybe Brooke's roommate remembered something.* The dorm wasn't far out of the way. She turned around and headed toward it.

The dorm was downright depressing with its unpainted cinder block walls and flyers stuck haphazardly every few feet. A few students hung out in the lobby and she felt eyes following her as she turned to the stairway. She felt like an upscale restaurant amidst a lot full of food trucks.

Brooke's hallway smelled like stale beer. Music blasted through the door.

"Who is it?"

At least she'd taught the roommate a lesson about safety. "It's Dr. Blake."

"Can I see some ID?" Before Jenna could respond to the snide remark, the door swung open. "What do you want? I'm heading home for the MLKing long weekend." She scratched Bijou behind his ears.

"Do you know where Brooke kept her camera?"

"I haven't seen it lying around. Check her drawers."

Jenna felt strange going through Brooke's things, but if she found the camera, she'd assume Brooke had gone on an early morning photo shoot in the woods. "Is this her dresser?"

"Yeah."

She pawed through the nightshirts and sweatpants but didn't find a camera. She proceeded to check the other drawers. "I don't see one. Where else might she have stashed it?"

"I'm not her mother, how should I know? Try

under the bed."

Jenna stuck her hand under the bed and grabbed something that crackled when she squeezed it. A single bag of Nacho Cheese Doritos. *At least the bag is closed.* She envisioned reaching into a sea of orange crumbs and considered herself lucky. She pulled out a box of half-eaten chocolate-peanut butter girl scout cookies—Tag-a-longs. Last time she'd bought a box she demolished it in one sitting. *Who leaves half a sleeve?* She swore the joke about girl scout cookies containing crack just might be true. Definitely addictive.

"Did you find what you need? My parents are expecting me for dinner."

She heard her back crack when she wriggled out from under the bed and pulled herself upright, bracing against the bed. "No camera."

She felt a lump under the comforter and pulled it back. "Hey, is this Brooke's purse?"

"Guess so."

"Would she have gone out and left it here?"

"She hardly ever carried it on campus. She kept her university ID card in a pocket on her phone. No one carries around a purse anymore."

"I don't see a camera" She unzipped the purse. "And her car keys are in here. She must not have planned on going far." *The photography theory makes sense.*

"Guess not. Anything else? I'd like to get on the road and beat the Friday traffic heading out of town."

"No, that's it. Here's my card in case you hear from her."

"Do you think something's happened to her?"

Probably. Otherwise, why has she disappeared

without a word to anyone? "I hope not. Her parents are putting together a search party tonight and I know they're posting flyers."

Chapter 8

Once back at home, she made herself a cup of coffee in the Keurig and tried calling Max once more. When he didn't pick up, she tore into a bag of M&M's from the pantry and guzzled them down in record time.

"Bijou, if you see me trying to call Max, remind me not to, okay?" She gave him a dog treat from the jar on the kitchen counter. *I should check the area hospitals. Why didn't we think to do that already?* She called three different hospitals. Brooke wasn't in any of them. *Is that good news or bad news?*

Her heart felt like a belt had tightened around it. One more call had to be made. Jenna's fingers shook while dialing the number for the morgue. Sweat beaded on her forehead, though the house was at its usual arctic temperature. *Hold? Are you kidding?* Didn't they know better than to play pop songs over the phone in a morgue? The music stopped. Before she could request the information, she was again put on hold.

"Hello? Yes, I'm still here." She'd lied and said she was looking for her daughter. "Are you sure? No one fitting my daughter's description any time this past week?" Jenna unclenched her fists.

Bijou barked at the door that led from the kitchen to the garage. Rarely did she go into the garage. When she had a few dollars to spare, she'd replace the broken automatic door opener and no longer have to wipe snow off the windshield or freeze while carrying in groceries. Giles had promised to fix it, along with the doorbell, the leak in the guestroom shower, and the ripped screen on the patio door.

She smiled. "Who am I kidding, Bijou? Even if he were alive, these things wouldn't be fixed." Giles was a master procrastinator. Tears streamed down her cheeks like a sudden downpour on a sunny day. In the beginning, she imagined the grieving process would mean graduating from one phase to the next. Instead, she bounced around from sadness to anger to denial. *I hate him for what he did...I never got closure...they never found the body.*

Her phone rang, jarring her into the present. *Maybe it's Max.*

"Jenna, it's Hayley. Do you want us to pick you up on the way to the search party tonight?"

"Um, that would be great."

"Are you okay? You sound like you've been crying."

"I'm okay."

"Dress warmly. It's supposed to get below freezing tonight."

"Thanks. Text me when you're getting close and I'll be outside."

She was grateful to have taught in the classroom next to Hayley when they were both new to the profession. Hayley only stayed in the classroom for a short time before moving on to the university position. She'd gotten Jenna the job at Monk Haven after the shooting.

She glanced toward the door and then back to the freezer. She'd have to go through Giles' things if she had hopes of ever parking in the garage. *I'll go through that box before dinner.*

Bijou followed her into the garage, sniffing at everything in this unchartered territory. Tools hung from a peg board against one wall. Giles' bike, swim noodles, and a few folding lawn chairs leaned against it. Jenna opened the cardboard box, giving herself a paper cut in the process. She took out a plastic drawer divider with staples, paperclips, and rubber bands neatly in place and thought about the last time Giles closed the drawer. She could feel the warmth of his strong hands as if he were there beside her.

She lifted out a large trophy and remembered the night the school won it at the marching band competition. Then she picked up a manila envelope full of photos from concerts, the school holiday party, football games...

She pulled out a sweatshirt from Oxford University. Giles didn't go to Oxford, but with his British accent, he amused himself by allowing people to assume he did. She snuggled her face in it. There was a bag of toiletries in the bottom of the box—deodorant, a toothbrush, toothpaste, hair gel...She had an identical stash in her desk drawer in her office.

Bijou barked at the garage door leading to the outside.

"What do you hear, boy?" She listened and thought she heard a car pulling away. *No way Hayley and Oliver are here yet.* Probably her imagination. She stood on her toes and looked out the garage window. *No one's here, relax.* She repacked the box, taking the sweatshirt inside with her. If she washed it, she could wear it, but she wouldn't dare throw it in the washing machine. It smelled like Giles, even after all these months. The Giles she fell in love with.

Inside, she made herself a peanut butter sandwich. Afterward, she pulled on jeans over thermal underwear, a heavy flannel shirt, and thick socks. When Hayley texted, she scooped up Bijou and met them in her driveway.

Cars lined the street leading to the university. Jenna worried about her agoraphobia making an appearance, but if she stayed sandwiched between others, she assumed she'd be okay.

"Quite a turnout," said Hayley. "I even saw Delores when I was getting out of the car. And there's Kyle and Ross."

Kyle, dressed in a wool coat with earmuffs and a plaid scarf, handed them flashlights. "Brooke's parents mapped out grids of the area. We're about to start looking." He petted Bijou. "And this little bloodhound wanna-be will be a huge asset."

"Love her doggie jacket," said Ross. "And she looks cute with the bow."

"It's a he," said Jenna. She reached down and yanked off the bow, sticking it in her pocket.

Flood lights illuminated the search area. They made their way to the white canopy and signed their names on a roster. The sun had gone down and it was noticeably chillier. Brooke's parents had copied a series of grid maps, which they laid out on a folding table. Oliver sifted through as if the particular area mattered and eventually picked one up. An assortment of whistles on lanyards were strewn across the table.

Oliver said, "Jenna can come with us. I've got GPS on my Apple watch. Come on."

"What if someone finds her and she's dead? Can you imagine how awful her parents will feel?" said Hayley.

"I don't mean to sound blunt, but at least they'd have a body to bury." Jenna scanned the ground with her flashlight. "It's doubtful anyone could survive four nights out here." She shined her light downward to the road below the edge of the woods, where a mute police jeep crawled along with its lights flashing.

"The sooner they find a body," Oliver said, "the sooner the police can start their manhunt."

"If she's dead, I hope they catch the son of a bitch." Her muscles tensed, thinking about the school shooter escaping. To this day, he hadn't been caught and was probably living on a beach in the Caribbean.

Deep in the woods, Oliver kept a close eye on his GPS, directing them at every turn. "Aren't those her parents wandering around?"

"Yes," said Jenna. "I guess after they got everyone started, they couldn't help but join in the search. I mean, their daughter might be out there." They nearly collided with them.

Brooke's mother hugged Jenna. "Thank you. With this huge turnout, I know we'll find our baby."

Jenna thought so too, but assumed it'd be a body if they found anyone in these woods tonight. "We'll do our best."

Brooke's parents turned down one path; Oliver directed his crew down another. A man in an orange vest carrying a walkie-talkie passed by. They'd passed a woman in an identical vest earlier. Jenna assumed they were trained in search and rescue, or they'd simply stepped up to the part.

Hayley looked at the map over Oliver's shoulder. "Shouldn't we turn left here, according to our map?"

"No. We turn right. Besides, everyone else seems to be headed in that direction. Let's follow my GPS." She trudged along, blindly following Oliver through the scratchy trees, over patches of dirty snow.

Jenna's feet ached, even with the cushioning from her thick socks. Her boots weren't designed for hiking miles through the woods and she lagged slightly behind her friends, aiming the flashlight back and forth in a rhythmic pattern. She was about ready to suggest turning back when something caught her eye.

Holding the flashlight steady, she walked toward it. A rock the size of a large grapefruit blocked her path. She bent down for a closer look. *Blood? What is a bloody rock doing in the middle of the path? It can't be. Is it the murder weapon? Smack in the middle of the trail and no one found this?* Dizziness overcame her. Fighting to steady herself she, blew her whistle. "Over here. I found something." Bijou barked.

Haley sprinted over. "What did you find?"

"I hope I'm wrong, but is this blood?"

Oliver and Hayley both aimed their lights at the rock. Hayley said, "We must have walked right by it and didn't notice."

Oliver inspected it closely. "It looks like blood. Where did you find it, Jenna?"

She pointed to the spot. "Right there."

"Let's put it back where it was. The police will want to see exactly where you found it."

"Leave it here? You're sure?" Part of her didn't want Detective Russo knowing it was she who found the murder weapon. He already treated her like a suspect.

"Yeah." He snapped a picture with his phone. "Come on, we may be close to finding something. Jenna, check over by the ravine. Hayley and I will search behind those trees." They picked up the pace.

Jenna felt dizziness wash over her when Bijou barked and tugged on his leash. She took a deep breath and steadied herself. "Bijou, did you find something?" He led Jenna to the edge of a ravine overlooking the road below. "Oh, my God." She yelled, "Come here, quick." Her legs shook as if they were about to collapse.

"What?" said Hayley, rushing back.

"Aim your light. Is that what I think it is?"

"It could be an animal carcass," Hayley said.

"Wearing a parka?" said Jenna. She blew her whistle to signal others in the search party. "We have to go down and look."

"It's too dangerous," said Oliver. "There's a road down there. Better to drive around. I'll notify the paramedics."

"But by the time we go back and get the car...I'm not waiting."

"Good luck getting service," said a man in an orange vest. He mumbled into his walkie-talkie. Something about spotting a body, needing assistance. "I'll go take a look. My car is just around the bend." He headed away from the ravine.

"I'm going," said Jenna. Hayley and Oliver tried to stop her. She handed the end of Bijou's leash to Hayley.

The man in the orange vest whipped around. "Hey, it's too dangerous to maneuver in the dark. Come with me to the car." When Jenna ignored him, he followed her on foot. She heard him mumble "over and out" into the walkie-talkie.

Oliver said, "It's too steep. If you slip, you'll make twice the work for everyone."

Jenna ignored them. She scooted sideways as the path narrowed. She took a misstep and almost fell, but managed to grab onto a tree limb. Oliver and Hayley followed her but couldn't quite catch up.

"We told you it was dangerous," said Oliver.

"Too late to turn back now." Regaining her balance, Jenna inched forward. Her toes felt numb while her arches continued to ache.

Jenna was thankful to hit level ground and brushed the bits of dead leaves off her jacket. She could no longer see the road from this level, hidden by a tangle of branches and snow-covered pine needles. The man in the orange vest was right behind her and pulled a flyer out of his pocket. He ran over to the body. "It's her."

"Is she…dead?" asked Jenna. She already knew the answer.

The man bent down and felt for a pulse, then nodded. "Looks like she's been here a while."

Hayley and Oliver emerged from the brush. Hayley, gasping for air, pulled out her phone. "I've got service."

From behind the trees, Delores emerged. "I already went for help. What took you so long?"

What's she doing here? How did she happen to be down here when the search party concentrated on the woods above?

Having heard the whistle and being in better shape than most of the searchers, Kyle and Ross scooted down the path. Sometime later, Brooke's parents pushed through the brush, coming from the adjacent road. Kyle ran over, blocking the view of the body. He put his arm around Brooke's mother. "Be prepared. It may not be good news."

They stomped through the brush and worked through the tangle of bare branches concealing the body.

Brooke's mother screamed and ran to her daughter's side. "My baby! My poor baby."

Her husband bent down beside her and listened for breathing. He sobbed into his wife's shoulder. "She's dead. She must have lost her footing."

Brooke's mother teetered and grabbed onto her husband's arm. "She must have been taking a picture for her class. I'm going to be sick."

Jenna knew it wasn't an accident. The parents hadn't seen the bloody rock. Besides, if Brooke were in the process of taking a picture, where was the camera?

Jenna heard a siren. Minutes later, Detective Russo appeared. "Back away from the scene." He briefly examined the body, then called for backup. The man in the orange vest was already on the walkie-talkie, calling for an ambulance.

Kyle took a branch and drew a line around the area. Hayley and Oliver shooed people back. Bits of sleet fell from the sky.

Jenna said, "Detective Russo, I have important information." Her voice trembled both from the cold and from the sight of Brooke's frozen, lifeless body.

"I'm a little busy, Miss Blake."

She blurted out, "I found a bloody rock up there." She pointed. By this time, Oliver and Hayley were beside her.

Oliver said, "I've got GPS. I can show you exactly where it is."

Detective Russo stopped. "You found a bloody rock? You, her friend, noted the coordinates. Quite the coincidence."

"This is a search party. We were searching."

"Show me." He motioned to two officers who had followed him into the woods. "Take care of this."

The officers taped off the area while Jenna and her friends weeded through the brush to the road and got into the detective's car. A helicopter whirred in the distance. At the top of the ravine, Jenna retraced her steps. She couldn't find it. Had she imagined it?

Oliver said, "Here's the rock. Come here. We didn't want to get prints on it."

Detective Russo pulled on a pair of blue latex gloves, bent down, and examined it. He looked up at Jenna.

"How is it with fifty or so people searching, you are the one to have found the murder weapon?"

"We followed the grid pattern we were told to follow. Oliver has the map. He led the way."

"It was pure chance?"

"What else would it be? You can't seriously think I had anything to do with this?"

"Did you encourage or even suggest the idea of a search party to the parents?"

"I don't believe what I'm hearing you imply."

"Yes or no?"

"It was their idea."

"And you encouraged them?"

"I didn't discourage them. You didn't want to help them."

"I'll need you to come to the station with me."

"Why?"

"To make an official report. You found the body, and apparently the murder weapon as well."

Hayley and Oliver overheard. "Excuse me," Oliver said, "but can't it wait until morning?"

"No. The sooner the better before the details fade."

"I don't have my car," Jenna said.

"I'll have an officer take you home afterward."

"No, we'll drive you," said Oliver.

"Good. We need statements from everyone who was there tonight, anyway."

They hiked back to where Oliver had parked. Once inside his car, Jenna said, "Am I in trouble? He's acting like I killed Brooke."

"He's eating crow for not taking the missing person's report seriously. He's trying to pin it on someone. He has no basis to charge you."

Hayley said, "Maybe we should call our lawyer, just in case."

"Now you're scaring me. You think I need a lawyer?" She tried calling Max. He was once on the police force and would know whether or not she was in trouble. No answer. Frustrated, she threw the phone into her purse.

Oliver pulled in front of the police station a short while later. The area was deserted this time of night, especially since the roads were getting icy. They went through the front where Detective Russo was waiting.

"I'll take your statement first, and afterward your wife's. Ms. Blake can wait in the conference room. The officer will show you where it is."

She followed the detective to a windowless room

with a metal table and two metal chairs. *Conference room? Who's he kidding? I've seen enough crime shows.*

"Wait here. Do you want water or coffee?"

So you can get my DNA? "No, I'm fine."

Even with her coat on, Jenna shivered in the stark, gray interrogation room. She hugged Bijou. It seemed like an eternity before the detective strutted through the door holding a manila folder and an evidence bag. She wondered if keeping her waiting was part of his strategy. *I'm not guilty, so why am I scared?*

The metal chair screeched like nails on a chalkboard as Detective Russo took a seat across from her, folding his hands on the table. "Tell me how you knew Brooke."

"I didn't really. She was a student but it's early in the semester and I'd hardly spoken to her."

"Why did you start asking about her and contact her parents if you didn't really even know her?"

"Her friend came to me, concerned. Brooke had missed a few classes, and no one had seen her for a few days. I came to you but you didn't take me seriously." She emphasized 'you'.

"Why did you suspect foul play right away? What made you think she hadn't gone away on her own? She was twenty-one, a legal adult."

"Well, I guess I didn't suspect anything at first, but her friends were concerned, and then I saw her purse and keys in the dorm room. Her car was in the lot. If she wanted to get away, she'd have taken her car, right?"

"You went to her dorm room?"

"To see if her camera was there. She'd been taking

a photography course and I thought she may have been taking photos when she…when she was in the woods."

"Did you find a camera?"

"No."

Detective Russo shook his head while jotting down notes. Jenna heard him mumble 'unbelievable' under his breath. He slapped the notebook shut and leaned back in the metal chair, crossing his arms. "Let's talk about Isabel Hernandez."

"What about her? I never met her."

"Do you know how Isabel Hernandez was killed?"

"No. The news hasn't given out many details."

The detective stood up and walked around the table holding a plastic bag in front of Jenna's face. "This is the scarf we found tied around Isabel's neck. Recognize it?"

Jenna gasped. "It's…it's my scarf."

"It's the scarf the killer used to strangle Isabel—we got back preliminary DNA results. The killer snuck up behind Isabel, looped the scarf over her head, and pulled it tight." He mimed the action as he spoke. "Poor girl must have reached up, tugged for her life trying to release the scarf, all the while choking for air. I'll bet she tried to scream, but of course, she couldn't. Her veins popped. There were little red dots—reticular hemorrhaging, we call it in our line of work. She struggled so hard, her capillaries burst."

The blow-by-blow made Jenna nauseous, but she wasn't about to let detective Russo see it. "Did you match the DNA to the killer?"

"We matched it all right. Matched it to DNA you'd sent to one of those ancestry kits. Matched it to your DNA." He pounded his fist on the metal table. Bijou yipped. The vibrations crawled through Jenna's forearms, up into her body.

"Mine? That's impossible." She felt the room spinning around her, thankful to be seated. Bijou licked her hand.

"You took it to the student union building with you when you went to meet Isabel. Or, perhaps you were wearing it and it was a weapon of convenience." His voice grew louder; his speech cadence quicker.

"Are you crazy? I haven't seen that scarf in years. For all I can remember, I'd given it to Goodwill. And what motive do I have for killing a complete stranger?" She worked to control her breathing. Detective Russo was not going to see her break down.

"Your DNA on the murder weapon that killed the first victim, and now you find a dead student in the woods—just like that." He snapped his fingers. "Brooke had to have seen you the day she was killed. After all, she swiped her ID card in the student union coffee shop right around the time you were supposed to meet Isabel. Perhaps she witnessed you murdering her. When she confronted you, you knew you had to kill her too."

"You're making all this up. I don't have a hint of a motive."

"Oh, we found a connection. And it's a good one."

An angry woman burst through the door. "I'm her lawyer." She turned to Jenna, jaw set, eyes on fire. "Stop talking."

"I didn't call a lawyer."

"Your friends Oliver and Hayley called me." She leaned over the table until her face was close to the detective. "What evidence do you have to hold my client on a murder charge?"

"She's just here for questioning."

Jenna said, "He says they matched my DNA to DNA found on the scarf that strangled Isabel Hernandez."

"Let me see the DNA report." She held out her hand to the detective.

"It's not here."

"Because you don't have it. No way you did a DNA test and searched ancestry databases in this short of a time. You're bluffing."

"It's her scarf. She admitted it." He leaned back in the chair, tipping back on the legs.

"But you have no physical evidence and no motive. Do you have a witness? Someone who saw my client murder Isabel Hernandez?"

"No. Not yet, anyway."

"You can't charge her and you can't keep her. Come on, Dr. Blake."

Detective Russo stood up, scraping the metal chair legs on the floor. Jenna jumped. "You better believe I'm building a case. Your client is guilty, and it's a matter of time before she's arrested."

"Come on. Don't say anything until we're outside." Jenna followed the attorney out of the police station. She spotted Oliver and Hayley waiting in their car for her.

Jenna whispered, "He had DNA that matches mine. How's that possible?"

"He's bluffing. If he did, he'd have arrested you."

"I did use one of those ancestry kits."

"Doesn't mean anything. They use that line all the time now. Is it your scarf?"

"Yes, but I haven't seen it in years."

"Then how are you sure it's yours? Could be an identical or similar scarf. The police can't prove it belongs to you."

"But I admitted it was mine."

"Read my lips. It's not your scarf. You were under duress. You'd just discovered a dead body, after all. He can't hold you to your saying it's yours. Come on. If you need me, call. Without physical evidence or a witness, he doesn't have a leg to stand on."

Jenna knew one thing for sure. She may have misplaced the scarf, but seeing as it was knit by her dead grandmother, she never would have given it away. How on earth did the killer get ahold of it? And without DNA, how did Detective Russo know it belonged to her?

Chapter 9

The glaring red numbers on the clock radio taunted Jenna. She should be sleeping, but the harder she tried, the more elusive sleep became. *Why did I admit the scarf was mine? How did I fall for the DNA bluff—I know they can't get DNA matches by snapping their fingers. It's Saturday. Thankfully, I don't have to work.*

She rolled over on the mushy old mattress. *Is it legal for law enforcement to search those DNA databases, or are they covered by the same privacy laws as medical records?*

Bijou, who'd been sleeping at the foot of the bed, awoke and licked her face to say good morning. He'd made a huge difference in her life, giving her a reason to get out of bed after the shooting and especially after she became a grieving widow. If she'd opted to hide under the covers all day after Giles' death, the dog would have died of starvation.

Where did the detective find the scarf, and how did he know it's mine? Wait. Her grandmother had knitted her a matching hat, and she always wore them together. The last time she saw the set was in the cedar chest in the master bedroom.

"Can we do this, Bijou? I have to pull myself together. I have to find the hat."

She tightened the belt on her flannel robe for extra warmth over the thermal pajamas and slipped her feet into wooly slippers. "Come on, Bijou."

The old-fashioned phone on the nightstand rang. Her heart skipped a beat. It took a moment to connect the sound to the phone and pick up the receiver. "Hello? Hello?" She hadn't realized the landline was active, and certainly hadn't received a single phone call on it until now. "Who is this?" Click. The line went dead.

She and Bijou crept over to the steps. For a moment, she lost her nerve and turned to go back into the living room. *No, I have to see if the hat is still upstairs.*

One step yielded a mournful creak. She jumped, squeezing Bijou to her heart. Bijou yipped. "Sorry, buddy. I knew that stair squeaks. I should have stepped over it." *I'm okay. I'm breathing fine. I'm calm.*

She took it slowly until reaching farther up the staircase than she'd been since Giles died. Her eyes floated up, down, up again. With her left hand anchored on the wall and Bijou over her heart, she reached the landing.

She stood facing the wooden door. The previous owners had installed a padlock, which they never used. After Giles died, she locked it. Locked away the memories. Reaching into the vase on the hall table, the key clinked against the glass as she retrieved it. *Right where I left it.*

Trembling, she lost her grip on the key while trying to insert it. The walls pulsated, and the floor felt like the earthquake simulator at the Museum of Science.

I just can't. Rubbing her face in Bijou's fur, she took a few deep breaths. *Floor, key, door. Breathe in, breathe out.* Her eyes closed. *I can't do this.* She turned around and started down the staircase. Bijou barked, then licked Jenna's face as if to encourage her not to give up.

"Bijou, I can't. It's too painful to think about." He licked her face again. The stakes were high. If she couldn't explain why her scarf had been used to murder Isabel, she'd be the one behind a locked door. Locked cell was more accurate. She shuddered at the thought of an open toilet and a bed lumpier than the one in the guest room.

She turned around. *I'm going to do this.* She marched back up the steps, the key still in hand. The lock didn't turn at first. She jiggled it back and forth until it yielded.

The sticky wooden door creaked open with a slight push, unleashing musty air seizing its freedom. The early morning sun peeked through the grimy window. She faced the thrift store bed covered with a yellow and blue quilt they'd received as a wedding present and smiled at the memory. Her eyes fell to the antique chest at the foot of the bed.

Pushing up the lid, the scent of cedar filled the room. Gently, she lifted out her frayed baby blanket, a high school track t-shirt, and her scratchy netted ballet tutu. The object in question came to view. Loose knit, topped with a pom-pom…she held up the matching hat her grandmother had made.

Brushing it against her cheek, something scratched her face through the wool. *Of course! The hand-sewn nametag. To Jenna, love Grandma Walensky. That's how the detective knew it was mine. Any detective worth his salt could easily have determined Walensky was my maiden name.*

At that moment, a car screeched outside. She scrambled to the window in time to see a dark sedan pull away. It looked like the one she thought had followed her previously. When she tugged at the window, it lifted easily in spite of its inactivity. Realizing it had been unlocked, panic sizzled through her like lightning. Her own cowardice may have compromised her safety. All those months she lived with her parents, this place sat empty. Anyone could have taken a ladder, crawled in the window, and stolen everything. Luckily, she'd left nothing of value. Nothing of monetary value, anyway. And there was the padlock. It came in handy after all, confining the intruder to the bedroom.

On the way out of the room, she stared at the ruffled pillow on Giles' side of the bed, shuddered, and closed the door behind her.

Going down the steps was easier than going up. She hoped she'd be able to sleep in her own bed soon—maybe even tonight. Every muscle ached after sleeping downstairs in the guestroom all these weeks.

The doorbell rang. Jenna startled. The doorbell? Wait. The doorbell didn't work. That's why visitors knocked with the brass knocker. It hadn't worked forever. She crept to the door, pulling her robe tighter. She closed one eye, squinted through the peephole, and let out the breath she'd been holding.

She opened the door. "Max? Where have you been?" Her words sounded accusatory, though she hadn't meant them to.

He took a step back. "Whoa. I'm sorry. I had something I had to do. Should I have asked your permission first?"

Fair enough. "I tried calling and texting. I left messages. We found Brooke's body in the woods last night."

"Really?"

"Brooke's parents organized a search party. I found a bloody rock. Then I spotted her body in a ravine."

"Slow down. *You* found Brooke's body? Your missing student?"

"Yes."

"Damn it. Another dead girl. I wish I'd been there with you."

"Yeah, me too. They think *I* did it. Detective Russo dragged me down to the police station after I found the body." She realized she had known Max not even a week and yet he felt like an old friend. He owed her nothing.

"Hang on. You found Brooke's body and the detective thinks you killed her?"

"What is it with him? It's like he decided I was guilty the first time he saw me."

"You look like his ex-wife. And she was also a college professor."

"What?"

"Yeah. She cheated on him, got pregnant with another guy's kid, and took off. But first, she tried to scam him into thinking the baby was his so he'd have to pay child support."

"Sounds like a reality show. *The Real Wives of Monk Haven Cops.* Guess that's somewhat of an explanation as to why he seems to hate me."

"Rewind to where you found Brooke's body and he thinks you killed her."

"Yeah. Detective Russo thinks I killed Brooke *and*

Isabel. He made up a story about having my DNA on the murder weapon. My scarf was used to strangle Isabel and the lawyer said not to admit it."

"Whoa. A lawyer?"

"Someone Oliver knows."

"And you said *your* scarf killed her? How did your scarf…Are you sure?"

"It's mine. My grandmother made it. I have no idea how it wound up around Isabel's neck. I checked upstairs and the matching hat is in the cedar chest."

"Maybe you dropped it."

"I haven't worn it in ages and when I did, I always paired it with the matching hat. The hat is in my cedar chest in my room." Her face pleaded for an answer.

"Why are you looking at me like that? You think I have the answer?"

"You're a private investigator, aren't you?" As soon as those words left her mouth, she realized how ridiculous they sounded. "I'm sorry. I didn't get much sleep last night. Besides, it may be my fault. The window in the master bedroom was unlocked. Anyone capable of climbing a ladder could have snuck in and stolen it."

"Someone stole your grandmother's hand-knit scarf to frame you?"

It sounded stupid when she said it out loud. "I told you I didn't get much sleep."

"Have you had breakfast?"

"Not yet. I'd offer to make you something but the cupboards are bare."

"I wasn't looking for you to make breakfast. Santiago Salas, Isabel's fiancé, wants me to meet him at the Monk Haven Café. You're welcome to join us."

"We've already met. He wouldn't mind?"

"Isabel wanted to tell you something right before she was murdered. You might be the key to finding her killer."

"I'm sure it's awful having your fiancée murdered without a clue as to motive." *Kind of like having your husband commit suicide two years after an inciting event you thought he'd made peace with.*

"Get dressed and we'll go over."

She heard the phone ringing in the guestroom. She must have left the door open.

"Is that a phone? Are you going to get it?"

She was reluctant, but the ringing persisted. She ran over to the phone. "Hello? Hello? Who is this? You have to stop calling me." She slammed down the phone.

"What was that about?"

"I'm getting prank phone calls. Twice this morning."

"Do they say anything?"

"No. I heard breathing earlier this morning. I didn't even know we had a landline."

"You don't need a landline. Cancel it. And for now—" He pulled the phone out of the phone jack. "—problem solved."

"I feel like I'm being watched or targeted. I'll bet someone snuck into my house through the upstairs window. In fact, I don't remember plugging a phone into the guestroom jack before Giles died."

"Throw on some clothes and I'll take a look."

Jenna changed into a pair of jeans and a new sweater. With an unexpected urge toward vanity, she took a moment to wash her face and put on lipstick before going back out.

"Max?" She peeked out the front door.

"I'm out back. Come over here."

She walked around back.

He rubbed his hand on the outside wall. "When was the exterior painted?"

"That's one thing Giles managed to do before he…it was painted a little over a year ago."

"See these black marks going up the side?"

She squinted and had to practically touch her nose to the wood before she saw them. "Yes, I guess so."

"I think someone used a ladder to get to the window. Is that the master bedroom up there?"

"Yes, it is."

"Do you own a ladder?"

"There's one in the garden shed."

"Show me." He followed Jenna to the edge of the lot where a rusty storage shed was partly open. A padlock hung open on the door.

"The lock! We kept the shed locked. Giles worried neighborhood kids might go in to play or steal something. He always locked it."

"You're not crazy. Something is going on and you need to be careful."

"Can you check one more thing?"

"Shoot."

She still cringed at the word. "The doorbell never worked. Even the real estate agent pointed it out when we looked at the place."

"Want me to see if I can fix it?"

"Oh no, I wasn't hinting. Today it worked. You rang the bell. I don't know how it's possible."

"Let's take a look." He followed her around the front and pressed the button. "Works fine now." He ran his finger around it and looked underneath.

She said, "It looks new, doesn't it? See, the white plastic is clean as snow while the door itself is in need of pressure cleaning."

"You're right."

"The retired couple two houses over kept an eye on the place while I was staying at my parents."

"There you go. I passed an elderly man on the road on the way here. Speaking of going, we're going to be late. Come on."

She got into the dark blue, four-door Honda Accord in the driveway.

Chapter 10

Saturday brunch at the Monk Haven Café meant a long wait for a table, but Santiago Salas had already been seated and motioned them over. Max started to introduce Jenna.

"We've met. Glad you could join us, Dr. Blake."

"Jenna. I've been trying to figure out why Isabel left me that note. I have nothing new since the last time we spoke. I'm still as puzzled as you are." The waitress offered coffee and Jenna held up her mug.

His eyes were moist. "I'm in the process of going through Isabel's things." He pulled a pink diary from his satchel. "I found this on Isabel's nightstand."

Max took it and flipped through the pages. "It's in Spanish."

"Spanish was her native language, though she spoke flawless English."

Jenna said, "Can you translate the parts you think may be relevant?"

"Yes, I marked them. Here she says: '*I can't tell. Too embarrassed. Is it my imagination?*'"

"What's that mean?" asked Jenna.

"I have no clue." He flipped through the diary. "'*He touched me through my shirt. I don't know if he meant to. It was my fault. The neckline was too low.*'"

"Does it give any clues as to who she's talking about or where it happened?" Max asked.

"She says something about being cornered in the small room. He tried to kiss her. She says she didn't stop him."

"So it could have been a coworker." Max sipped his coffee.

The waitress brought food to the table but no one seemed to notice.

"Is there a possible connection to the campus? Perhaps he was a student at Monk Haven University, or he worked there and somehow connected to Brooke as well."

Santiago said, "Isabel didn't work in an office. She didn't have any co-workers."

"How would she have met this boy?" After another sip, Max placed the coffee cup on the table.

Jenna thought of a dozen ways before Max answered. Santiago seemed a little naïve given his age.

"They could have met at the gym or a coffee shop. Even online."

"I still don't understand why she wanted to meet with you on the campus grounds," Santiago said.

"I haven't a clue. I don't have any male students—just my TA, Kyle, but trust me, it wasn't him chasing after Isabel or any other female."

Max leaned forward. "Did she ever work on campus?"

"No. She was a freelance translator. She worked out of her apartment."

Max said, "Do you have a list of clients? If she was doing freelance work, perhaps some of her clients wanted to avoid working with legitimate agencies."

"Legitimate agencies? Are you insulting my fiancé?"

"No, I swear I didn't mean for it to sound that way. I'm saying, if someone involved in less than legal business needed translations done, he might opt for a freelancer rather than going through a translation firm."

"That's true. Isabel shared as much."

Jenna pulled the edges off her toast. "Like Max said, can we get a list of clients?"

"I have Isabel's ledger right here. She kept a record of hours for billing purposes, and there's a client contact list in front."

Max took the ledger and flipped through it. "Looks like she built a lucrative business."

"She was very good. Got a lot of word-of-mouth referrals. Oh, and I found a scrap of paper with a phone number. It was in her purse. I tried calling it but it was out of service. Here."

"I can try to trace the number," said Max. "Anything else you can tell us? Anyone who may have wanted to hurt Isabel?"

"There was an ex-boyfriend, before she met me. She said he called and sent her gifts constantly, but after we got engaged, I think he gave up."

"Do you have a name?"

"Ronald something."

"It's worth looking into. See if you can come up with a last name. Maybe she has an old card or letter from him."

"I don't think she would have saved it but I'll check."

"We'll do whatever we can to put the pieces together and find Isabel's killer." Otherwise, she'd remain Detective Russo's number one suspect.

Santiago picked up the check. "Thank you, both.

I'll look for Ronald's last name and go through more of Isabel's things."

After Santiago left, Max said, "Do you have plans this afternoon?"

"Only a nap. Why?"

"I need to relax. Want to come with me to my favorite spot?"

"Where's that?"

"You'll see. Come on."

"I don't know. I think I need to catch up on my sleep. Besides, I have a pile of laundry overflowing onto the floor."

"You can do it later. Please. I don't want to be alone right now."

"Why don't you want to be alone?"

"I…I can't talk about it. Not yet."

Normally, she wouldn't consent to accompany a new acquaintance to an unknown location, but her gut dictated she could trust him. "Okay. For a little while." Jenna followed him into his car, peppering him for information. "Is it outdoors or indoors? It isn't a shopping mall, is it? I don't do well in open spaces."

"You'll see." He drove away from the town, taking a mountain road toward a well-known ski resort.

Butterflies fluttered in her stomach. "I don't know how to ski."

"Me neither." He continued until he came to a gravel path blocked with a chain.

They hadn't passed a single car since turning onto the mountain road, though it wasn't exactly cause for alarm. *Who comes up here in the middle of winter?* "It says it's closed."

He hopped out of the car and unhinged the chain,

then hopped back in. The scene reminded her of a Ted Bundy documentary she'd watched recently and a chill crept up her spine. Had her gut been wrong to consent to this?

"Not anymore." He continued on the gravel road, tires crunching over the gravel and dirt. She was glad her seat belt was fastened as they rolled over significant pieces of rock. His Honda handled the off-road driving like a pro. He pulled into a clearing. "We're here." He walked around and opened her door for her.

Jenna relaxed as she drank in the aroma of pines while her eyes surveyed the area. Wooden picnic tables, brick barbecue pits, and mesh trash cans. *I think this is where Hayley and Oliver go to picnic in the summer. She said something about a waterfall.* They'd passed a sign for a waterfall earlier on.

In the warmer months, she imagined it buzzing with people, but in this cold, it was as barren as Antarctica—minus the penguins. *No wonder the road was closed.* The sky was vivid blue today and the sun, warm and visible, yet it was still the dead of winter.

Max rotated slowly, arms reaching outward, face to the sun. "I love it up here. Most of the winter the road is inaccessible but not today."

He grabbed a blanket from his trunk. "Come on, just down the path." His gait was just short of a skip.

This is a little creepy. What am I doing here? Unless she attacked him and grabbed his keys, she was pretty much stuck. *And the blanket? If he wanted to, he could smother me, roll me up in it, and bury me in the woods.* She slapped herself. *You are watching too many true-crime shows.*

"Jenna, come on. You have to see the view."

Putting her imagination to rest, she and Bijou caught up to him. "This is one of my favorite places in the world. I come here to think."

She hung onto his arm, not to be romantic but to prevent a panic attack being in the open clearing. She felt her pulse rate quickening and tried to slow it down with a deep breath. Surprisingly, it worked. She looked at a panoramic view from the top of the mountain. Pine trees, snow-topped mountain peaks, rooftops of cabins in the valley below... "It's so peaceful." She meant it.

"Hard to imagine the other side of this mountain is full of skiers. There's a ski lodge but it's overpriced and hard to get a reservation. I prefer bringing a picnic. If we hadn't just eaten, I might have suggested giving it a try."

"It is gorgeous, but a little cold for a picnic, don't you think?" Her teeth chattered.

"Nah. And not too cold to enjoy the view. I keep this thermal blanket in my trunk for emergencies, but it will do nicely for our afternoon outing. Come on."

She glanced into the trunk. No duct tape, no clear sheeting. Nerves relaxed.

Behind a clump of trees, an old-fashioned wooden swing overlooked the valley. He motioned for her to sit next to him. Then he spread the blanket over their laps. *Is he coming on to me? It's been so long, maybe I missed the signs.*

"Bijou seems warm enough. You okay?"

She relaxed into the gentle motion of the swing. "I'm more than okay. I needed a change of scenery."

"I used to come hiking up here with my daughter. After the hit and run, it was the only place I found peace. If I'd found it sooner, maybe my life wouldn't have gone so horribly off the rails."

"Off the rails? We all go a little off the rails when we lose someone we love. I can attest to that."

"It was bad. I started drinking. My temper got out of control, and I was kicked off the force. Can you top that?"

"I had a full-blown panic attack in the middle of teaching a class and was forced to take medical leave and live with my parents for months."

"But did you get thrown in jail for beating up some guy at a bar?"

"No. You win."

A while later, Jenna said, "What was her name?"

"Her name?"

"Your daughter."

"Taylor."

"Taylor. Pretty name."

"It's her mother's maiden name."

"This had to be awful for her mother, too." She knew the death of a child broke up many couples and wondered if that's what happened.

"She and I were divorced long before Taylor's murder. She lives out in California. We don't speak."

"I'm sorry."

"Like I said, the divorce had nothing to do with Taylor."

They swung back and forth, lulled into relaxation by the rhythmic motion. Jenna took in the view and relished the warm sunshine on her face. Bijou had fallen asleep. Moments of blissful peace.

Max's voice crashed the silence. He sounded as if he'd swallowed venom. "I'm going to find the bastard who ran her over. When I do, he'll wish he'd been run over by a car." He pounded one fist into his palm. His veins popped out of his forehead. She hadn't seen this side of him previously.

"Um, have you made any headway finding him?"

"Not yet." He gathered the blanket and stood up. "Let's go."

Chapter 11

The rest of the weekend flew by in a whir of laundry, dishes, and catching up on schoolwork. Before she knew it, Friday afternoon bled into Monday morning. Delores was the first face Jenna saw when she got to campus. She wanted to confront her about the cactus but on the other hand, not mentioning it would get under her skin more than any words she could say. It was too late to pretend she hadn't seen her.

"Jenna, how was your weekend?"

For an older woman, Delores was in good shape. Jenna didn't doubt her ability to climb up a ladder to a second-story window, motivated by visions of knocking her out of the running for the tenure track position. Jenna had to quit once before over emotional issues. Easy target.

Not this time.

She willed her mouth into a smile. "Great. Yours?"

"Spent it working. I'm editing a paper I'm submitting to *Campus Educator*. We both know how the university loves it when faculty members publish in peer-reviewed publications. Have you published anything recently?"

"The article I'm working on now will change the face of education. You'll see. I'm not supposed to talk about it. Editor's orders. Now, excuse me. I have work to do." *I wish I had a camera to capture her face right now.* She walked into her office. Kyle was sitting at the desk—rather on her desk.

"I'm glad you're finally here. I couldn't wait to tell you about my idea for a research topic." He leaned back, taking in the whole picture. "You look like the cat who just swallowed a canary. What's going on?"

"I just had a little fun watching Delores squirm. You'd have loved it."

"Are you all right after finding Brooke the other night? I heard Detective McDreamboat questioning you like you were a suspect or something."

"I had to go down to the station. Even have a lawyer now."

"No way."

She regretted telling Kyle the moment the words left her lips. "I don't want that made public."

Kyle mimed zipping his lips. "Your secret is safe with me."

Hayley knocked as she came into Jenna's office. "Sorry I'm late."

Kyle said, "How did the blood test go?"

"Keep your voice down. I told you I don't want anyone to know."

"But for sure you told Jenna."

"I thought I was the only one around here who knew," Jenna said.

"Kyle figured it out and can't keep his mouth shut." Hayley set her bag down on the chair.

"Not nice. I'm here to support you. You'll be a great mom."

Hayley shook her head. "Are you happy with the lawyer we called? If not, we can find you someone else. Oliver has contacts." She looked at Kyle, then Jenna.

"I'm sure he knows all about it."

"He nailed it before I took off my jacket."

"Delores was one of the first people at the bottom of the ravine Friday night," Kyle said.

Hayley said, "I know she's awful, but a murderer?"

"If she had it in her, she'd have strangled *me* with the scarf, not Isabel," said Jenna.

Kyle jumped off the desk. "She was strangled with a scarf?"

"My scarf."

"Oh, girl, the plot thickens. I think someone's framing you big time, and I may have something to help us."

"Help *us*?"

"Ross and I found something after you spotted Brooke's body and everyone raced down the hill. I know we should have turned it over to the police…"

"Spill it," said Hayley.

"We found a camera. I'm sure it belonged to Brooke."

Jenna grabbed his arm. "So she *was* taking photos for her photography class. You kept it? Why didn't you give it to the police?"

"I don't know. We were going to give it over, but when we heard McDreamboat roughing you up verbally, we thought we'd hang on to it. Though being manhandled by that Italian stallion wouldn't be so terrible, come to think of it."

"Kyle, stay on point."

"Anyhow, Ross and I have a theory. We think Brooke saw something out in the woods and that's why she was pushed into the ravine. We have to get the film developed."

Hayley said, "You're an idiot. Withholding evidence will land you in jail. Don't you ever think before you act?"

"We were just trying to help."

"Now that you told us, we can get in trouble, too." Hayley huffed. "You're unbelievable."

"Where's the camera?" Jenna asked. "I have a friend who is a private investigator. He's working for Santiago Salas."

"Santiago who?"

"Isabel's fiancé."

"What if the fiancé murdered her?" Hayley said. "I mean, what better way to cover your tracks than to hire an investigator to 'find the killer.' I saw it in a movie once."

"I don't think so. He seems genuine."

"Does he have an alibi?"

"I didn't ask."

Kyle cleared his throat. "Do you want to see the camera?"

"You brought it here? To campus?" *Where was my head when I chose him for the assistantship? He's nuts.*

"I was going to show it to you." He opened the closet and pulled out a plastic bag. "See?"

Jenna examined it. "The lens looks like a kaleidoscope."

"And the neck strap is torn," added Hayley. "Like someone ripped it off her neck. You should bring it to the police."

Jenna said, "Put it back for now. Class starts in ten minutes." Once again, she wasn't in the mood to teach. She'd have to keep her head clear and focus on the job or she'd be in trouble. Should she trust the police?

They'd find it quite the coincidence that she knew anything about the camera. Even if Kyle turned it in, they knew he was her assistant and would be suspicious.

"You can get things started." She needed time to think, and lagged behind him on the way.

While Kyle started the class, she texted Max. He'd already tried tracing the number on the paper Santiago gave him and determined it was a burner phone. Dead end. He was in the process of searching for 'Ronald,' Isabel's old boyfriend. Her student, Sadie, tapped her on the shoulder.

"Dr. Blake, have the police found Brooke's killer yet?" Her voice cracked as she wiped a tear.

"Not yet, but they will. You didn't have to come to class today. I know you and Brooke were friends. I'd have excused the absence."

"A few of us are going to put up a make-shift memorial where she was found."

"The police have it blocked off. It's a crime scene."

"Then we'll get as close as we can." Jenna's eyes fell on the bouquet of wildflowers on the floor next to Sadie's backpack while the student spoke. "She had her whole life ahead of her."

"I know. Life just isn't fair sometimes."

Kyle motioned for Sadie to come back to her group.

"You'll make sure they find the person who did this, won't you?"

Now she had to save her own skin in addition to wanting the police to catch the bastard who killed an innocent young lady. "I'll keep on the police. Don't worry."

Max texted back. —See you tonight at the grief group.—

She'd take the camera and give it to him tonight. Kyle was way too impulsive for his own good. He had messed up big time by stealing evidence. *Can't turn back the clock. I hope something on that camera makes it worth the risk he's taking. Then again, what risk? This is going to fall back on me.*

Jenna took over the second half of the class, then returned to her office. She got through some paperwork and caught up on email, then took a break and knocked on Hayley's door.

"Hey, come on in. Are you okay?"

"Not really. That idiot detective is trying to pin the murders on me. I know it looks suspicious, but I'm as puzzled as he is. How did I wind up in the middle of all this?"

"The lawyer Oliver hired is the best. If you wind up needing her, I mean."

"What on earth was Isabel going to tell me? I'm positive I hadn't met her. And I didn't know Brooke before she showed up in my class. I couldn't even put a face with the name until I saw a photo."

"I'll bet Brooke was just at the wrong place at the wrong time."

"Better than thinking there's a serial killer out there. I hope her photos hold answers. I'll give Max the camera tonight."

"Max. It sounds like you like him?"

"What?" She hadn't analyzed her feelings toward him. She barely knew him. "I mean, he's a nice guy. I like talking to him."

"What does he look like?"

"Really?"

"Humor me."

"He's tall. He could use a haircut. Looks like he's wearing a thick, blond mop. He has deep, crinkly eyes."

"Deep set, you mean?"

"No, deep like he's been through a lot. Deep like a dam holding back a flood of emotions. Like he has a lot to share if he'd ever get past his anger over his daughter's death. She was killed by a hit-and-run driver."

"The two of you might be good for each other."

"I'm not ready to date or anything—not by a longshot."

"I didn't necessarily mean dating. I meant as a friend."

She had to admit it felt good holding onto Max's strong arm and sitting close on the swing—but she'd admit it only to herself. It was too soon.

"Are you starting a new cycle of fertility treatments?"

"Yes. Round two. I'm still beaten down from round one."

"You can handle it. Think positive. Let me know if you need me to cover a class or give you another shot."

"If IVF doesn't work out, it's over for us."

"I know what you said about adopting, but if things don't work out, maybe you'll feel differently down the road."

"Even if I did, adoption is off the plate."

"Because of the money?"

"No. You can't say anything if I tell you something very private, okay?"

"Do you even have to ask?"

"No, I trust you." Hayley whispered, "Oliver has a criminal record. From years ago."

"Really? I can't imagine it. He's such a nice guy."

"Well, he didn't murder anyone or anything."

"What did he do?"

"I'd rather not say."

"If it wasn't a violent crime, I'll bet it won't matter. It wasn't, was it?"

"Of course not, but it's still a criminal record, and no adoption agency is going to overlook it."

"It's going to work out one way or another. I feel it."

"Thanks."

Jenna scooped up Bijou. "I'm heading home. See you in the morning."

"Oh, by the way, we have a department meeting Friday morning. Just in case your email was intercepted by our friend Delores."

Jenna drove home processing what Hayley said about Oliver. He was a loving husband—Hayley became a different person when they got together. No more brooding and depression. And if it weren't for Oliver, she never would have met Giles. He and Giles went to school together in London when they were growing up. He and Hayley arranged to have them meet. *The right person can turn your life around. No. I'm not going to cry. I'm not going to think about Giles.*

When she pulled into her driveway, something looked off. When the headlights shined on the garage door, she saw an opening at the bottom, like it wasn't flush to the ground. The garage door opener had never worked, yet Giles insisted she keep it in the car and he'd fix it. It hung from the passenger side visor and had become invisible over time to the point it hadn't occurred to her to remove it. She pushed the button and her jaw fell to her lap. The garage door opened.

Disbelief paralyzed her and it took a moment to process what had just happened. She pressed the button again and watched the door close and lift. Reluctant to trust it, she closed the door again, then turned off her engine, walked around, and entered through the front door. All she needed was to pull in and have the car trapped in the garage.

She flicked on the lights and made herself a cup of chamomile tea, thinking Max would have a laugh if he saw her drinking it. The garage door opening gave her a chill. *Maybe it was frozen or something and worked itself out. I hadn't tried using it since we moved in. What if all along I could have been using it?*

Then she thought about the locket. Did Giles purchase it? She'd been through this with herself already. Their anniversary had been coming up when he died. Maybe he kept it at school so she wouldn't find it. Maybe one of his students found it or stole it from the band room and had second thoughts.

"Come on, Bijou. We're going upstairs." She took a breath like a swimmer about to dive under the water. She'd already conquered this. She could do it again. *One foot in front of the other.* She clutched the banister and didn't look back. *Two more steps, one more step...Made it.* She imagined giving herself a high-five.

The padlock she'd removed sat open on the hall table next to the key, the symbolism not escaping her. She creaked open the bedroom door, flicked on the lamp, and made a bee-line for the small filing cabinet in the corner by Giles' side of the bed. The spy thriller he'd been reading before he died sat on top of the cabinet, a frayed bookmark at about the halfway point. His reading glasses had fallen on the floor next to the bed.

She pulled on the drawer. Locked! *Where did he keep the key?*

She hadn't emptied his dresser drawers. Pulling open his underwear drawer, she took out a soft t-shirt and buried her face in it. She wasn't sure if it was her imagination, but she could still detect Giles' scent. She found an open black bottle of Drakar Noir cologne, hair gel, and a comb mixed in with the clothing, but no key.

Her mind wandered to the day Giles proposed. It was right after school had let out for the summer. They'd been on a picnic by the waterfall, the sun had warmed her arms and she was glad she'd chosen a sleeveless top. The ring sparkled, its multi-facets like a prism, separating sunlight into the colors of the rainbow. That's where he...she touched the ring she still wore...where he...*No. Don't.* She shut the drawer. *I came here for a reason, and it wasn't to cry over a trip down memory lane.*

She moved on to the night stand next to the filing cabinet. She opened the top drawer, pawed through his dress socks, and found a small key.

Please be the one! Her fingers trembled and she almost dropped the key behind the nightstand. Regaining her grip, she jiggled it into the lock. *Voila.*

Now what? Folders for insurance papers, health records, old tax forms...two entire folders were full of receipts. She spread the contents on the bed.

Restaurant and hotel receipts from recruiting trips he'd taken, a receipt for the big screen TV, one for a new garage door opener. *I guess he realized the old one was beyond repair. Too bad he never got around to replacing it. Had he?* Now she wondered if he had fixed it before his suicide. She doubted she'd tried it in the interim—until the other day.

Then she found a receipt for the local jewelry store, where they'd gotten their wedding bands. It was for a purchase made three years ago. It had an item number and a price, but didn't list the name of the item. She glanced at her watch. Too late. The store would be closed now.

What else is in here? He saved everything. She found a receipt from a gun store. He had wanted to start hunting when they were first together, but he'd seemed to have lost interest. Was it for protection? He once mentioned safety was a concern being far from your neighbors and flanked by woods.

What was he doing with a gun? A chill ran down her spine. They found his car parked on the bridge. They assumed he had jumped to his death. His body had never been recovered.

She searched the closet, under the bed, the filing cabinet…no gun. Bijou barked.

"Okay, I know. Dinner time." She shoved the receipts for the jewelry and gun into her purse to deal with tomorrow. She went downstairs and filled the dog food bowl, then made herself a grilled cheese sandwich. She'd have to eat quickly to make the meeting.

Chapter 12

Jenna slipped into the grief support meeting just before it started. Max moved his coat off the seat next to him, motioned to her, and whispered, "Everything okay?"

If she had a nickel for every time someone asked her if she was okay, she'd be rich by now. She did her best to hide her annoyance. "I'm fine. Did you find Isabel's ex-boyfriend?"

"Ronald? I did. I'm meeting with him tomorrow. He seemed both surprised and sad that Isabel was dead. He hadn't heard. Want to come?"

"Sure, if it's after school."

"Four o'clock. By the way, I had a friend develop the film. Wait till you see the photos."

The leader began. "Good evening. Tonight I want to address seasonal depression. Winter is prime time for depression under normal circumstances, but with the losses you've all suffered, it must be especially difficult. Anyone want to start?"

The widow who'd given away her husband's things last week spoke first. "It has been harder lately. I don't like driving at night when it gets dark so early, and if the weather is bad, forget it. I've been a hermit since before the holidays. When I first lost my husband, my friends made a point of dropping by and taking me out for meals. But now? I feel abandoned. Dinner time is the loneliest part of the day. You know what? I don't even want to go out anymore. Who needs them?"

The leader said, "What do you do to cope when you're eating dinner alone?"

"Other than cry? I mostly eat in front of the TV, go to bed early, and try to sleep away the evenings."

The young gym rat said, "It's not too cold for a brisk walk if you bundle up. Exercise gets your endorphins going."

Max rolled his eyes; Jenna leaned on her elbow and hid her smirk behind her hand.

The widow said, "My street is dark. I'm afraid to go out alone by myself, especially after those two girls were found murdered."

"Both murders took place in the woods behind the university," Max answered, "so it's unlikely the killer is roaming the town looking for random victims. You're more likely to slip on the ice or be hit by a snowmobile. You never know."

The gym rat seemed to perk up even further. "You could go out in the mornings. It'd set the tone for your entire day as it does mine. I take an eight-mile sunrise run most mornings before I hit the gym."

Jenna looked at the poor widow's sad eyes and spoke up. "I'm glad exercise works for you, but it's not the answer for everyone. I wouldn't be going out in the cold and in the dark to walk. Exercise isn't a panacea."

"A what?" The gym rat looked and sounded confused.

Millennials. I guess big words use up too many characters on Twitter.

The moderator addressed him. "Let's examine Jenna's comment. Does exercise completely keep you from missing your mother?"

He wiped his face on his sleeve. "I make myself so tired I can't think. If I'm busy, I can't think about her."

The moderator turned to Jenna. "How do you cope?"

"Well, I keep busy with my job and I have my little buddy here." She snuggled her face in Bijou's fur. "Having a therapy dog has made a huge difference." She turned to the widow. "Have you considered getting a pet?"

"I don't want to go out at night to walk a dog."

Duh. She just said as much. "Then maybe a cat. Just as affectionate, but less work."

"I'll give it some thought."

The moderator said, "Jenna, have you made any progress with your agoraphobia?"

"I've mostly avoided open areas. I did manage to go upstairs to the master bedroom for the first time since I lost Giles."

"That's literally a huge step."

The widow said, "I thought agoraphobia meant you couldn't leave the house?"

"It's a less common form. It started after the school shooter came through the open media center where I huddled in the corner with my class." She could still feel the indentations of the little barrettes on her inner arm. She'd squeezed Janelle so tightly, both to comfort and to keep her quiet.

The moderator said, "You've had two huge tragedies in a short time. You're doing remarkably well."

Jenna had spoken more than she normally did at these meetings. It was getting easier to talk about her feelings. She felt thankful for making progress, even though she back-slid periodically.

After the meeting ended, Max suggested coffee at the Monk Haven Café.

"Yes, that would be nice. I can show you what I found."

"Me, too."

The night sky was clear, with a full moon the color of new-fallen snow. Jenna thought to outsiders, they looked like any normal couple strolling down the sidewalk. The scars they'd both endured were hidden deep, which was both a blessing and a curse. Some days, she needed empathy; mostly she wanted normalcy. They hustled to the café and slid into a booth.

Max started. "My friend developed the film from the camera. There were mostly nature scenes—animals and trees. Fits with the course she was taking. But here." He pulled out a blurry photo. "It's time-stamped right around the time of Isabel's death."

Jenna looked at the photo, then put on her reading glasses and looked again. "Is this what I think it is?" Her whole body shook.

"It looks like a person strangling another person with a scarf. Too bad it was taken from the back. You can tell that's Isabel, but the attacker is wearing that damn ski mask."

"He's not too much taller than Isabel. Are you sure it's a man?"

"Hard to say with the unisex parka and the hood pulled up. I suppose it could be a strong woman."

"But not me, right? This proves I didn't kill Isabel."

"You're what, five foot four on your tip toes? This photo puts you in the clear, at least for Isabel's murder."

"And Brooke was murdered because she witnessed the crime? Now what? The police need to see this, yet we can't tell them Kyle took it from the crime scene. And I need for them to see it's not me in the picture so I'm off their suspect list."

"I'll get it to them without giving Kyle away."

"How? They'll see the film has been developed!"

"I've got a few friends left on the force who can make sure it isn't traceable back to anyone. What did you want to show me?"

The waitress poured two cups of coffee. When she walked away, Jenna pulled the receipts out of her purse.

"Here's a receipt from a jewelry store. It could be the locket, though it doesn't say. There's just an item number." She handed it to Max.

"It was purchased three years ago. Wouldn't he have given it to you back then?"

"I know. I wondered the same thing. If it's even the locket we're talking about. Giles bought me a set of diamond earrings three years ago."

"For that price, they'd have to have been cubic zirconium. What else have you got?"

"A receipt for a gun." She handed it across the table. "Giles had talked about getting a gun and taking up hunting back when we were first married."

"This is one bad ass gun he bought. Did you find it?"

The couple at the table across from their booth turned to look. Jenna whispered across the table.

"I didn't find one. Is it a hunting gun?"

"I'm not sure."

Jenna caught something in the way he said it. "What aren't you telling me?"

"Nothing. Did he have a safety deposit box?"

"Not that I knew about. I haven't received any bills or anything. They cost money, right?"

"You're right. Did you find a permit?"

"A permit?"

"He'd have to have gotten a permit to purchase the gun legally like he did."

"I'll have to look. And there's something else. Remember the doorbell? How it suddenly started working?"

"Yes, I was the one who rang it."

"The garage door opener has been broken forever. Today, when I pulled into the driveway, I noticed the garage was open a tad. I pushed the button in my car and the door opened."

"That's freaky."

"I found a receipt for a garage door opener in Giles' things. It's dated from before he died. He may have fixed it and I didn't notice. But the doorbell's another story." She had an idea. "You didn't sneak over and fix those things to help me out, did you?"

"And not take the credit? Never. But maybe someone did."

"Like Hayley's husband? He and Giles were good friends."

"I don't know. Ask Hayley. Want to get some baklava to go? We can drive up to my spot and sit on the swing."

"Sure."

Max paid the bill and handed Jenna the white paper

bag with the baklava. Max drove them out of downtown and up the mountain to the lookout spot. With the headlights on bright, he easily undid the chain and they drove through to the picnic area. It was a little too open for Jenna this time and she grabbed onto Max's arm. By the time they reached the swing, she'd settled down. The only light came from the full moon and sky full of stars.

Jenna scanned the sky. "Absolutely beautiful. Everything is so much brighter and clearer away from town."

"Look over there. See those three bright stars? That's Orion's belt. Orion was a hunter."

"Where?"

He put his hands on her face and gently guided her gaze. "Right there. Look to the left and that's Sirius." Her skin warmed under his hands.

"I see it. The really bright one, right?"

"That's it." He pointed to the sky. "Use your imagination. Think of Sirius as a dog's collar. Can you picture a dog?"

"Yes."

"That's Canis Major. If you go back to Orion's belt and go the opposite direction, you can see Taurus the bull."

"How did you get interested in astronomy?"

"My grandfather was a big space buff. He used to take me to the planetarium and had a good telescope right in his backyard."

Jenna shivered and he put his arm around her. She snuggled into him feeling safe and peaceful. Bijou had fallen asleep next to her, covered with the blanket. They sat in silence looking at the stars. She drank in his woodsy scent and felt the prickle of his five o'clock shadow against her cheek. Her mind was quiet; her heart fluttered, but not from fear. Her skin tingled in a way she hadn't felt in a long while. She snuggled closer and closed her eyes.

Bijou leaped out from the blanket, barking wildly.

"What is it?" said Jenna. She jumped up and looked around. Max was on his feet in a flash.

"Stay right here. I saw something behind the trees."

She tried to hold onto Bijou but he broke free and ran ahead of Max.

Max pushed aside the branches, using his phone as a flashlight. Jenna ran to him. She wasn't about to stay vulnerable alone by the swing.

The branches rustled. Max took off into the woods. Without his flashlight, the only light came from the night sky. She shivered and her heart beat fast under her jacket, like a wild animal trying to claw its way out.

Mountain, stars, moon. Breathe in. Breathe out. She wished Bijou would have stayed with her instead of running after Max. *Swing, branches, snow. In for two, out for four.*

She heard a car beyond the trees, revving its engine. Although paralyzed facing the openness, she forced herself to try to move, but couldn't. Her legs were like iron chains tethering her to the ground. Hyperventilating in the cold night air burned her lungs. She spotted Max emerging from behind the trees. Max, out of breath, jogged in from the woods holding Bijou.

"You okay?"

"I am now. What happened? Did you see anyone?" Her legs freed and they worked their way back to the swing.

"Damn it! I saw someone running through the woods. I tried to follow, but I lost him."

"I heard a car peel out."

"Me too. Come on. Let's see if we can find tire tracks or footprints. Get out your phone and turn on the flashlight."

She did as told, and they went back into the woods. She grabbed his hand like a mountain climber whose life depended on not letting go. A layer of re-frozen snow covered the ground making it difficult to find footprints.

"Wait. What's this?" She fingered a piece of fabric caught between pine needles. "I'll bet he snagged his jacket while running."

"I doubt anyone else has been through these woods recently so it's a fair bet." He separated the material from the needles and inspected it with his flashlight. "Looks like plaid flannel." He put it in his pocket. "Looks like it may be one of those hunting jackets. Too thick for a flannel shirt."

They followed the semi-path until they came to a slushy clearing. Jenna looked down at faint lines in the snow. "Aren't these tire tracks?"

"Yes." He took several pictures with his phone. "Maybe this will tell us something."

"Let me see the fabric again." He took it from his pocket and she examined it. "Isn't it the same print like in the blurry photo?" It was honestly hard to see clearly, but she hoped it was true.

"I think you're right. It's a common plaid print but it could mean the man in the blurry photo was here tonight following us."

"Or the woman." Jenna's teeth chattered. She still

had Delores in the back of her mind. "Can we go? I'm freezing."

"Of course. Sorry our peaceful outing ended like this."

"We'll do it again."

Chapter 13

After school the next day, Max picked up Jenna shortly after she got home. She'd had just enough time to change into stretchy jeans and a green sweater, to scarf down a handful of Oreos, and refill Bijou's water bowl. When the doorbell rang, she jumped. Although she'd been expecting Max, she still hadn't gotten used to hearing the sound of the doorbell. He looked kind of cute, with his messy mop of hair and a hint of reddish–blonde stubble on his face.

"Ready to go?"

"I am. Do you think we'll find out anything?"

"If I didn't, we wouldn't be driving out there. We haven't had much to go on."

Max drove past the university and to the outskirts of town. Then he pulled into a newish cluster of condos and looked for the address. Jenna spotted it first. Ronald lived on the ground floor of a three-story building. A holiday welcome mat, muddy and wet, covered the stoop, and a dried-out wreath hung from a long nail on the door.

Ronald invited them in. He was clean-shaven, wore wire-rimmed glasses, and looked to be in his early thirties. Was that how old Isabel was? She couldn't tell from her photo. In spite of first impressions, the tastefully decorated living room convinced Jenna he'd found either a wife or a girlfriend since breaking up with Isabel. She spotted a wood-framed wedding photo on the wall, confirming her theory.

They followed Ronald to the dining room table. Jenna smelled fresh coffee, which he promptly offered them.

Jenna said, "I appreciate you taking the time to talk to us."

"Were you a friend of Bela's?"

"A friend of Isabel's? No, I never even met her. She had set up a meeting with me but never showed up. I have no idea what she wanted to see me about."

"We were hoping you could fill in the blanks," Max said.

"I couldn't believe it when I heard Bela was dead. We'd been out of town visiting Tory's parents. Just got back yesterday and heard your message." He directed his explanation to Max.

"Two girls have been murdered on the Monk Haven U campus. The working theory is that it's either a serial killer, or the second victim witnessed Isabel's murder."

"I don't know what to say. Everyone loved Bela, and I'm not just saying that because she's dead." He reached out to pet Bijou.

"Any ideas at all?"

"Well, she did translating for some shady characters. I met one once. Bela said he dealt in illegal imports and exports. She attracted those types of clients. They knew she wouldn't go to the police. You knew her visa had expired, right?"

Jenna nodded. "We did." *Seems like everyone but the authorities knew it.*

Max sipped his coffee. "And you hadn't seen

Isabel since you broke up?"

"No. It's been years. I'm married now, and last I heard, she'd moved on and had a new boyfriend."

Max asked, "Where were you when the murder occurred?"

"Pardon me? You can't think I have anything to do with this."

Jenna put down her mug. "Max, that's rather abrupt. He's trying to help us."

"Sorry. I'm just trying to be thorough."

"I'm hardly a possibility. I loved her once."

"I heard a little stalking was going on." *Is he trying to tick him off?*

"Stalking? I tried to win her back for a while but realized it was fruitless. Anyway, I met Tory a few months later. And, I wasn't even in town when Bela was killed. You said she was murdered on Monday when you called me."

"That's right."

"I was two hours away visiting Tory's folks. Her parents will tell you. So will the neighbors. Want to check my toll receipts?"

"No, not now, anyway. If you can think of anything, let us know. Any other clients who may have been after her?"

"She didn't tell me any names or anything."

"Okay. Thanks for your time."

Jenna mouthed 'Thank you' as they left.

Once in the car, she said, "You sounded like an ass the way you accused him of being involved in Isabel's murder."

"I didn't accuse him. Sometimes you have to prod in order to get the information you need."

"They teach you that at private eye school? He was perfectly willing to help us. You can't still think he had anything to do with Isabel's murder."

"No. But I'll check the alibi just to be sure. I'll also see what I can find out about her clients. Maybe Santiago can help with that."

The week flew by. Jenna taught her classes, met with Kyle about his dissertation topic (or lack of one) and double-checked her spam folder to be sure Delores hadn't done any more damage. She had to do some convincing and wait for university approval, but a locksmith did change the lock on her office door for her.

It was Friday, and Jenna hoped to see more of Max over the weekend. They'd been texting and talking daily since their 'date' after the grief support group and their meeting with Ronald. She'd dropped the swatch of plaid fabric at the police station Tuesday morning and hadn't heard back from Detective Russo. Not that she expected to. He probably shoved it in a drawer and didn't give it a second thought. Hayley had been out sick for a few days, but today she'd returned.

"What did I miss while I was gone?" said Hayley.

"It's been quiet here. I'm glad you're feeling better."

"Should have sucked it up and gotten the flu shot, but I hate needles."

Remembering the hormone shot she'd given Hayley, Jenna laughed. "I'm sure the needle they use for a flu shot isn't nearly the size of the one you've been poked with for the fertility treatments."

"You're sure? That means you haven't gotten a flu shot either."

"Never. I hate needles. Besides, I have a strong immune system. Speaking of which, how's the new round going? Did being sick interfere?"

"No, still going ahead. At least I was home and didn't have to stop at the lab for bloodwork on the way to school. Maybe being more relaxed will help."

"I'll bet it will."

"Oliver must be so disappointed in me. He's always wanted to be a father."

"You'll get through this together."

"I feel like I deceived him. When he married me, we'd talked about having a family and now I can't get pregnant. I'll bet he's having an affair. Maybe that's why he's spending so much time at work these days."

"Seriously? You don't believe that."

"I wouldn't blame him. Even if it's not another woman, I think he's avoiding me. He never traveled this much."

"Nonsense. Lots of couples have trouble conceiving, they just don't talk about it. I've known Oliver longer than I knew Giles. He thinks you walk on water."

"Thanks for the pep talk." She hugged Jenna.

"Yeah, well, what are friends for?"

"Ah, enough mushy talk. We sound like a sappy chic-flick."

"Changing the subject, is there any possibility Oliver could have gone to my house to repair my doorbell or garage door opener?"

"Huh?"

"Both haven't been working since before Giles died and I know I mentioned the garage door in front of him when I was over at your house after the holidays.

He and Giles were like brothers. Maybe Giles asked him to look out for me, you know, after he was gone."

"If he thought Giles was planning to kill himself, he'd have stopped him. Oliver has his moments, but he's lazy as hell. I highly doubt he'd have snuck over to your house to make repairs without asking you first. Besides, he'd have wanted the credit if he took the time to play Good Samaritan."

"I know. Sounds ridiculous."

"Are you sure the doorbell didn't work? When was the last time anyone tried it? Maybe it had been frozen and then the ice melted out of it."

"I don't know. I suppose the few people who come over knew to knock."

"And the garage door? Maybe it was stuck or something."

"No. I'm sure it wasn't working."

"How about the new man in your life? Maybe he's been playing hero."

"What? We're just friends."

"Keep telling yourself that."

"No, I don't...Okay, maybe a little, but it hasn't even been a full year since Giles died."

"I'll bet he made those repairs."

"I don't think so. He seemed genuinely surprised when I mentioned it."

Jenna heard clumsy footsteps approaching. Moments later, Delores stood at the doorway fanning a journal. "My article is out. Hot off the press. Want a copy?"

Hayley said, "If I'm going to make time to read, it has to be something interesting."

Jenna would have snapped back with a bitchy

remark but was focused on Delores's jacket. Red plaid. Like the swatch they found stuck to the tree.

"Well, Jenna? Maybe you should take my example and get something published if you have ideas about getting the tenure position."

"I already have the position." She didn't, but couldn't help herself. It was fun watching Delores's face turn the color of her jacket. "Is that a new jacket? I didn't know you hunted. I've never met a woman who hunts."

"I can out hunt, out fish, out shoot any man in the state. Not for the faint of heart. Don't suggest you try it or you might have another one of those breakdowns." She looked at her watch. "I've got to get this over to the dean. Toodles."

Kyle came in as she was leaving. "What did the bitch want?" He said it loudly enough to be sure Delores heard it. She could have heard it on the next floor with the volume he'd used.

"To brag about her article."

"If she wrote an article, I'll bet it's plagiarized. Want me to check?"

"You've got more important things to spend your time on, but thanks for the offer. Do you happen to know what kind of car Delores drives?'

"A black Explorer, why?"

"Not a sedan?"

"More of a Jeep, but the new models do look more like cars."

"I think she followed me and Max, and I think she broke into my house."

"Seriously? What did she steal? I'm going to confront her and make her fess up. Then I'll drag her sorry ass down to the police station."

"Nothing is missing as far as I can tell, but she was either looking for something or simply trying to spook me."

"You know she copied your office key and left the note. I'm sure that's what happened."

"Isabel was strangled with my scarf. Someone broke into the master bedroom but it had to have happened before the murder. The matching hat was still in the cedar chest."

"So she snuck in, stole the scarf, and used it to kill Isabel? That's your theory?"

It sounded a little far-fetched when she said it out loud. She weakly replied, "Yes." She looked for Kyle's reaction.

"She's certainly strong enough. And she wants your job really bad."

"And when I got to the bottom of the ravine where Brooke was found at the search, Delores was already there."

"I know. I was there. You think she killed Brooke, too?"

"She knew right where the body was. Oh, and just now, she was wearing a red plaid jacket. When Max and I were at the lookout, someone followed us. We found a piece of fabric matching her jacket stuck in some branches."

"You and Max were up at the lookout? In the middle of winter? You go, girl."

Feeling like a silly schoolgirl, Jenna felt heat rush to her face. "Stop. It wasn't like that."

"Uh huh. Did you notice if her jacket was torn? Can you find any evidence at all that she was in your house, followed you, or that she left the note?"

"I dropped the piece of fabric at the police station but haven't heard anything. We kept our ladder in a locked shed. When I went out there, the padlock was open."

"So, fingerprints?"

"I can't imagine she didn't wear gloves. Besides, she didn't have the key, unless…"

"Unless what?"

"Giles had hidden it under one of those fake rocks on the side of the shed. She could have easily found it had she been looking."

"Tell you what. I'll get a look at the jacket for starters."

"How?"

"Seriously? I think I want a copy of her article ASAP. After all, I'm sooo impressed. I'll head over to the supply closet—I mean her office."

"Thanks, Kyle." She checked her watch. "We're going to be late for class. You're a bad influence."

Class was uneventful. Afterward, Max called and asked her to meet him at the café. When she arrived, Santiago and Max were seated across from each other in a booth near the window.

"Hey, Jenna. Glad you could meet us here. Santiago has information to share and I thought you'd want to hear it, too."

Santiago shook her hand. "I was going through more of Isabel's things and I found a printout of texts. Look."

—*Meet me after school. Can't get you off my mind.*
—

—*No. I'm going to tell the police if you don't leave*

me alone.—

—Can you say 'illegal'? If you go to the police or tell anyone, I'm spilling the beans. Coming?—

—I'll be there. God will punish you for this.—

Jenna sat back against the booth. "So Isabel was being harassed by someone. She wanted to report it but this person knew Isabel was illegal and threatened to have her deported if she did. Meet me after school? Was it a Monk Haven student?"

"*Spilling the beans* doesn't sound like an expression a millennial would use. Besides, Isabel wasn't a student. It doesn't make sense." Santiago pushed back against the booth.

"It does if it was a professor." Max sipped his coffee.

Santiago said, "As far as I know, she had no connection to the university."

"Except, she came to find me and set up that meeting."

"And the other girl who was killed? The one they found in the woods?"

Brooke could have simply been at the wrong place at the wrong time."

"You're saying she witnessed the murder? She was collateral damage?"

Max said, "Possibly. You're sure Isabel never mentioned a professor from Monk Haven U? Perhaps she did translations for him."

"Or her." Jenna's phone vibrated. "It's the police station."

"Get it," said Max.

"Hello. Yes, detective. You did? Uh huh. It matched. Okay. Did you do anything with the fabric swatch I dropped off? Okay." She slipped the phone back into her purse.

"What did he want?"

"The blood on the rock matches Brooke's. That's not a surprise. Like I thought, he's done nothing with the swatch from the tree."

"I'll keep looking through Isabel's things. It's difficult emotionally, but we have to find out who did this to her." Santiago grabbed the check. "My treat. We'll be in touch."

After he left, Jenna said, "Want to meet for dinner? It's been a long week."

"I'm sorry, I can't. I have plans."

She wanted to ask what plans but refrained. "How about tomorrow night?"

"I'll be out of town. We'll talk Monday at the grief meeting. Maybe we can get coffee afterward."

Jenna felt like the kid not picked for the dodgeball team at recess. Max laughed when they were together. He was opening up to her. She thought he enjoyed spending time with her as much as she did with him. *Stop thinking like that. It's not like he's a boyfriend. He's barely become a friend.* "Okay, then. See you Monday."

She picked up Bijou and went home, exhausted. Her back ached every morning when she woke up on the lumpy guest room bed. She made a decision. *I'm sleeping in my own bed tonight.*

Chapter 14

When the sun peaked through the blinds in the master bedroom, it took Jenna a moment to realize she wasn't in the guest room. Her back didn't ache and her legs weren't stiff. She'd stayed on her own side all night long as if waiting for Giles to crawl in next to her. She imagined how it was when they were first married and they'd cuddle under the covers, neither wanting to leave the warmth. Her body shivered while walking to the closet.

She opened the closet and grabbed a favorite flannel robe. It smelled a bit stale, but a shot of Febreze would bring it back to life. She browsed through the dresses and sweaters that had been left in the closed closet all year. A favorite blue rayon dress and a cashmere sweater smelled especially musty. She tossed them on the bed to drop off at the cleaners.

She scooped up Bijou and went downstairs for breakfast. Maybe she'd pick up some groceries while she was out. The Raisin Bran was past its shelf life, and the milk was on its way to being expired. She poured dry food into Bijou's bowl and filled his water.

Bijou barked. "Okay, Okay. Let's get you out for a walk." She put her coat on over her pajamas, slipped into her furry boots, and wriggled Bijou into his new puffy jacket. "Let's go."

She was passing the neighbor's house when the

143

retired couple waved. "Morning, Jenna." The man bent down stiffly to pet Bijou.

She hoped they didn't notice she was wearing pajama pants. "You two are up early on a Saturday."

"Who can keep the days straight? They're all the same, if you ask me."

"Honey, you sound like we don't have a life. We're volunteering at the homeless shelter today; tomorrow we're meeting Saul and Penny for a matinee and dinner. We have plans nearly every day."

"Yeah, just griping."

"What do you do at the homeless shelter?" Jenna ruffled Snoopy under his chin.

"I mostly do handy work. Repair sticky doors, help paint the rec room. Mabel helps prepare meals."

"That's great. Two good Samaritans. Aren't many like you left."

Mabel shivered. "It's brutal when you stand still. Not enough meat left on these bones. Sykes is cold, too."

Sykes, that's his name. "Go on. I'm catching a chill myself. Have a great day."

She and Bijou were nearly finished with their walk when it dawned on Jenna. Her neighbors were good-hearted people. *I'll bet he's the one who replaced the doorbell. Then again, Mr. Price took a while to straighten up after petting Bijou. The doorbell wouldn't have required any bending or heavy lifting. Mrs. Price is from a different generation. I doubt she'd know the first thing about repairing a doorbell or garage door opener.* She kept the internal debate going all the way home.

Back in her bedroom, she fished through her side

of the closet and picked out a few favorite items to have cleaned. The others would have to wait if the Febreze didn't do the trick. Paying to have her clothes cleaned was not a priority with the electric and phone bills already late.

She got to the dry cleaner shortly after it opened. The stuffiness of the overheated shop made her dizzy. She hung on to the counter while she loosened her scarf and waited her turn. Chemicals were terrible for the environment, and she rarely picked fabrics that needed special care. The rayon dress had been a birthday present from Giles.

"Good morning, ma'am." He took the items from her. "Been here before?"

"I think so."

"Can I get your phone number?"

She gave it to the clerk.

"Giles Blake, is that correct?"

She couldn't remember Giles ever dropping off dry cleaning. She couldn't even picture an item of clothing he owned that would have needed special care. The shirts he wore to school were wash and wear—wrinkle-free, even. She imagined him in her favorite—the light blue dress shirt with his music note tie. That was just for special occasions, like school concerts. Mostly, he wore pullovers with dark jeans or khakis. *Stop. It's not the time to get emotional.*

The clerk typed the order into the computer and tagged her clothes.

The chemicals stung her eyes like freshly cut onions. At least she had a plausible excuse for the tears trickling down her cheeks. Tears of sadness—tears of anger, snuck up on her at random times.

The door jingled behind her, and the brisk air cleared her head. She spotted the jewelry store canopy a few doors down. Christmas colored window paint advertised outdated holiday sales. Inside, she browsed through the glass cases while waiting for the owner to become available.

"Sorry for the wait. Lots of post-Christmas resizing and exchanges. What can I do for you?"

"Can you tell by this receipt what item was purchased? It's only got an item number and the date's worn off."

"Hmmm. Let's check." He entered the number into the computer. "Not from last year's inventory."

"It may have been purchased quite a while ago."

The owner continued searching. "Got it. It's for a gold locket. We don't carry it anymore. It was popular back a few seasons ago."

"Do you have a picture?"

He turned the computer screen so she could see. "This one. Came in silver, too. I can order it for you." It was a perfect match to the one that was in the package Isabel sent her.

"No, thanks. Can I take a picture?"

"Sure."

She snapped a photo of the computer screen. "Speaking of resizing, my wedding ring has gotten a little tight. If I drop it off, can you resize it for me?" She'd prefer melting it down for the gold but hated taking up the jeweler's time without the promise of business.

"With my eyes closed. Drop it off. May take a bit longer than usual, like I said. Especially with Valentine's Day coming up."

"Great. Thanks for your help."

Back in her car, she took a moment to digest the information. Giles bought that expensive locket, but not for her. He was having an affair, but with whom? Did his lover mail it to tip her off to his infidelity? Why now?

She could kick herself for not trusting her earlier instincts.

He *had* been a little distant even before the shooting. And though she'd buried her suspicions since his death, there was the scent of perfume on Giles' jacket. And all those after-school meetings? And the night he didn't make it home at all? Car trouble. She'd been suspicious enough at the time to look for a repair bill or tow truck receipt but hadn't found one.

She worked the tight ring off her finger and tossed it into her purse, with no intention of ever putting it on again.

Back in the car, she took a moment to collect herself before attempting to drive home.

Wait. Is that Max across the street? She squinted, as if that would compensate for needing distance glasses. One more unaffordable expense. When he crossed and came closer, she knew it was him. It caught her off guard. She debated jumping out and saying hello, but he'd made it clear he had plans.

He walked into the florist shop. *Who is he buying flowers for?* This was her day to feel rejected. He lied about having plans, and it stung. Had she not been mulling over Giles being unfaithful, she most likely would have shrugged it off.

She ducked down and waited for Max to come out of the shop. He was carrying a dozen roses. He had plans all right.

She waited until he was out of sight, then pulled out. Overheated, over-emotional, and lonely, she called Hayley, hoping they could get together this weekend.

"Jenna, I'm sorry, but we have tickets to see *Hamilton* in the city. We're getting ready to leave in a few minutes."

"I forgot it was this weekend. Have fun."

"Maybe tomorrow? Is everything okay?"

"Yes, of course it is. We'll talk soon."

Chapter 15

The loneliness gnawed at her stomach. Every time she believed past events remained in the past, she was reminded there was still a long way to go. Besides feeling lonely, anger pulsed its ugly head. Angry that Giles had been cheating on her. Angry for having missed the signs. All she wanted to do was take a long nap and stop thinking. First, she picked up the sledgehammer and whacked at the kitchen/ dining room wall. Her arms ached and her legs were sore, but when she stood back to admire her work, she realized three-quarters of the wall stood strong. *All that work and this is how far I got? Breaking through this wall is going to take longer than I thought.* Exhausted, Jenna curled up under the afghan and took a nap.

Later that afternoon, the doorbell rang, startling her. She wiped the sleep from her eyes and found Detective Russo standing at the door.

"Sorry to bother you at home, but the DNA results are back."

"And?"

"We'll need a cheek swab from you. We have to, umm, eliminate you."

"So maybe someone else left their DNA on the scarf. The murderer maybe? You said you already had my DNA on the scarf. Don't you remember? The ancestry kit?"

He didn't respond to the comment about the DNA kit. "If it doesn't match, it gives you an out."

"Seriously? You still think I killed Isabel?"

"I don't like to make presumptions without evidence to back them up."

"Excuse me? How can you possibly…"

"It's standard procedure. Elimination DNA."

"Do you have a warrant?"

"As a matter of fact, I do."

"You come to my house on a weekend to get my DNA, which you lied and said you already had. I would have come down to the station during normal business hours."

He ignored her comments. "Did you lend out your scarf?"

"No. And I can't remember the last time I wore it."

"What about Santiago Salas?"

"Isabel's fiancé? I'm certain I didn't lend him my scarf." He appeared less than amused.

"How do you think he's taking Isabel's death?"

"He seems genuinely distraught."

"Could he have stolen the scarf?"

"No." It came out snappier than intended, but the detective was getting on her nerves. "I didn't meet him until after Isabel's murder. Besides, he hired a private investigator. He wants this solved."

"Or he wants someone to help cover things up. Someone who used to be a cop and knows how to tamper with evidence."

"Max? I don't believe that for a moment. Where's the motive? And what motive would Santiago have had for killing Isabel when they were about to be married?"

"I'm not at liberty to discuss it."

"Just get the cheek swab over with. I have things to do." She thought about what Max said about the detective's ex-wife and how she looked like her. *Maybe I should cut him some slack.*

Detective Russo opened his bag and brushed his hand against her lips as he guided the swab into her mouth, twirled it, and sealed it in a plastic tube. The lights flickered. The house plunged into darkness. Jenna screamed.

Detective Russo put a stiff arm around her shoulder. "It's okay. Power went out, that's all. The wind nearly blew my car over on the way out here." He reached into his coat pocket for his phone, then with the flashlight app, went to the window. "Can't see any other houses from here so I don't know if it's just your house or the whole area."

"I have a flashlight in the kitchen drawer. I'll get it."

"We'll need more if you've got them." He followed her. "Where's the fuse box?"

"In the garage." She pointed. "Through that door."

He drummed his fingers loudly on the door frame while waiting for her to find the flashlight, then stepped into the garage. She stayed at his heel while he fiddled with the box. "Have you been having problems with your electricity?"

"No."

"Why didn't you convert to a circuit breaker system? These old fuse boxes are more likely to cause fires."

"It's one of those things Giles had on his to-do list. The real estate agent told us the wiring was the original from back in the seventies."

She watched the detective's chunky fingers delicately examine the parts. The heart tattoo on his wrist looked as though it were pumping when he tugged on the fuses, and she wondered if that was the intention.

"Hmm."

"What do you mean, hmm?"

"Has anyone been in here recently?"

"No, why?"

He extracted a small fuse and showed it to her. "This is the wrong size, and it looks brand new compared to the others."

"Maybe Giles replaced it before he…"

"How long has he been gone?"

"Close to a year."

"No, this had to have been done recently or your house would have burnt to the ground already."

Alarm coursed through her. "What do you mean?"

"Anyone knowing about fuses never would have replaced this with the wrong size. It's dangerous. Who else had access to the garage?"

"No one. I mean…"

"What?"

"See the garage door opener over there? It never worked. Then out of the blue, I came home and the door was open a crack. I used the remote in my car and it worked."

"Has anyone been in here?"

"I told you, no."

"This entire past week, no one but Max has been here?"

"Just Max. And you of course."

"What did I tell you about Max not being who you think he is?"

"He didn't do this."

"Who else? Any deliveries or repairmen?"

"My friend Hayley and her husband came over for pizza last weekend."

"Did either of them go out there?"

"No. Can you fix the problem?"

"I'll need a new fuse. The hardware store's closed until morning. You're stuck for now."

"I have to stay here in the dark all night?"

"Or go to a hotel."

She was near enough to prime skiing that hotels in winter were way past her budget. "I'll stay here."

"I can drop you off at a hotel. It was freezing in this house *before* the electric went out."

"I've got blankets."

"Suit yourself." He started to leave but paused with his hand on the doorknob. "I'll light you a fire if you want. You got any wood?"

"Yes, on the back porch." She was grateful for the offer.

"I'll bring it in." He followed her outside. "Do you have any friends you could stay with?"

"With the dog? I don't know. I can try Hayley." Then she remembered Hayley and Oliver had gone to the city to see a play.

"Call her while I get the wood together."

"I forgot. They're spending the night in the city."

"Anyone else you can call?"

She thought about Kyle, then remembered he was staying at his boyfriend's place. "No."

The wind howled and she jumped when a large branch hit the roof and tumbled to the ground.

"It's just a branch. You outta get that tree trimmed

before it damages the roof."

An animal howled in the distance. Jenna screamed.

The detective sighed. "Do you want me to stay on the couch tonight?"

The offer took her aback. She was about to say no, but imagined being alone, hearing every sound, and having a panic attack. She weighed it against spending the night with the arrogant detective. "Okay. I'd appreciate it."

The wind whipped through the naked trees. Jenna cowered, then grabbed an armful of logs and Detective Russo grabbed two more.

"Freezing rain. Not a night to be out driving, anyhow." Once inside, he tossed a log into the fireplace and lit the kindling.

"Good thing I have a gas furnace," said Jenna.

"You need electricity to work the furnace. It's going to get cold, even with the fire."

"Want some coffee?" asked Jenna.

"Cold coffee? No thanks."

His chestnut eyes reflected an old soul in the softness of the fire's glow. He could have left her stranded. Instead, he lit a fire and volunteered to keep her company. Maybe he wasn't as much of an ass as she'd thought.

She wasn't particularly fond of small talk, and it seemed he was even less so. Nonetheless, she felt the need to fill the uncomfortable silence. "You live alone?"

"Yep."

"Do you want a glass of wine?" She remembered a bottle she'd gotten as a gift which had become a fixture in the fridge over the last year or so. *Does wine go bad?*

"Okay." He glanced at his watch. "Technically, I'm off duty now."

She took the flashlight and felt the heat evaporate as she left the living room. She fumbled in the dark and managed to find a corkscrew and two tumblers.

"I don't know if it's any good. I rarely drink." *Especially now that I'm taking anti-anxiety drugs. Alcohol and drugs, not a good mix.*

"It will warm us up." Bijou jumped up on the couch. "How long have you had this dog?"

"Since shortly after the school shooting. He's been a life-saver."

"Your husband is the one who jumped off the bridge, wasn't he?"

He could use some sensitivity training. "Yes. He committed suicide."

"Didn't you notice he was depressed or anything?"

Like I haven't blamed myself a million times for not picking up the clues. "No. In fact, everyone who knew him commented on how well he was doing. He even went back to work at the school where the shooting happened. I couldn't do it."

Jenna felt the soft, blond strands of little Ryan's hair with his head cradled against her neck. She remembered his heart beating in his little chest. *Shush. It's going to be okay. Goodnight comb, goodnight brush...*soothed by a childhood story, though no longer a baby.

"Ms. Blake?"

"Um, no, I couldn't. When the gunman burst into the media center and I was huddled with my students, responsible for their lives...I couldn't go back. It was the worst fear I'd ever felt."

"Good thing you found another job."

"My friend Hayley got me a job at the university. I was settling in, doing okay, until Giles jumped off that bridge."

"But you continued working. That's the best remedy."

"I took some time off. My parents babysat me. They were afraid I'd follow in Giles' footsteps. I came back to town after the holidays to start the semester."

"Must have been tough." Detective Russo added another log to the fire. His face softened in the glow of the flames. "But you're good now."

"Good? I mean, a few weeks into the semester and I get that note from Isabel, and then find Brooke's body. It's a miracle I've been able to keep working."

"Got to pay the bills." He gulped his wine.

She was feeling the effects of the wine. "It's not like Giles left me with life insurance money or anything. Even if he'd had a policy, without a body I'm not sure they'd have paid out." She poured them both another glass.

"Suicide's an exclusion in any case. Have you thought about selling this place?"

"All the time, but the market is terrible right now. Even if I could sell it, it would be at a loss. What's your story?"

"What story?" he asked.

"Are you originally from here?"

"Grew up in Brewster. Went straight into the academy after high school."

"So you always wanted to be a cop?"

"Guess so."

It wasn't easy getting a two-way conversation

going. At that moment, an explosion shook the walls.

"Oh, my God." Jenna was back in the media center, guarding the children, hearing the gunshot. They ran to the front window. Detective Russo held her back. "There's fire!"

"Where's your fire extinguisher?" asked the detective.

"Um, in the kitchen."

"Get it, quick."

She groped along the wall until she found it. She wasn't even sure if it worked. Had they bought it when they moved in, or was it left over from the previous owners? She made her way back to the living room. "Here."

"Stay here. Call 9-1-1." He ran out the front door. Bijou barked at the window, relentless as paparazzi at the Oscars. She moved away from the window so she could be heard over him.

The 911 call picked up. "This is an emergency. There's a fire on my front lawn. No, I don't think it will reach the house. I'm inside. Send a firetruck. Hurry."

She opened the front door and watched Detective Russo attack the fire with white foam. She yelled, "They're on the way."

"Did you ask them to send a unit?"

"No, should I?"

"Call the station. Tell them I need them out here stat."

Chapter 16

By the time she heard sirens, Detective Russo had successfully put out the fire with the kitchen extinguisher. A patrol car pulled in front of the house.

Detective Russo tossed the empty fire extinguisher on the ground and directed the patrol unit. "Collect any evidence you can find. I'm going to interview the neighbors. Jenna, go back inside and wait."

Jenna? I guess almost being set on fire together puts us on a first name basis. Though, I don't even know his first name. She watched him head down the road, knowing her neighbors were already in bed. With the distance between houses and given the late hour, she doubted he'd learn anything.

The patrol officers, evidence bags in hand, systematically inspected the front lawn. Once or twice they bent down and picked up potential evidence. Jenna squinted but couldn't make out what they put in the bags. Bijou had calmed down, and they watched out the window until the detective returned.

"Did my neighbors see anything?"

"Are all your neighbors in bed by nine p.m.? I didn't know Hudsonville had its own retirement village. They were all fast asleep and annoyed when I knocked."

"All of them? You mean the retired couple a quarter of a mile to the left, and the young man in the farmhouse a half mile in the other direction?"

"I use the term neighbors loosely. And I didn't even ask if they had security cameras."

"And?"

"No one noticed anything suspicious. Or anything at all. Like I said, they were all asleep."

The two officers came inside. "We didn't find much. Looks like some kind of homemade pipe bomb or souped-up firecracker."

"Get it back to the station and tell the lab I said to rush it through."

"Anything else?"

"That's it for now."

"I'm glad you were here," Jenna said. "I'd have freaked out if this happened and I was here alone."

"All part of the job."

She knew it wasn't. He'd gone above and beyond tonight, earning her respect.

"Try to get some rest on the sofa. I'll keep guard."

"You think whoever did that will be back tonight?"

"Doubtful, especially if they heard the sirens and saw the patrol car. I'm more concerned with keeping the fire in here going." The detective poked at the logs in the fireplace. "You'll freeze if it goes out."

Detective Russo stayed overnight, tending to the fire and keeping guard as promised. She felt every ounce of her body wanting to drift off to sleep but couldn't get her mind to cooperate. Lacking the energy required to keep a conversation going with the detective, Jenna closed her eyes, thoughts fired up as if on steroids.

I'll bet the same person that broke my window is upping his game. Or her game. She hadn't ruled out

Delores. *Isabel is dead. Brooke is dead. I'm in the crosshairs for both of their murders. If the killer wanted me dead, surely he or she could have done it by now.*

She must have fallen asleep. When she awoke, the blanket from the rocking chair was tucked in around her. She craved coffee.

"Ms. Blake, I'm going to run to the hardware store and get the fuse taken care of. I'll call the station on the way and see if we got anything off the evidence regarding the firebomb."

"Jenna."

"What?"

"You can call me Jenna You did last night."

"Okay. Jenna." He ran out the door without a reciprocal offer. He was still Detective Russo to her.

Although it was freezing, at least she had sunlight. She bundled up and grabbed the dog leash from the peg near the door. While walking Bijou, she tried to fit the puzzle pieces together—for the thousandth time.

Just when she'd pulled herself together to go back to work, everything tumbled. From the anonymous note, to Isabel Hernandez's body discovered in the woods. *I'm no closer to answering that question than I was when the detective first told me.*

Bijou tugged at the leash, and Jenna realized she'd stopped walking.

"Bijou, how did I wind up in the middle of all this? Is Delores setting me up so she can get my job?"

Bijou barked as if to answer. By the time they returned, Detective Russo was gone. He'd fixed the fuse, turned on the lights, and cranked up the heat. She was alone again and in need of a distraction.

In daylight with the electricity back on, Jenna felt

brave. She took a deep breath. One foot in front of the other, she marched up the stairs, determined to sort through Giles' things and start a Goodwill box.

Opening the closet, Giles' scent still lingered. She sifted through his work shirts and trousers, stopping occasionally to rub her face in his scent. Most of his wardrobe was folded in the dresser drawers, as she'd taken more than her share of the closet. She fought to hold back tears. *It's time to move on.* Then she threw the blankets and boxes out of the bottom of the closet. That's when she noticed a shoebox buried under an extra blanket.

When she opened the lid, her heart skipped a beat. A camera. Not their family Sure Shot Canon, or any other camera an adult would likely use. It was a small, square, turquoise camera like the kids used. She supposed he took it away from one of his students, though why bring it home?

Then she remembered how the school required confiscated electronics to be locked in the school safe. Giles often stayed late—past when the school office closed. He never had the chance to return it.

Her phone rang in her pocket. Startled, she jumped and bumped her head on the edge of the closet. "Hello?"

"Ms. Blake? It's Santiago Salas. I tried Max but he hasn't picked up or returned my voicemail."

"He's on a job this weekend. Can I help you?"

"I found something. The most recent translation Isabel was working on."

"What was it?"

"Forged paperwork. Immigration papers translated into Spanish. One of her clients was fleeing the country.

She made several notations, like she was going to point them out to whoever her client was. She was helping someone escape the country and start over in Colombia."

"That could be motive. Maybe he was worried she'd turn him in. Do you see a name?"

"The name on the immigration papers is John Talbot. Might as well be John Doe. You know he didn't use his real name."

"Where was he going to work? Do you have the name of the company?"

"I do, but I can't figure out what sort of business it is. I was hoping my private investigator could do that."

"If I hear from him, I'll let you know ASAP."

"Thanks. I'll keep searching through the files."

The next morning, Jenna slept through the alarm, having taken half of a sleeping pill when she found herself unable to quiet her mind at 2 am. Needing to hurry to avoid being late, Jenna forced her hair into a low ponytail, threw on black pants and a pullover sweater, and grabbed a Pop-Tart to eat in the car.

Jenna parked and hustled to class, where the students were already waiting.

Of course Kyle is late again.

"Take out your homework. You are going to trade your lesson plan with the person next to you. Using the rubric that was included in your readings this week, evaluate your neighbor's plan and offer constructive criticism. If you were subbing for that teacher, is the plan clear and easy to follow? Does it address multiple learning styles? Is the standard you are teaching clear?"

"Dr. Blake, did you hear? Another girl is missing."

"What? No, Sadie. They searched the woods

behind the student union building and last I heard, they didn't find a body."

"They didn't find Brooke right away, either."

Another student said, "It's just a rumor. I also heard two professors were missing and a TA was stabbed in front of the library last night."

Another said, "I heard a security guard had his throat slit in the arboretum. You know that didn't happen. I walked right past the arboretum on the way to class just now. I didn't see any blood or yellow tape anywhere."

"Rumors have a life of their own. Besides, the campus is crawling with extra security, and I saw maintenance installing a security camera right outside this building. Keep being cautious, but try not to worry. Trade papers and take out the rubrics."

She got the class started, then circulated while the students worked. Kyle strolled in fifteen minutes later.

"Before you say anything about my punctuality or lack thereof, I have news."

"What news? And it'd better be good. You're never going to make it in the job world if you can't be on time for work. Not to mention you'll need recommendations, and you're getting a reputation."

"I examined Delores's jacket. You know, the plaid one."

"Tell me it was torn." Her tone changed, sounding less like a disappointed parent.

"Sorry, but no. I even looked for stitching to see if it had been resewn."

"So it wasn't Delores out in the woods. Someone else tore a plaid jacket on the trees."

"All info is useful, right? If the hypothesis isn't

supported—"

She finished the sentence that was her mantra. "Go back to the drawing board and form a new one."

"I got a better look at her car. It could pass for an Explorer. It could still be her."

"Thanks, Kyle. What we need is an alibi—or lack of one. What was she doing the day Isabel was murdered? She doesn't have class on Mondays, does she?"

"No, but she has closet hours, I mean office hours, on Mondays."

"I'll see what I can do."

After class, Jenna headed back to her office, still taking the more sheltered but longer route to avoid the open quad area. *I'm going to work on conquering that next.* She noticed new flyers on practically every available surface warning the students to lock their doors and walk in groups.

She'd checked her phone at least a dozen times for a message or call from Max, but there was nothing. *His own client can't reach him when he has important news to relay. Glad he makes enough money to blow off a client.* She doubted that was true. He was way overdue for a haircut and wore the same pair of jeans every time she'd seen him. She knocked on Hayley's partially open door.

"You look awful. Are you sure you're over that flu?"

"It's the hormones. I'm moody all the time, and gained seven pounds. All I want to do is take naps. If this doesn't work, I'm going to shoot myself."

"Hayley!"

"Oh, I'm so sorry. I didn't mean it." Her face

blushed red as a ripe tomato.

"It's okay. I understand. You're sure Oliver's record is a deal breaker? What about adopting from overseas?"

"I'm sure. And even if we had the money for a foreign adoption or a private one here in the states, I'm sure it *would* be a deal breaker. Would you let your baby go to someone with a record?"

"If they knew the circumstances…"

"No."

"What about a surrogate?"

"Same problem. And I'd worry constantly she'd change her mind even if we could afford it."

"Well, then we'll keep praying it works out. You have two more shots at this, right?"

"Yes. I wish I could settle down. I'm scared being stressed is hurting my chances. Maybe I'm not meant to be a mother."

"Stop the pity party."

"Easy for you…I'm sorry."

Jenna took a deep breath. She'd lost her baby the night of the shooting, and with forty on the horizon, knew it was unlikely she'd have another chance.

"You're still seeing that private investigator, right?"

"I'm not *seeing* him. We're friends, or so I thought. He's been MIA all weekend. I'll see if he shows up at the grief support group tonight."

"Let me know what happens. I have a student meeting in a few minutes. Catch you later."

Chapter 17

When Jenna walked into the grief support meeting, the aroma of coffee and the sight of glazed donuts gave her hope she'd be able to stay awake. Max walked up behind her.

"Good idea." He grabbed two donuts and poured himself a coffee with his free hand. "I need this tonight."

She didn't respond, nor did she wait for him. Her warm feelings toward Max had cooled significantly from the moment she had seen him buying flowers for God knows who.

Max sat next to her and leaned over to her. "Ready for more advice on sweating out your problems?"

"I suppose." She didn't look at him.

"What's wrong?"

"Nothing." She took a bite of the donut. She couldn't help herself from oozing out passive aggression. "How was your stakeout?"

"Stakeout? I wouldn't call it a stakeout. Just legwork on a case."

"And you couldn't answer your phone? Your client tried to reach you all weekend."

"To be truthful, I forgot it at home."

Does he seriously think I'm that stupid? He started to say more, but she put a finger to her mouth and whispered, "She's getting ready to start."

The gym rat spoke first. "I've taken positive action in my mother's memory. I'm organizing a 5K to raise money for ALS." He opened up a t-shirt with his mother's picture on it that advertised the first annual Maria Gigliotti run for ALS.

The organizer ran a hand across the t-shirt. "Beautiful. That's a wonderful way to pay tribute to your mother's memory."

The widow said, "I'm in. I can't run, but I can walk."

Max whispered, "Like that will make everything better. I can't walk but maybe I'll crawl."

Jenna gave him a harsh look, folded her arms, and turned full attention to the speaker.

He put his hand on her shoulder and whispered in her ear. "What's wrong? Something's bugging you."

"You shouldn't be mocking the poor boy."

"Mocking? Okay, fine. I'll zip it."

Both the widow and the gym boy turned to look.

"I'll help you out on race day," Max said. "I can register people or hand out t-shirts and water— whatever you need."

"Thank you. I appreciate it," said the boy.

Jenna whispered, "Nice save."

"Anyone else want to share?"

Jenna raised her hand. "I went upstairs and slept in my own bed for the first time since Giles died."

"That's fantastic. How did it feel?"

"More comfortable than the guest room bed, that's for sure."

The other participants laughed. Max clapped his hands in silent applause and nodded at her.

"And something else." She cleared her throat and

took a dramatic pause. "I think my dead husband was cheating on me."

The room fell silent. She looked from face to face—shock, surprise, pity...all the emotions she felt when she'd first come to that conclusion.

The gym boy broke the awkward silence. "How do you know he cheated?"

"I received a gold locket in the mail. At first, I thought Giles had ordered it and it got lost, or maybe he had it sent to the school. I figured it was a surprise for me."

The moderator said, "But you found that not to be true?"

"That's right. I found a receipt and went to the jewelry store where it had been purchased—more than three years ago. Surely he'd have given it to me if it was meant for me. The coward had two years between purchasing the locket and killing himself."

The gym boy said, "Maybe he forgot about it."

"He was cheating, I'm sure of it," said Jenna.

"How does that make you feel?" the moderator asked. "When someone we love dies, we often put them on a pedestal—think about all the good things. It has to be difficult finding out these things now. Especially since you never had the chance to confront him."

"I feel disappointed, gullible—and angry. Our relationship wasn't what I thought it was. All the more reason to keep moving forward."

"Good outlook," said the moderator. "It'll be a few steps forward, then one or two back, be prepared. But you're going in the right direction."

When the meeting ended, Max asked Jenna to get coffee. She was still angry but needed his help. "Okay, but you're buying."*If I drink much more coffee, I'll never sleep. It won't matter that the bed is comfortable.*

Once settled in a booth with baklava on the way, Max said, "How was your weekend? Other than finding out about Giles. I'm sorry I wasn't around to help you through it."

No, you were with your girlfriend, whoever she is. "Where do I start? Detective Russo came by for a cheek swab."

"A cheek swab? Did he have a warrant?"

"He did. I mean, I would have cooperated in any case. I want this solved as much as anyone, and I know I'm not guilty."

"Next time, don't be so willing to cooperate. Call me first."

"Like I didn't try? Did you check your messages over the weekend?"

"I'm sorry. I didn't have service where I was. Anything else I should know?"

Another lie. He said earlier he left his phone at home. "While the detective was here, a fuse blew and knocked out my electricity. He thinks someone deliberately changed the fuse so it would blow."

"Do you think it was Delores?"

"No. Remember the swatch of plaid fabric stuck on the branch?"

"Of course. The fabric didn't match?"

"It wasn't torn."

"Who else would want to mess with you?"

"I don't know. I'm just glad Detective Russo spent the night with me. It was dark and freezing cold until he fixed the fuse in the morning."

"He spent the night?"

Jenna had to admit she was enjoying this. "Yes. He's got a soft side under the harsh exterior."

"Don't let him fool you. He was a real bastard when I worked with him. Verged on abusive. It's no wonder his wife ran off with a professor."

She heard the contempt in his voice. "Our next move is to work on our fairly non-existent suspect list. So far, we don't have motive. I'd be inclined to go along with the coed killer hypothesis, but she was specifically coming to meet me. Her note said it was a matter of life and death."

"That's a figure of speech. If Isabel walked through the woods to meet you, perhaps the killer was lying in wait. The second girl was found in those woods as well. Maybe that's his hunting ground."

"*Is* his hunting ground? You think he'll do this again?" She thought about how she'd tried to reassure her class this morning.

"If it is a serial killer, he's still out there, and he's not going to stop."

"I'm going over to Santiago's tomorrow to brainstorm. How did I wind up in the middle of all this?"

"Because of the GPS and the other victim being your student."

"Yes, and someone's messing with me. I thought maybe our neighbor was doing the repairs, but he wouldn't destroy the fuse like that."

"Maybe he thought he was helping. What about your friend's husband, Oliver? Didn't you say he and your friend were over for pizza last weekend?"

"Yes, but I'm sure it wasn't him." She flashed back to the conversation about Oliver having a record. "And

I know I've been followed. And don't forget the hang up phone calls."

"Make a list. Besides Delores, who has a motive to hurt you? Could the fuse box have been an accident?"

"No. The detective said it had to be deliberate. Oh, and someone threw a firebomb on the lawn."

"What?"

"Oops. Guess I forgot to mention it."

"First thing tomorrow morning, I'll set up a meeting with Santiago and look into your friend's husband."

Chapter 18

Jenna stopped by Hayley's office in the morning. "How was your grief meeting? Did your friend show up?"

"I told them how I'm now able to sleep in my old room."

"That's huge."

"My back thanks me, to be sure. And I told them about the locket I received and how I think, how I *know*, Giles was cheating on me."

"I'm sorry I couldn't talk longer last night. You know I'm in your corner, right?"

"Yes. Getting a filet out of the oven before it burns takes precedence over comforting a messed-up friend." She was trying not to sound sarcastic, but by looking at Hayley's lips pout, she was sure it had come out that way. "And yes, Max was there. It was hard to stay mad."

"Mad for what? Because he didn't call you while on a stakeout, or because you caught him buying flowers?"

"It wasn't a stakeout. And I caught him in another lie. He said he left his phone at home. Later, he said he didn't have service."

"And how do you know the flowers didn't have something to do with his job?"

Now she's defensive because of my stupid comment

about the steak. "Okay, so maybe I overreacted." *To all of it.* "I want to ask you something."

"What?"

"Oliver and Giles were good friends. Is it possible Oliver has been looking out for me and making repairs on my house?"

"Without telling you? We went through this."

"You remember after Giles died? Oliver offered to do all sorts of things to help, but I told him flat out I didn't want him taking on the burden. It was shortly after he started his new job."

"He and Giles went way back. Friends since boarding school—I can see how he'd want to look out for you with Giles gone. He was sincere when he made the offer, but you turned him down. Why act now if he didn't act sooner? And without asking you? Besides, he's busier than ever with work."

"It's been a cold winter. And the anniversary of Giles' death is coming up."

"I did mention how you wanted to sell the house, but it was falling apart. And Oliver is really good with handy work."

"Last weekend when you guys were over for pizza, did you see him go into the garage?"

"No. Wait. You asked him to go out there and bring in a carton of soda."

"I'd completely forgotten."

"What are you thinking?"

"The garage door opener started working shortly afterward. Maybe he fixed it."

"I'll ask him."

"I don't want him to be embarrassed or anything. What if he didn't do it?"

"You can't have it both ways."

Kyle opened the door with a dramatic gesture. "I brought lattes. And you'll love this, Dr. Blake. They're offering a discount if you bring your own mug." He set the coffees on the desk. "One for you, one for you, and one for the environment."

"I feel like a proud mother," said Jenna. She sniffed the latte. "Peppermint mocha. I'm in heaven." Bijou jumped up on her lap and tried to get a sip.

"I hope I'm not interrupting."

"Since when has that been a concern?" said Hayley. She shook her head and half-smiled.

Kyle said, "I almost forgot. Did you see the news this morning?"

Jenna finished her sip of latte and said, "What news?"

"They caught a drug dealer who was selling on campus. Fentanyl. It's the new heroine."

"The one they thought was responsible for the football player's overdose last spring?" asked Hayley.

"That's him. And the two girls who were at the frat party a few months ago."

"How'd they catch him?" said Jenna.

"Forged documents. The translator had sent them to the police is what I heard."

"Translator?" asked Jenna.

"Yeah. He was trying to flee to South America, but he didn't speak Spanish well enough to fill out the paperwork. That's what I heard."

"This sounds crazy, but Isabel Hernandez did freelance translations. What if she worked for this drug dealer and then threatened to go to the police when she realized what he was up to?"

"Or, he didn't want any loose ends," said Hayley.

Kyle said, "You think she sent those documents to the police before she was murdered? How about asking that hunk of a detective who's been hanging around?"

"He's not going to discuss a case with me or any other civilian."

Hayley said, "What about Max?"

"Max? I don't know. Maybe. If Isabel did the translating and turned him in…" She remembered what Santiago told her about forged documents and sketchy foreign job applications.

"There's motive for murder," said Kyle.

"That doesn't explain why she wanted to talk to me the day she was murdered. I had nothing to do with forged documents or a drug dealer."

"Correlation doesn't mean causation. Isn't that what you always say?" Kyle sipped his coffee.

"I'll see if Max can find a link between the drug dealer and Isabel."

Jenna went into her office and pulled up the news article about the drug arrest. Kyle was right. The authorities said he was heading to South America and the police had been after him for some time. She called Max to tell him the news.

"I heard it this morning," said Max. "It crossed my mind about the translations as well. There aren't a lot of Spanish speakers here."

"Can you find out for sure?"

"I'm meeting with Santiago Salas later this afternoon. Want to come along?"

"Yes, please."

"Monk Haven Café. Three-thirty."

"Right after my class. Perfect."

During class, Jenna glanced at her watch every few minutes. Time seemed to stand still. *If I end class early, the students will be happy, but administration won't.* Nonetheless, she wound up stopping fifteen minutes early. Grabbing her jacket and dog, she rushed out the door before the students and was the first to arrive at the café.

Max arrived a few minutes later. "It's cold out here. Let's go in and get a table. Santiago runs on Cuban time."

They entered the restaurant and she sat next to him in a booth by the window.

"If Isabel did the translation for this drug dealer and turned him in or threatened to, we have motive. But what was my part in all this? Why did Isabel want to see me? And how does Brooke figure into this?"

"There's Santiago now." Max waved him over.

"I brought the client records you requested." Santiago handed Max a large accordion file. "I think she kept records on her computer as well, but these are assorted documents I found in her office."

"I'll go through these," Max said. "I'm thinking perhaps Isabel did translation work for the drug dealer who was arrested this morning."

"Ricardo Florez?"

"That's the name. Did you run across it?"

"I didn't have time to look. I gathered up the papers and brought them over. There's a lot."

"Was she the only translator in town? This is a thick file."

"Remember, she was illegal. Her clients thought she wouldn't run to the police."

The server turned up the TV.

"That's the campus," said Jenna. "Oh, my God. Looks like another student has gone missing. How's that possible?"

"They're dubbing the guy the co-ed killer. Three murders." Max hit his palm on the table for emphasis. "Now they've got a serial killer on their hands."

"A serial killer? They said this girl is missing. They haven't said anything about finding a body."

"Looks like the serial killer scenario is getting legs," said Max.

Jenna leaned in. "Did the girl go missing before or after Florez was arrested?"

Santiago said, "I'm not sure."

"If it was after, that gives him an alibi and blows the translating motive out of the water."

Jenna shuddered. "It could have just as easily been me if we're talking about a random serial killer."

Max put his hand on her shoulder. "But it wasn't."

"I'll keep translating Isabel's diary," said Santiago.

"I thought we were on the right track, but now? This just got a whole lot messier."

Chapter 19

Jenna fell asleep to the drone of the TV news discussing the co-ed killer. When she woke up in the morning, a different news reporter was talking about fear on campus due to the presence of a serial killer. *Just the publicity the campus needs. A serial killer.*

The thought sent a shudder through her body. Although the latest victim's name hadn't been released, she worried it was somehow going to come back on her. They still hadn't said anything about finding a body. *I'm sure they scoured the woods where they found Isabel and Brooke. This is awful, but I'm glad this girl has nothing to do with me. At least I hope she doesn't.*

Max called while she was scooping up the last bit of oatmeal.

"Hey, Max. Did you find out something since last night?"

"No. Look, I'm going to push Santiago to fast-track those diary translations."

"To link the drug dealer with Isabel's murder?"

"Yeah. If he was Isabel's client and she threatened to go to the police, that's motive right there."

Bijou begged to lick the oatmeal bowl. "Why would Isabel risk turning him in with her own security at stake?"

"I don't have an answer. The media is latching on

178

to the serial killer theory. I'll bet ratings are through the roof."

"They haven't found a body, so they can't call it a serial killer. It has to be three murders to be considered serial."

"I've got to go. I'll talk to you later."

Jenna picked up the bowl to put in the sink, then noticed dust from crumbling sheetrock on the tile under the wall. She picked up the sledgehammer and gave the wall a few whacks. She'd been making slow but steady progress—though she was tired of staring at the eye sore and breathing in cement dust. At least she was able to see through from the kitchen to the dining room now without standing on a chair.

After sweeping up the mess, she changed into corduroys and a tunic-length sweater—a Christmas gift from her mother. A few months ago, she'd have spent the day on the sofa in pajamas, despite prodding from her parents.

Bijou was curled up on top of the afghan. *What if I let him stay here and sleep instead of making him go out in the cold? I love him, but I don't need him like I used to.* Grabbing her keys, she headed to the door, then stopped short of opening it. *I can't do this solo. It's making me queasy just thinking about it.* She grabbed the leash and walked back to Bijou, sleeping like a baby on the sofa. Looking at him and glancing at the door, she clutched her keys and took a few deep breaths. *I've made it this far. I can do this.* Kissing Bijou on the head, she said, "See you later, buddy" and left the house.

Jenna pulled into the faculty parking lot right behind Hayley's black Toyota. Hayley walked with her into the building.

"Hey, I asked Oliver about the repairs. He says he wished he'd have been that considerate, but he can't take the credit."

"You're sure he's telling the truth?"

"Why would he lie about it? If he had taken the time to make those repairs, it'd have earned him major points. Like I said earlier, he would have told me. Besides, he's awful at keeping secrets, so it would have slipped out. What do you think about the third girl who's gone missing? They haven't released her name."

"Honestly? I'm glad they can't connect her to me. Of course, I hope they find her alive despite the serial killer hype. How are you feeling?"

"Hopeful. The hormone levels are where they should be and I'm having an ultrasound next week. Fingers crossed. Hey, where's Bijou?"

"I left him home."

"Really? Just like that?"

"Just like that. I'm feeling stronger than ever. This weekend I'm going to finish boxing up Giles' things and I'll send them off to Goodwill. I'd better drop this stuff off and get to class. We'll talk later."

When she got to the classroom, Jenna was surprised Kyle had beaten her there. About half of the students were missing.

"Where is everyone?" she asked.

"Everyone's scared. I heard a lot of parents already picked up their kids and won't let them come back until the co-ed killer is caught."

"We don't know even know if the cases are related."

"Seriously? Three murders on our campus in the

span of a few weeks? If they aren't related, there's something in the water. No way three different killers are in town simultaneously."

"The third girl is *missing*. No one said she's dead. They haven't found a body last I heard."

One of the students came up to them. "I might not make it to class the rest of the week. I'm too scared to walk on campus, so I'm going to fly home."

Scared in broad daylight? Then again, Isabel was murdered during the day. "If you stay out of the woods and walk in groups, you'll be fine."

"I can't. Whenever I think about those girls, it freaks me out. They should close the school until they catch the killer."

"If you let fear drive your decisions, it can really derail your life." *Says me, who has dizzy spells when walking across open spaces.*

"I'm not taking any chances. As a matter of fact, I'm leaving now." She walked over to the desk, grabbed her backpack, and walked out.

"Kyle, this is going to be horrendous."

"Going to be? You don't think two dead girls, most likely a third, isn't already horrendous?"

"I didn't mean it that way. Come on. Let's get started with the students we have."

Throughout the day, Jenna checked for a text from Max or Santiago. She'd hoped continuing to translate Isabel's diary would yield a clue. Nothing. She monitored the news, waiting to hear if they'd discovered a third body. Again, nothing. *There's still hope the third girl is alive.*

After school, Bijou greeted her at the front door, tail wagging.

She ruffled his fur. "I missed you, too." He licked her face. *Someone cares if I'm here or not.* "I love you, buddy. What would I do without you?"

She grabbed a handful of cookies, popping them into her mouth on the way upstairs. She changed into fleece leggings and slipped on Giles' Harvard sweatshirt. Giles loved wearing that sweatshirt and had no qualms nodding and smiling if anyone commented on what a fine school he'd graduated from. *Liar.*

From there, her thoughts turned to the gold locket Giles purchased, not for his wife, but for some woman he'd been carrying on with. She ripped off the sweatshirt and tossed it into the Goodwill box, replacing it with the fleece top that matched the leggings.

Anger fueled an urge to rid all traces of Giles. She opened his dresser drawers and threw his clothes into the cardboard box without a second thought. Then she opened his side of the closet.

Goodbye belts. Goodbye suits. Goodbye shoes underneath the suits. She picked up an expensive pair of Italian loafers he'd bought on a whim, and held them up, contemplating whether they'd fit Kyle. *He'd love these.*

She pulled out the cedar shoetree. *These are in mint condition. I only remember him wearing them once, to a friend's wedding.*

Her phone rang.

"Hi, Hayley."

"Hey, I need a friend."

"You and me both. Are you okay? It sounds like you've been crying."

"How does someone sound like they were crying?"

said Hayley.

"You sound hoarse, and the sniffling between words kind of gives it away."

"I'm so depressed."

"About the fertility stuff?"

"Yeah. I wish I could fast forward past the treatments and have a baby in my arms. I'm on edge and tired all the time. Oliver's going out of town on business again. Can you help with the shots?"

"Of course."

"How are you doing?" asked Hayley. "You said you needed a friend also."

"I was getting rid of Giles' things."

"Must be sad."

"More angry than sad. I can't believe he cheated on me."

"You're not sure he did," said Hayley.

"Then who was the necklace for? I'd better get back to it before I run out of steam. See you in the morning."

She couldn't focus on making dinner. Tried to remember if Giles ever mentioned a previous school, but couldn't. *If I call Elmwood, will they tell me the information he listed on his employment application?* They'd already be closed for the day. She called Max.

"Hey, Jenna. What's up?"

"I need your help."

"Go on."

"I've been going through Giles' things. First, the locket I got in the mail. Giles bought the locket three years ago. It obviously wasn't meant for me."

"You suspected that."

"Yes. At first, I assumed he'd been having an

affair. Now I think it was worse. I think he was carrying on with a student. Like he was a sexual predator."

"Seriously? Did I hear you right?"

"I found pictures of half-naked tweens taken in the band room and the camera that took them with Giles' things. And he has porn sites bookmarked on his computer."

"Lots of men, not me of course, look at porn sites. It doesn't mean he was a predator. And he's not here to defend himself regarding the photos. High school girls go out in public with their bare stomachs and shorts so short you can see their butt cheeks. Not that I look."

"It's more than bare midriffs."

"Wow. That's a shocker. I guess you can never really know someone, even if you're married to them for…how many years was it?"

"Don't make me feel more foolish than I already do."

"I'm sorry."

"Noted. Can you investigate his prior work history and see if this happened before? I don't know all the private eye shortcuts."

"What's the difference? He's dead now."

"Are you kidding? I have to know."

"I hate to see you dragged under by this. I'll see what I can do."

"How's your other case going?"

"Which case?" asked Max.

"The one that took you out of town last weekend." *The one that required you to buy roses and lie about leaving town.*

"It's coming along. I'll get back to you on the work history."

She took Bijou for a walk, watched a little TV, then heated up a frozen veggie burger.

Chapter 20

When Jenna got to school the next morning, flyers of the missing girl had already been slapped on every door and light post she passed. *So she was…so she is a student.* Despite privacy issues, her picture and name were all over campus. Natalie Johnson. Smiling and clutching a fluffy poodle, which reminded her of Bijou. She couldn't help putting herself in the shoes of the girl's poor parents. *I hope beyond hope she'll turn up safe and sound.*

Kyle met her in the hallway. "I hear they're organizing a search party later this afternoon to find Natalie. Want to join? I think I'm going to."

"Really? The last thing I want is to find another dead body. I think I'll skip it."

"I have news." He clasped his hands together, looking like he was either praying or trying to stay warm.

"From the look on your face, I'm assuming it's good news." He followed her into her office.

"Ross proposed last night. We're getting married!"

"Kyle, that's great news! When's the big day?"

"We're aiming for summer. I've always wanted to be a June bride." He mimed putting on a veil.

"I'm thrilled for you. You know, you could get a healthy start on your dissertation by then if you set your mind to it. Then you could spend more time enjoying marriage."

"I know. I've narrowed it down by topic choices. I'll show them to you by the end of the week."

"Okay, then. Looks like the thought of being a married man is already changing you for the better."

"What can I say? I'll see you in class. Do you think it's okay to tell the students?"

"Like you could keep your mouth shut even if you tried. The way you're glowing, they'll figure something's up."

He practically skipped out of the office as Hayley passed him at the doorway.

"What's with him?"

"I'll let him tell you himself."

"Okay. Can you help me with the hormone shot?"

"Oliver's off already?"

"Yeah. Before I woke up. He had an early flight."

"Shut the door and hand over the drugs. By the way, did you ask Oliver about Giles' work history?"

"He said he'd worked at a few schools but he couldn't remember the names. Sorry."

"I've got Max working on it. He's paid to find out these sorts of things."

"You're going to pay him?"

"Well, no. It was just…do you think I should offer to pay him?"

"Not if he didn't ask you to. He's your friend, right?"

"I think so." She wasn't sure of her judgement regarding men anymore.

"Are you joining the search party this afternoon?"

"I wasn't planning on it. I'm afraid of what I might find."

"There's nothing connecting this girl to you, right?"

"Nope. At least not yet. I've never heard of her, nor have I received an anonymous letter asking to meet." She didn't mean to sound as if she were taking this lightly.

Later that day, Max got back to her.

"I found Giles' prior employer."

"That was quick."

"He left in the middle of the school year. Strange, right?"

She couldn't totally agree, since she'd practically done the same last semester. "Not typical."

"Anyway, of course I had to do some digging. He was fired for misconduct while working at a music store many years ago. Did you know he worked in retail before becoming a teacher?"

"No, I didn't. Turns out there's a lot I didn't know about him."

"He had been written up and warned by HR before it happened."

"Let me guess. Sexual harassment?"

"It went a little further. It never went to court, but I checked bank records."

"And?"

"Giles made a significant withdrawal from his bank account before leaving town."

"Hush money?"

"Or a settlement."

"I'm not surprised—not anymore."

"Something else. He was fired from two other schools before coming to Elmwood. Actually, he was fired from one. Technically, he resigned from the other, but there was a police report showing he'd been named in an attempted rape case. The girl was a student teacher at the school."

"This just keeps getting worse. I thought I knew Giles, and it turns out my judgement was completely off."

"These types are first-class manipulators. Don't blame yourself."

"A manipulator, a predator, and a coward. A true triple threat. I should have never let his suicide derail me. He wasn't worth it."

"At least you know the truth."

"Thanks for the info."

"Not a problem. You want to get dinner tomorrow night?"

"Sure. Time and place?"

"I know a nice Italian place near the overlook. We can go for a walk afterward if the weather holds up."

"That would be nice. Thanks again."

She monitored the search for Natalie Johnson, checking the newsfeed periodically. Nothing.

Chapter 21

Jenna was pulling on her pajamas when the phone rang.

"Dr. Blake, it's Santiago Salas. I found something. It's important."

"What did you find?"

"The diary I've been translating? It didn't belong to Isabel. It belonged to her younger sister."

"You're sure?"

"Positive. The more I read, the less it sounded like Isabel. Isabel marked certain passages. And she had a slip of paper stuck between two of the pages. It looks like a phone number. It's hard to read—Isabel had the worst handwriting. I think it says detective something."

"A police detective?"

"I don't know."

"What were the entries about?"

"Looks like Isabel was going to the police over something that happened to her sister. I can't explain it over the phone. I'll have to show you."

"Okay. Call me back tomorrow and we'll set a time and place. And you should call Max."

"I tried. I was starting to tell him when he got another call and had to take it. Sounded like an emergency."

"I hope he's all right. I just spoke to him earlier. Anyhow, try him again tomorrow."

"I will. Sorry for bothering you so late."

"I was up. Not a problem."

In the morning, Jenna turned on the news first thing. Nothing about finding a body.

Arriving at school earlier than usual, she noticed a light under her door. Jenna's heart pounded. *Why did I leave Bijou at home? I'll contact security. But if someone is in the office, I don't want to give them a chance to escape.* Taking a deep breath, she pulled the mace out of her purse and opened the door cautiously.

"Delores! What are you doing sneaking around in my office? How did you get in here?"

"I wasn't sneaking. I just stopped in to deliver these minutes from the department meeting we had yesterday."

"What department meeting?" She was ninety percent sure Delores was lying, but part of her wondered if she'd missed something. "And how did you get in here?"

"The custodian let me in. Well, if you don't want them, I'll be going." She clutched the folders to her chest.

"Not so fast. Let me see that folder you're carrying." *So much for having the lock changed. I'll have to have a talk with Vincenzo. He should know better.*

"Out of my way." She clutched the folder tighter and pushed forward. Jenna grabbed her arm.

"Give me that folder."

"Not a chance." Delores broke away and waddled down the hall. Jenna considered calling security, but what would she say? Technically, Delores didn't steal anything, she was leaving something. What had she intended to leave? Another anonymous note?

What if Delores had set up the first meeting, the one with Isabel? *She knew Brooke was my student. Delores didn't know Isabel, but what if we got it backward? What if Delores planned to frame me for killing Brooke, but Isabel got in the way? But the handwriting...and the GPS...*

Settled at her desk, she rested her aching head face down on her folded arms until she felt her blood pressure get back to normal. She combed through the papers on her desk. Kyle had left her a list of potential research topics. She'd left it front and center to go over this morning, and it was gone. Nothing made sense. Why would she care about a TA's research topic?

I'll bet Delores has her own baggage. A criminal record maybe? Would the university have hired her if she did? One more thing to ask Max about.

She grabbed her phone and, although he'd said he was an early riser, was half-surprised when he picked up on the first ring.

"Jenna, what's up?"

"A couple of things. First of all, I'm at work. When I got to my office, Delores was here. She concocted a story about leaving me a folder but wouldn't let me see it."

"Why does she have a key to your office? Didn't you have the lock changed?"

"The custodian let her in."

"Did she take anything?"

"From what I could see, she took my TA's list of possible research topics. I have no idea what she's planning on doing with it. Can you do a background check on her for me?"

"Text me her full name."

"Also, I talked to Santiago Salas last night. He was trying to reach you. He thinks the diary belonged to Isabel's sister, not Isabel. And he found a phone number in the diary. He'll be contacting you."

"I'll get an early start on all this. We're still on for dinner, right?" asked Max.

"I'm looking forward to it."

During the day, everyone from custodians to freshmen took a stab at being an armchair detective, speculating on the identity of the co-ed killer and why Natalie's body wasn't found in the woods where the other two had been discovered. Barely twenty-four hours had passed and Stockholm syndrome was being tossed around as the most popular theory, with alien abduction running a close second. *Stockholm Syndrome? As if Natalie had bonded with her captor in this short amount of time? No way.* During lunch, she listened to a local psychic being interviewed on a podcast.

Flyers papered the walls, and a local news crew had set up in the quad, cornering passing students. "Do you feel safe with a co-ed killer roaming your campus?" *Brilliant. Anything for a story. Get these kids more hyped up and scared than they already feel.*

Jenna called Kyle to request a duplicate topic list.

Kyle squealed through the phone. "That bitch took my topic list? I made a detailed outline of three possible topics—even started drafting an abstract for one of them."

"She walked out with a folder, and the list that was on my desk when I left yesterday was gone. I'm guessing she took it, but I can't figure out how she plans to use it, unless it is another way to make me think I'm losing my mind."

"This is dire. An approved topic must be original research. She could rush to publish any one of my choices. She could set me up for plagiarism. You're my chair. It would come back on you."

"That woman must have no life. She seriously needs to find a hobby."

"And I think she has something to do with the murders," added Kyle.

"You think she'd go that far?"

"In a heartbeat." She pictured Kyle snapping his fingers. "Think how quickly she showed up when you discovered Brooke's body."

"Anyhow, get me a copy of your topics. This means you'd better get moving on the dissertation before Delores beats you to it."

"Very funny. I'm aiming for approval before spring break. Ross and I have wedding plans to make during the break and I want a clear conscious."

"I'll hold you to it."

She had no desire to teach, especially without Kyle to pawn off the direct lecturing portion of the class. The students were kept busy planning lessons on climate change. Unlike some other states, New York was progressive enough to mandate it as part of the public-school curriculum.

While they worked, she overheard talk about the co-ed killer and speculations on who it might be. One girl made a case for it being a disgruntled ex-employee. Another insisted it was linked to a recent prison escape. Jenna feared it was more personal. Someone targeted Isabel, and Brooke was collateral damage because she witnessed the murder. The third missing girl so far hadn't turned up dead.

After class, Santiago called her.

"The number in the diary was for a police detective. Either she had something to report, or her sister did."

"Did you talk to the detective?" asked Santiago.

"She couldn't tell me anything because of confidentiality issues. Even if they are both dead. Did Isabel ever say anything about being stalked?"

"No. And we were together practically twenty-four-seven. I'd have noticed. This had to be something regarding her sister."

"But her sister died, right? How long ago did she die?"

"A few years ago. But wait. When Alicia died, their mother packed her things and put them in storage before abruptly moving back to Guatemala. Isabel got a notice that the company was changing ownership and opted to collect Alicia's things rather than pay the increased storage rental fee."

"So she only recently found the diary."

"Yes. If something happened to her sister, Isabel just found out a week or so before she herself was killed."

"Did Isabel ever mention her sister having a boyfriend?"

"We had dinner once with Alicia and a boy named Cooper, I think it was. They seemed close, but I didn't keep up on the details."

"Keep working on the diary. I've gotta go."

Jenna went home, walked Bijou, and got ready to go out to dinner. Finding out all the awful dirt on Giles somehow gave her the freedom to entertain the possibility of dating again, guilt-free. After a second shower, she styled her hair into a half twist, then chose a sweater dress, pairing it with cable knit tights and boots. *A touch of lipstick, a squirt of perfume, and I'm ready to take on the night.* She was taking one last look in the mirror when the doorbell rang.

"Wow, you look beautiful."

Jenna blushed like a teenager on a first date. "Thanks. You don't look half-bad yourself." Max's hair was neatly brushed, and his face newly shaved. She smelled aftershave, or was it cologne? In any case, he smelled delicious.

"Are we taking Bijou?"

"No. I think he'd be more comfortable here rather than braving the cold."

"He pointed at the crumbling wall between the dining room and kitchen. "Looks like you're making progress."

"At the rate I'm going, this mess will be gone before you know it."

She followed him to his car, where he opened the door like a true gentleman.

"I haven't heard anything about finding the third girl."

"No, and I was just listening to the news. I talked to Santiago. The number found in Isabel's things was for a special victim's detective. That means…"

"I know. He called me."

"And did he tell you Isabel's sister had a boyfriend?"

"Cooper Flavin. I already tracked him down. Haven't spoken to him yet. Maybe tomorrow."

Max pulled in front of Casa Roma and turned the car over to the valet. The building looked like a medieval castle with vertical iron bars on the front windows and a row of white lights on either side of the steps leading to the front door.

"Valet parking? Fancy."

"I'm splurging. Besides, it's cold out." Max rubbed his hands together as if counting on friction to warm them up. He guided her inside, his hand resting lightly on her shoulder.

It took her a few minutes to adjust to the dim lighting. The aroma of garlic bread wafted toward the entrance. The hostess led them to a table covered in white linen with a stubby candle in the center. Nearly every table was taken, mostly by couples, old and young alike.

"This place is gorgeous," said Jenna. "I can't remember when I last had a first-class meal."

"You said you didn't eat meat, so I figured you can't go wrong with pasta."

"Italian's my favorite, and I'm starving."

"Me too. When my daughter was little, we used to make pizza together on Friday nights. My ex-wife worked late on Fridays and Taylor liked the idea of surprising her with dinner. I bought the dough pre-made, but she loved sprinkling on the cheese and watching it bake."

"Sounds like a nice memory."

Max picked up the wine list. "Red or white? Or do we assume red because we're eating Italian?"

She felt comfortable enough to tell him something she only divulged to Hayley. "I shouldn't. I'm on anti-anxiety drugs." *And I didn't handle the wine so well the night Detective Russo came over.* She looked at his face for a sign of disgust, but saw none. "My doctor says give it a little more time and he'll start weaning me off them."

"I get it. I've still got a bottle of Xanax in my medicine chest for those times I get into a dark place over Taylor."

They ordered the special—Mama's rolled eggplant. While eating their salad, Max's phone buzzed. "I'm sorry." He looked at the phone number. "I'd better take this. I'll be right back."

Jenna finished her salad, then went to the restroom to check the mirror for any leftover lettuce bits on her teeth. She passed by Max, huddled in the hallway with his back to her. She stopped for a moment, unable to resist eavesdropping.

"I told you, there's still a chance. As long as she's breathing, there's a chance."

Jenna ducked around the corner.

Max said, "I'm not giving consent. How many times do I have to say it? She's comfortable. They said that last weekend too but she was fine. I was there all weekend with her. Don't dare. You need my signature and if you try to…" He put the phone back in his pocket.

Jenna gave it a few minutes before going back to their table. The food was waiting.

"Everything okay?"

"Yeah. Fine." He cut his eggplant as though sawing through a slab of wood. Then he shoveled bites into his mouth, hardly stopping to chew.

"You can talk to me. I promise I'm trustworthy."

He put down the knife and fork and looked into her

eyes. His were moist, like he was fighting tears.

"It's Taylor. I lied when I said she was dead."

"What?" But the grief support group…the things you shared about losing her…"

"I did lose her. She's been in a vegetative state since the accident. The doctors say she's brain-dead, but I can't give up on her. My ex-wife keeps hounding me to let them pull the plug."

"How long can she remain on the ventilator?"

"Indefinitely, I suppose. They called Patrice because she got an infection from her feeding tube—again. Patrice wants to give up."

"And you're not ready."

"No. I go sit with her most weekends. I bring her roses—they were her favorite. I read to her, tell her about my life. I read about this girl who was in a coma for ten years and suddenly woke up. And then there's this thing called locked-in syndrome, where the person is really alive with thoughts and everything but their body seems dead."

She felt like a heel thinking the roses were for a girlfriend. "I sympathize with you. At least you're able to see and touch her."

"I can't let go of her."

The server came by with a dessert cart. Jenna was deciding between the tiramisu and the cheesecake when Max waved him away and asked for the check. There were tears in his eyes.

"Are you still up for a walk?"

His voice cracked. "Do you mind if we skip it?"

"Of course not."

"Want to pay a visit to Cooper Flavin tomorrow?"

"Isabel's sister's boyfriend?"

"Yeah."

"Tell me what time and I'll be ready."

Chapter 22

It took Jenna a while to fall asleep. *Poor Max. What an awful position to be in, deciding if and when to end your own daughter's life.* She wasn't sure how she'd react if placed in a similar situation.

Max arrived mid-morning. She took Bijou along, even though she didn't need him the way she used to. Bijou proved himself over and over again to be a great icebreaker. Max drove toward the campus. Neither discussed his daughter.

"Where does this guy live?"

"In a student apartment complex near the campus. He's a senior at Monk Haven U."

"And he'll be awake at this hour?"

"He set the time." His navigation system guided them around the school. Max pulled into a brick apartment complex with a rusty bike rack and student cars, most of which looked to be at least a decade old. "Here we are."

As they walked to the door, it took every ounce of restraint for Jenna to leave the recyclable beer cans and empty cigarette packages on the frozen ground. *Don't these kids know it's their world they are ruining? They're the ones who are going to be underwater and dealing with record temperatures.*

Max knocked on the door. A young man wearing gym shorts and a t-shirt opened the door. Once the outdoor air blasted him, the student hugged his body.

He had the manners to shake their hands and introduce himself, something Jenna found rare in these millennials. "Come in." He tossed a pile of papers off the sofa. "Have a seat."

Max started. "Like I said on the phone, I think Isabel Hernandez's murder may have something to do with her sister."

Jenna said, "Her sister set up a meeting with me right before she died."

"About Alicia? What'd she say?" asked Cooper.

"She didn't. She never showed up. We found Alicia's diary. It appears she was being sexually harassed, perhaps by a teacher."

"Wow. That makes sense. Alicia and I broke up weeks before she died. I'm not sure I can help you."

"What makes sense? Was there a change in Alicia's behavior? What caused the breakup, if you don't mind me asking?"

"She was acting weird right before she called it quits with me. I knew something was bothering her, but she didn't want to talk about it."

"Weird, how?"

"Quiet. She didn't want to go out of her own house. Stopped taking my calls, stopped posting on her social sites."

"She broke up with *you*? It was her idea?"

"Yeah. Said she didn't want to be in a relationship anymore. She acted, I don't know, depressed, I guess, is the right word."

"How soon before she died?"

"Maybe a week or two. I still can't believe she's gone."

"You don't know if she was getting unwanted texts or phone calls or anything?"

"No. I know she was skipping school a lot, which wasn't like her. Her mother caught on and said she'd drag her back to Guatemala if it happened again. If only she'd skipped school that day, she'd be alive."

Jenna assumed she'd been hit by a car or involved in a car accident. Max had warned her not to bring it up. When he spoke to Cooper, that's one thing he said he wasn't willing to talk about.

She knew all about 'if only.' She'd played that game a million times. If only she hadn't taken her lass to the library that day. If only she'd realized Giles was on the verge of suicide... "You can't go there. You'll drive yourself crazy."

"Anything else you can tell us?" asked Max.

Cooper reached down to pet Bijou, who had been sniffing and exploring since they'd arrived. "Sure. There was one more thing. I don't know if it's related or just a coincidence."

"What's that?"

"After she broke up with me, I drove to her house to try and talk to her. I couldn't change her mind. Then, the next morning, I went out to the driveway and all four of my tires were punctured. It was an old car and all, but still, who'd do that?"

"Do you think Alicia punctured them?" asked Jenna.

"No. Why would she? She's the one who called it quits, and she just wasn't like that."

"Okay. Here's my card in case you think of anything else," said Max.

Cooper put it in the pocket of his shorts and went

back inside his place.

Back in the car, Jenna said, "Do you know how Alicia died?"

"No. When I first mentioned her death, Cooper went ballistic. He couldn't talk about it. Said it was horrible."

"Do you think it was some kind of accident?"

"He mentioned something about school, right?"

"Something like that. I've seen people speed through those school zones. Kids these days walk with their heads buried in their phones. It's an accident waiting to happen."

Jenna's phone buzzed. She looked down at the caller. "It's Detective Russo."

"Ignore it."

"I can't. Maybe he figured out how my scarf wound up around Isabel's neck."

"Don't let him bully you."

She answered. "Detective? Yes, the new fuses are holding up well. Thanks again. I know. When I get some extra money put aside, I'll definitely upgrade." *Unless the market does a turnaround and I can get rid of the money pit.*

"A wooden key chain with my name on it? Where? In the woods? Smokey National Park? Giles and I vacationed there before we were married. I haven't seen it in years. Where did you find it?…I'm coming now."

"What was that all about?"

"Someone found a key chain with my name on it in the woods near where Isabel was murdered."

"It said Dr. Jenna Blake on the keychain?"

"Well, no. Just Jenna."

"Who finds a key chain and brings it to the police?

Does he think you're the only Jenna in town?"

"No, but it sounds like the one I had. I lost it, I don't even know when."

"So now it turns up, conveniently with your name on it, right near where the body was found."

"Someone's framing me."

"Yep. The police combed that area after they found the bodies. They'd have found it earlier."

"You think Delores is doing this?"

"Can you think of anyone else with a motive to get you arrested?" asked Max.

"If someone wanted me out of the picture, they could have killed *me* instead of Isabel and Brooke. Why go through all this trouble?"

"If they got caught, they'd have faced the death penalty. This makes it harder to connect them with a murder, especially if there's no connection to the other victims."

"Sounds complicated," said Jenna. "The serial killer scenario almost sounds plausible."

"Then how did your keychain wind up in the woods? Did you use it for any type of keys? For your office or anything?"

"No. And it wasn't the whole chain, just the piece that came off." She had a thought. "It must have been Delores. Maybe I did have my old keys on that chain. In all the drama between the shooting, the suicide, and my breakdown, who remembers what those original office keys were on."

"We're almost at the station. Want me to go in with you?"

"Please do."

Max found a spot down the block from the station.

When they walked in, Detective Russo was waiting to usher Jenna into his office.

"What's he doing here? He's not a lawyer," said Detective Russo, motioning toward Max.

"Do I need a lawyer?" Her whole body tensed.

"No. At least not yet."

"Max is a friend. He's here for support."

"I thought you had the dog for that," said the detective.

She ignored the comment. "It's not a formal interview or anything, is it?"

"No," he grumbled, looking at Max. "You can bring in a chair from the next room, unless you want to stand." He reached over to pet Bijou.

Max complied. By the time he came back, the detective was already in action.

"You don't deny the keychain belongs to you, and again, your scarf was used to kill the first victim."

"I may have had my office keys on it at one time. I honestly can't remember."

"How do you think it wound up near the victim's body?"

"I think a jealous coworker planted them."

"A jealous coworker? Really?"

"The woman who took over my classes when I was on leave. She and I are up for the same tenure track position, but I'm the more likely candidate."

"She's framing you and murdered two, maybe three girls so she could get your job?"

Max broke in. "She had Jenna's office keys. She even made a secret copy and tampered with things in Jenna's office."

"First of all, you stay out of it. Secondly, it sounds

too bizarre to be true that this coworker would go through all that trouble to frame you. Why not kill you right off the bat?"

"It'd be too obvious. Everyone knows she's after my job. This way, the murders can't be traced back to her."

"Creative, I'll give you that," said Detective Russo. "All the evidence points to you at the moment."

"Is she under arrest?" Max jumped up, looking him straight in the eyes.

"Not yet, but the evidence is piling up."

"Are you even looking for another suspect?" said Max.

"Cool your heels. That's what got you fired in the first place." He turned to Jenna, his tone softening. "This isn't personal. It's not like I want to see you thrown in jail. I'll look into this coworker, but if I were you, I'd get back in touch with that lawyer I saw you with the night Brooke Adams was found."

"We're going now," said Max. "If you can't do your job, we will." He slammed the door shut. Jenna followed him back to the car.

"I'm scared. What if I get arrested?"

"You won't be arrested. All the evidence they have is circumstantial."

"Since when is DNA circumstantial?"

"It's your scarf. Your DNA belongs on your scarf."

"Maybe I won't get arrested, but if I lose my job over this, I'm sunk—whether or not I get convicted. I'll never get another job, and what will I live on? I can barely maintain that money pit of a house as it is."

"We're going to take the bull by the horns. First, we investigate Delores. Want to help?"

"Of course I do."

"Come on." He led her to the car, then headed away from the police station. Ten minutes later, he pulled into a quiet neighborhood off a mountain road. If you weren't looking for it, you'd never notice the turn. Jenna was pretty sure she'd never been anywhere near this area of town.

Max lived in what she could describe as a cottage. One-level, white stucco outside with dark green shutters framing the paned windows. He opened the front door and, while Jenna expected a sparse bachelor pad, a cozy floral sofa, an overstuffed club chair, and watercolor landscapes on the walls greeted her. The dining area flowed from the living room and opened into the kitchen, the way Giles had envisioned their kitchen/dining area when he started hacking at their wall. She had to admit it wasn't what she'd expected. She thought it would be more masculine and sparse—like Cooper's apartment.

"I'll take your coat. You can leave your boots here on the mat." He pointed to several different size pairs of slippers. "Help yourself. I keep them for guests. Guess it's a habit from living with my ex-wife. She was a fanatic about dirt." He slipped into a pair of plaid scuffs. "Do you want something to drink?"

"Not right now."

"My office is in here." He opened the door to what could have been a second or third bedroom. A large, antique desk with a rolling chair dwarfed one wall. A twin bed covered with a floral quilt hugged the opposite wall.

"Nice. It's very homey."

"We sold the family home when I got divorced. I

set this up so Taylor would have a place to stay when she visited."

"That's so sweet. It must be hard looking at it, though. Doesn't it make you miss her?"

"No, it makes me feel like one day she'll be here."

"For months," Jenna began, "I couldn't sleep in the master bedroom. It hurt too much to think of sleeping in there with Giles and now that he's gone…"

"We all handle things our own way. Come on. Let's boot up this computer and find everything there is to know about Delores." He opened what looked like a wooden wardrobe.

"Oh, my God. Looks like a complete spy headquarters in here!"

"Can't be a private eye without the most up-to-date tools. Let's put them to use."

Jenna watched him type Delores's name on the keyboard. The screen blinked as though it were thinking, and a few minutes later, Max said, "No criminal record per se, but she had a restraining order taken out against her two years ago."

"Who took it out?"

"Alexander Montalvo. Back seven years ago. His last known address puts him in Pikeskill."

"That's less than an hour away. Come on."

"Whoa," said Max. "How do I explain having this information? It's supposed to be confidential."

"Hmm. You're right, but I want to do *something*."

"Hold your horses. Let's keep digging." He rifled through folders in the two-drawer filing cabinet beside the desk. Then he went back to the keyboard. "I'm looking at her work history. She worked at the community college, but then there was a gap in the history. She received unemployment checks for some time before beginning at Monk Haven U."

"So she was fired from her first college teaching job. I knew it."

"Not so fast. Had it been for anything horrendous, she wouldn't have been eligible for unemployment. Her date of termination coincides with the end of a semester. May is generally the end of the spring semester, correct?"

She shook her head and squinted over his shoulder. "What are you looking at now?"

"Professional organizations, anywhere she had a membership."

"She was in the college teaching association up until she was fired from the community college."

"And it doesn't look like she rejoined. That doesn't mean much. Without a job, why did she need it?"

"For the networking opportunities. That's precisely when she should have paid her membership dues."

"Maybe without a job, she couldn't afford the dues. Some of those professional organizations have hefty fees. I pay a couple of hundred a year in dues to the league of private investigators."

"Where do we start?"

"Hey, do you know if she's married?"

"Seriously? Who'd..." She stopped herself from sounding like a petty, mean girl.

"Well, it's not the one who took out the restraining order, I'll confirm that." His fingers were busy on the keyboard as he spoke.

"How do you know?"

"Delores has no social media presence, but her hubby sure does. Look. Pictures of him and Delores on vacation. Look at the one with her holding up that giant fish in front of the boat."

"Wow. She's smiling. I can't say I ever saw her smile. Maybe a smirk, but never a true smile."

"And there are posts about happy anniversary, happy birthday."

"Let me see." She couldn't believe it was the same woman who was trying to steal her job. She kept scrolling. "Wait. Her husband was in a car accident two years ago and lost his job."

"Let me look something up."

Jenna waited while he typed and searched. "Find something?"

"He hasn't been able to work but had no disability insurance. They've been struggling. They're living on her salary."

"No wonder snagging my job is so vital to her. Not that I don't desperately need it. I can barely make ends meet since Giles died." A twinge of guilt shot through her.

"The other party in the accident was Alexander Montalvo. We just saw that name."

"The restraining order. Two years ago."

Max kept typing. "They went to court over it. Delores's husband claimed Montalvo went through a red light, but they couldn't prove it in court. And people think red light cameras are an invasion of privacy. If there'd been one, I'll bet he'd have won the case, providing he was telling the truth."

"Delores probably went ballistic and went after him. I can picture it," said Jenna.

"That explains the restraining order."

Jenna sighed. "I'm not getting the feeling she's our

killer, honestly."

"Yeah. I agree."

Max's phone vibrated. "It's Santiago Salas. I'll put him on speaker."

"Max, I found something really important in addition to something I saw the other day in the diary."

"What is it?"

"I have to show you in person."

"We can meet at the café."

"Too public."

"Come over here. I'm home and Jenna's here too. I'll text you the address."

"See you in twenty minutes."

Max ended the call. "Sounds urgent. Let's hope it's helpful."

Chapter 23

Santiago made it to the house in under fifteen minutes. Max hurried him inside.

"This is big news. Look what I found." He opened the diary.

"This is in Spanish. You'll need to translate it," Max said, pushing it back to Santiago.

"Of course. This is how the entry translates."

This is the worst day of my life. I did one of those drugstore tests. I'm pregnant. I'm disgusted. I wish I'd reported it earlier, but I didn't say no. We were drinking and it was partly my fault. Now, I'm going public. I confronted him over it and he told me to get rid of it. Disgusting. I can't tell my family.

Jenna said, "She was barely seventeen years old!"

Max said, "If she was only seventeen, it was statutory rape. She certainly wasn't at fault. He was the adult."

"When was this?" asked Jenna.

"Three years ago. It's the last entry in the diary. Right before she died."

Max said, "Maybe Isabel found out and confronted the man."

Jenna said, "Three years later?"

Santiago stood up and paced while he spoke. "Isabel had just gotten her hands on the diary. Remember, it had been in storage for three years. If the company hadn't raised the rental fee, it'd still be there."

"Isabel finds out, then she's murdered?" *If the company hadn't raised the rates, Isabel would still be alive. It doesn't seem fair.*

"If she threatened to expose the man, that's motive."

"How can we find out who this man is? Can you contact Isabel's mother in Guatemala?"

"No. I'm sure she knew nothing about this and if she finds out now—well, what's the point? It will break what's left of her heart."

"He was a teacher," Max said. "We know that. Let's figure out where she went to school. That's a starting point."

"Can you use your private eye skills to find out?"

"Private eye skills? You mean my expertise?"

"Sure. That's what I meant to say."

"I'll try, but those types of records are hard to get into because of privacy rights relating to minors. Do you know where she went to school?"

Santiago shook his head.

Jenna's phone vibrated. Elmwood Charter. Her old school. *Why on Earth are they calling, especially on a Sunday?*

She wandered into the next room. "Hello?"

"Jenna Blake?"

"This is she."

"I'm a parent volunteer calling on behalf of Elmwood Charter. We're inviting all teachers, staff, and students to attend the grand opening of the new music building. We're dedicating it to the victims."

She remembered, vaguely, talk about demolishing and rebuilding the structure where the fatalities occurred. "Um, when is it?"

"Wednesday night at 7 p.m. We sent you an invitation, but we hadn't gotten an RSVP, so I'm following up."

She didn't recall receiving an invitation in the mail. "Okay, I'll be there."

Her legs wobbled like jelly as she made her way back to the living room.

"You okay?" asked Max. "You're shaking."

"It was my old school. They're having a dedication and I'm invited."

She was mentally back in the media center.

It smelled like musty magazines and newly opened disinfectant wipes. The carpet was rough. It gave her a rugburn on her knees. She felt Ryan's warm breath on her arm, smelled the baby shampoo in his hair, felt him quivering as she softly whispered to him and Janelle. Good night comb, goodnight brush...The rest of the class crouched together in the storage closet. She told them not to make a sound. It was a game. She prayed they would stay quiet and not be scared. Her ears were on alert, but she never heard a sound. She couldn't cram another body into the closet. That's when she huddled with Ryan and Janelle under the plastic tarp covering the media cart.

"Did you hear me?" Max was staring at her.

"Huh?"

"I said, when is it?"

"It's Wednesday night. Want to come along?"

He nodded. "I'll pick you up."

"It's going to be a tough night, to be sure."

"All nights are tough," Santiago said, "ever since Isabel's murder. Whenever I have time to think, I fall apart. Dinner time is awful."

"Max and I go to a grief support group on Monday nights. That's how we met. Want to come with us tomorrow night?"

"Maybe. Can I let you know?"

"Sure. I'll give you a call tomorrow late afternoon and see how you feel."

Jenna went home, able to use her garage for the first time now that the opener was functioning and she'd cleared some space. She entered the kitchen through the adjoining door. "Bijou, Mommy's home."

Bijou ran to her, tail wagging a happy greeting. As soon as she was sure Bijou was no longer required to be by her side, she'd take him with her again. She was close to being at that point.

"I missed you. Let me give you some food and later we'll take a nice, long walk." His tail continued to wag as she poured food into his bowl.

She rifled through the stack of mail on the kitchen table. *Electric bill with a past due notice, a phone bill...a credit card pre-approval offer for Giles. How long will I keep receiving mail for Giles?* She wasn't clear why it bothered her, but seeing something so normal as a piece of mail with Giles' name when things were so out of whack upset her. She tore the envelope into little pieces and threw it into the recycling.

She confirmed not having received an invitation to the dedication ceremony. It had been three years, but the thought of going back felt like a storm waiting to strike. She'd lost touch with most everyone. Several faculty members and staff showed up at Giles' memorial service, but that was nearly a year ago. All the empty promises of 'let us know if you need anything,' and we'll get together for dinner soon' hadn't materialized. They wouldn't. Hayley was the only true friend she'd made in all the time she taught there.

Monday passed quickly. Hayley was in a hormone-induced foul mood, in contrast to Kyle's euphoria over the engagement rings he and Ross purchased over the weekend.

Kyle held up his left hand. "Isn't it beautiful?"

Hayley shrugged her shoulders. "It's a gold wedding band."

"Not just a gold band. Look closely at the etching around the edges."

"It's gorgeous," said Jenna. "Have you set a date?"

"Not yet. We're aiming for June. It depends on the venue and what dates are available."

"Venue?" said Hayley. "That's where you get to sample menus and cake. It was my favorite part of the wedding planning."

"I know exactly the cake I want. A layer of red velvet, one layer of German chocolate, and one layer of fun-fetti. With cannoli cream in between the layers."

"Cannoli cream?" said Jenna.

"Fun-fetti?" said Hayley

"To balance the chocolate. You know me. I'd never settle for plain vanilla." He pulled a folder from his backpack and handed it to Jenna. "By the way, here are the two topics I'm considering, complete with a sample abstract for both. I'd like feedback by the end of the day."

Maybe this whole marriage thing is what it took to make him grow up and be responsible. "I need time to read it. Day after tomorrow. And, Kyle?"

"Yes."

"I'm proud of you for buckling down and getting this done," said Jenna.

He winked at her. "You knew I would get to it. I'm heading to the library if you need me." He strutted out the door with his usual flourish.

"And I'm heading home," said Jenna. "See you tomorrow."

It had grown colder now that the sun was setting. The clock on the bell tower read 4:45. *Not even five o'clock and almost dark. Depressing. I'm ready for spring.* By the time she neared home, she needed the headlights.

True to her word, Jenna called Santiago before dinner, not really expecting he'd accept their invitation to come along to the grief group.

"I remembered, and I'd like to come along. If I don't, I'll sit here and drink myself to death. I feel so alone."

"I know how you feel. Dinner time is especially hard for me too. Giles and I always ate together."

"After dinner, Isabel would put on her glasses and spread her papers all over the kitchen table. I'd work on my laptop. Being together in the same room while we worked made it seem less like work."

"Do you want us to pick you up?"

"No, just send the address and I'll meet you there."

Jenna put on her jeans and a green turtle neck. When she saw the headlights through the window, she threw on her jacket and went outside. Max reached over and opened the door.

"I'm glad you talked Santiago into coming to the meeting."

"I didn't have to. He didn't want to be alone tonight."

"I feel like that myself many nights. I dream that Taylor is her old self and living with me. I think she'd love the room I set up for her."

"I'm sure she would." She cleared her throat, not sure if she should say anything, but she went ahead, anyway. "You have to be prepared in case it doesn't happen."

"I know. It's a long shot, but maybe somewhere a researcher is coming up with a way to regrow brain cells, or a device that lets us communicate with her."

Jenna reached over and squeezed his hand on top of the steering wheel.

Santiago met them outside the conference room. "What do we do?"

"We go inside," said Max.

"Let's get coffee and cookies and come sit with us," said Jenna. "Those are our usual seats." He followed their lead. "The woman in the denim dress is the leader. She's a nurse, and I think she's also a trained psychologist. She lost her husband on 911. He was a firefighter."

"Welcome," said the leader. "Hope you all had a good week. I see a new face. Welcome, sir. Why don't you introduce yourself?"

"I'm not much for talking in front of a group."

"I swear, no one bites," said the leader. "We're here to support each other."

"My name is Santiago Salas."

"Welcome, Santiago. What brings you to us?"

"My fiancée was murdered. They haven't yet caught the killer. I'm barely holding myself together."

Jenna whispered to Max. "If the gym rat tells him to start doing bicep curls, I'll go postal. I mean it."

"I'm sorry for your loss. We all understand what you are going through because we have all been in your position."

"We were shopping for a house. Our real estate agent called and said she found the perfect place, only it was two days after Isabel was murdered."

The widow said, "Two years since my husband died and I keep getting mail addressed to him."

"Two years?" said Jenna. "I'm sorry, I didn't mean to interrupt. I just got mail for Giles right before I came tonight."

The widow continued. "When I turned in the car he'd leased, I had to explain to the salesman why I didn't need to replace it. I broke down right in the middle of the showroom. The people in there were all staring at me."

Santiago continued. "I had put a deposit down on a honeymoon cruise to Bermuda. It was going to be a surprise. She died not knowing where we were going after the wedding."

"Things left unsaid or undone are hard," the leader said, "but I'm sure you said you loved her. That's the most important thing she needed to know."

"I went into her apartment to start clearing out her things and I couldn't stop crying. I wake up in the morning and reach over for her, then remember she's not just spending the night at her own place. I'll never wake up beside her again."

The gym rat said, "I can smell my mom's pancakes. Isn't that weird? Sometimes I wake up and feel like she has breakfast waiting downstairs."

Jenna whispered to Max, "He used to eat pancakes?"

Max smiled at her, then said aloud, "Not knowing who killed your fiancée must make it worse. I know how I feel, not knowing who put my daughter in the state she's in."

"I thought your daughter was dead?" When the leader questioned him, the others nodded in agreement.

"Technically. She's on life support, in a vegetative state. I can't give permission to pull the plug, though she keeps getting bedsores and infections. It's worth something to still be able to sit with her. Anyway, my point is, I have to know who did this to her. It's ruling my life."

Jenna squeezed his hand for the second time this evening.

The leader said, "Would it really change anything if you knew? It wouldn't bring your daughter back. Do you feel it would make your anger any less?"

"Yeah, I do."

"I know who killed my husband," Jenna said, "and it makes me angrier than anything. He did it to himself. He abandoned me, and now I'm finding out he wasn't at all who I thought he was."

"What do you mean?" said the widow.

"He was taking pictures of half-naked girls. He bought one of them a locket, which mysteriously wound up being sent to me. No picture, just the locket. I wonder if one of the girls he was harassing sent it to tip me off. Though it hardly matters now that he's dead."

"We tend to idealize the dead," said the moderator.

"I feel like such a fool. Why didn't I see the signs? All those mysterious overnight trips with the band.

Really? I should have known. And yet, I get upset seeing mail with his name on it."

"Emotions aren't meant to be logical." The moderator turned to Jenna. "You have to find what will give you closure. Maybe it's realizing it wasn't your fault what your husband did. You still loved him. There had to be some good memories. You still have a lot of living to do, Jenna."

She turned to Max. "Maybe it's letting go of your daughter and taking her off life support. Having a funeral and putting a loved one to rest brings closure to many."

"I'm not giving up on her."

The widow said, "And for Santiago, it's finding the killer, right?"

"That would be ideal, but what if it doesn't happen? Santiago, after time, you'll put yourself back together, even if the murderer is never found."

"I don't think so. I can't live like this."

"Yes, you can. One step at a time."

"*Mierde*! More clichés. I've heard enough." Santiago stormed out of the room.

The room fell silent. Then, the leader spoke. "Grief goes through stages, usually not in the textbook pattern and they're most often not linear. He's still raw. What's it been, a few weeks?"

Jenna nodded. She remembered what a mess she was for months after Giles killed himself. She couldn't even get out of bed. In comparison, Santiago was doing amazingly well.

The gym rat said, "Hope he comes back."

The widow said, "I hope they find whoever killed his poor fiancée."

Chapter 24

The gray Tuesday morning mirrored Jenna's gloomy mood. Although Bijou was no longer a necessity at work, she missed having him constantly at her side and decided to take him with her. When Jenna arrived at her classroom, a handful of students had shown up.

Kyle said, "They're scared. We're down to half the students we started with."

"I saw new flyers posted on the way in. And there was a segment on the evening news last night. Have you noticed a police presence? The reporter said there was increased security on campus."

"Can't say I have. Maybe her parents should organize another search."

"I think they've thoroughly covered the campus. If they go that route, they'll have to widen the search area."

Jenna released the students half an hour early. She'd be repeating much of the information once Natalie and the killer were found and the drama settled. Kyle walked her back to the office.

"Did you get a chance to look at my abstracts?"

"Yes. Solid work. I think the second topic will be easier to manage. There are already surveys out there so you won't have to invent one and go through the whole validation process."

"I was leaning toward it. I'll get started on the paperwork."

"Ahead of schedule? I'm impressed."

"Planning a wedding has lit a fire under my butt. All I want to think about is how chic I'm going to look in my white tux, which deejay to hire, and which white sand beach serves the best margaritas."

"You may have a small respite while your topic gets approved, but you have to know you have a ton of work ahead of you. Writing a dissertation is like pushing a boulder up Mount Everest."

"And it gets so you can hardly breathe. I know. If you said it once, you said it a thousand times."

Millennials.

Kyle moved to the window. "Do you hear something?"

"No." She joined him, peeking over his shoulder. "Wait. I see lights."

"Where?"

"Behind the parking lot."

"Let's check it out."

They grabbed their coats and headed outside. Kyle sped up the pace. "A news van. Channel 6. I wonder if they found Natalie's body."

A small crowd clustered around the reporter, who Jenna recognized from the local news. She scanned the group and spotted the associate dean and Detective Russo.

Kyle whispered. "I think they're getting ready for a press conference. I'll bet they found the body."

At the center of attention, Jenna spotted a young girl who looked familiar. She turned to the flyer posted on the building beside her. Natalie Johnson. Alive.

A second news van arrived while the first reporter made an announcement. "Moments ago, Natalie Johnson, suspected to be the third victim of the coed killer, came back to us." The crowd clapped and cheered. "Detective Russo, do you care to comment?"

"We traced her through an old acquaintance and were thrilled to find Natalie safe and sound at a ski lodge on the other side of town."

The reporter shoved the mike in front of Natalie. "The town is sighing with relief. Why did you disappear without telling anyone? You had us all worried."

"I wasn't aware I had to report my every move. I'm a legal adult. The pressure got to be too much. Especially with a killer on campus. I needed time to decompress and didn't want to worry my parents."

"Perhaps a phone call or text letting your parents know you were okay?"

"We had no internet or television at the lodge, and I was surprised when the detective showed up and told me what had been going on. I'm so sorry for causing all this worry."

Jenna moved closer to Kyle. "So much for the co-ed killer. Hopefully, things will get back to normal."

"Normal? We still have two unsolved murders. Have you forgotten?"

"I most definitely have not forgotten."

Neither of them had noticed Detective Russo standing over their shoulders.

"Forgotten what?" They spun around. Detective Russo looked from one to the other.

Kyle said, "Forgotten how there's still a murderer on the loose."

"About that." He looked directly at Jenna. "The blood on the rock you found matches the victim's, and the medical examiner confirmed it's the murder weapon." His tone was harsh, in contrast to the warmth which had begun to seep out the night the fuse blew.

"And?" said Jenna. "We figured as much."

"I can't get past how you knew exactly where to find the murder weapon. And how you're the one who convinced Brooke's parents to organize a search."

"I'm not the one who...I simply followed the map they handed me. Oliver had GPS on his watch so he led us around. That section of the grid could have gone to any random person."

"But it went to you. It went to the woman whose scarf killed another woman in those same woods on the same day."

"Same day? It's confirmed? Brooke was murdered because she witnessed Isabel's murder?"

"And you were at the scene of the crime and knew both victims." He reached into his pocket, looking like he was going to pull out a cigarette and give it a slow draw while she got nervous and talked too much. Instead, he popped a piece of Big Red gum in his mouth, dropping the wrapper on the ground.

"I didn't..."

Kyle interjected. "Brooke was on our roster but had been to class maybe twice. I couldn't have placed her if I ran smack into her, and my eyes are much sharper than Dr. Blake's."

Jenna gave him a look, not sure if he was helping or hurting her case.

"We found a partial print on the rock as well as on the piece from your keychain. We're running it for a match."

"And did you get back the DNA results on the scarf?"

"Still waiting. I'll be in touch."

After he left, Jenna picked up the gum wrapper and tossed it in the trash.

"I wish I had turned over the camera Ross and I found right away."

"You think? Why didn't you?"

"We were—I was—afraid it might look bad for you."

"What! Are you serious? You think I had something to do with those deaths?"

Kyle stumbled over his words, not something Jenna was used to seeing. "That's not what I meant. I mean, maybe you got into a fight or she threatened you. Isabel left you that note."

"I'm speechless. To think you could consider that a possibility is profoundly disturbing."

"I didn't mean…"

"Save it." She stormed away, shaking her head.

On the way back, she noticed many of the flyers had already been ripped from the trees and buildings. She picked several off the ground. *How hard is it to throw these in the trash instead of littering? Millennials. God forbid they lift a finger for anything except texting and taking selfies.*

She managed to get some work done, though her annoyance at Kyle entertaining the thought she might be guilty, gnawed at her. To an outsider, the vague connection to the victims, the fact that she was near the murder scene when the girls were killed, that she found Brooke's murder weapon…oh, and her scarf was used to strangle Isabel. *Oh, my God, it really does look like I'm guilty. Still, Kyle knows me better than that. Too bad he didn't leave the camera alone so the police would have the blurry photo of Isabel being strangled.*

She called Max. "Hey, did you come up with a plan to get the photo to the police?"

"Not yet. I haven't figured out how to get both the camera and the developed picture to the detective without it looking like we tampered with the evidence."

"How about mailing the photo anonymously?"

"I think it will look too convenient. And how will they know it's authentic? I have to think about it some more."

"You know they found Natalie Johnson alive."

"Yeah. It's been all over the news. I never thought she was a third victim in this whole thing."

"I'm glad she turned up safe. The detective was at campus talking to the press. He still thinks I'm guilty. I'm scared this is going to be pinned on me. They have a partial print on both the bloody rock and the keychain. Of course, my prints will be on them."

"Like I said, it doesn't mean anything. Your prints are supposed to be there."

"He's running them through a database."

"There you have it. You know the first thing he did was match them to yours. Obviously, he found other prints on those items, too. Want to meet for dinner?"

"Yes. I'll be done around five."

"How about I cook for you?' Swing by on your way home. Do you have to stop and feed Bijou?"

"Nope. I brought him along for the company today. Should I bring something?"

"I got it covered."

Jenna taught her afternoon seminar, then headed to Max's. When she pulled into the driveway, the light against the lacy curtains showed Max's silhouette setting the table inside the bay window. So domestic. So normal. As she knocked on the door, she smelled something wonderful—chili maybe?

"Hey, come on in. Dinner is almost ready."

She hung her coat on the wooden rack and followed him into the kitchen. "I didn't know you were a cook."

"Old family recipe. My mother's a Texan through and through. This recipe won her a blue ribbon two years in a row at the chili cook-off in Wichita Falls." He opened the fridge. "I know we aren't typically drinkers, but you have to have a beer with chili." He popped the cap off an amber bottle and handed it to her.

"Detective Russo is on my back. He keeps implying I had something to do with the two deaths."

"I'm sure he's getting pressure to make an arrest but he has nothing on you. Like I said before, the guy's a bully."

She took a sip of her beer. "Have you heard from Santiago since the meeting? I'll bet he's sorry he agreed to come."

"No. I'm glad he came. Even if he's not ready now, he at least knows the support group exists." His phone vibrated. "Speak of the devil."

"Santiago?"

He nodded and switched the phone to speaker. "Hello."

"Max, I found something important I think. It was in with Isabel's client files."

"What is it?"

"Looks like she was translating an employment contract from Spanish into English."

"That's what she did, right?"

"Mostly she took things written in Spanish and made them look correct in English—employment histories or job recommendations—stuff like that."

"You think it's significant?"

"She was working on it when she was murdered. Perhaps this client had something to do with it."

"Do you have any information about the client?"

"Only this. And I think it's the same client she was forging the papers for."

"Keep looking. It could be the lead we need."

He put the phone back in his pocket. "Finally, something."

"Should he go to the police with it?"

"With what? Tell them his illegal fiancée was translating a job contract for a client? Could be perfectly legit."

"Then why hire someone he knew would be discreet?"

"I'm still working on getting the photo from Brooke's camera in Detective Russo's hands. I think I've got a plan."

Chapter 25

Wednesday night arrived. All day, Jenna had trouble concentrating on work, knowing how difficult it would be going back to Elmwood Charter. She thought about skipping the building dedication, but her therapist encouraged her to go, noting it would be an important step in 'continuing the healing process.' Max had agreed to accompany her, which made it a bit easier to face.

Show time. Pulling into the parking lot, Jenna's heart raced and she wiped the sweat from her forehead.

"You okay?" Max chirped the lock as they walked toward the school.

"I'm glad you're with me. I haven't been back here since…"

"I've got you." He put his arm around her shoulder.

The front entrance had been repainted and a new, brighter welcome mat covered the area outside the door. Inside, Jenna looked through the window to the left at the media center. Any other day she'd have been safely upstairs in her classroom, but that day…it was their library day.

On Friday afternoons, the kids gathered on the primary colored carpet behind the circulation desk while the media specialist read them a story. Afterward, they wandered through the shelves looking for books to check out. That day, the media specialist had called in sick. Instead of canceling, Jenna took the students herself, not wanting them to be disappointed. She looked forward to their library time every week—a break in the daily routine. If only she'd kept the students in her own classroom…the shooter never made it down the primary wing…

Thinking of the past, the floor wobbled, and heat rushed through Jenna's body. She once fainted after giving blood and this feeling was similar. She grasped Max's arm with both hands.

"Jenna? Come on. Let's find a place to sit."

"There's no place. I'm sure the rooms are locked." She felt nausea overtaking her body as the room spun. She closed her eyes. *Breathe in, breathe out. In and out.*

Max put his arm around her, squeezing firmly enough to where she thought she'd regained her sense of balance.

"Looks like people are going out that door. Can you make it? Maybe there's a bench outside."

"Yeah. That's the way to the other buildings. The band room is…was…the first one." He led her outside

The biting air smacked her in the face the moment they exited. She looked across a flat grassy area sparsely covered with snow. It could have been someone's backyard or even a tiny park in the middle of town. "Wow. You'd never know there was a building here."

"There's a bench. Let's sit a minute." He gently helped her down to the metal bench and put his arm back around her like a weighted security blanket. "Better?"

The cold air helped. After a few minutes, she stood up, a little wobbly but better. "Yeah."

They continued to the new building, which stood bold and clean against the backdrop of the small campus. Three stories as opposed to the former building which had two.

A middle-aged woman in a quilted jacket came toward them. As they got closer, Jenna recognized a familiar face. A face she knew in miniature minus the wrinkles. One she'd never forget. The woman smiled and embraced her.

"Jenna, how are you?" It was the mother of one of the students she'd held that day.

"Hanging in there. How's Janelle doing?"

"She's thriving at the private Montessori school in our neighborhood. I keep thinking how it could have been her name on the plaque inside the office if it wasn't for you making sure she was safe."

In her mind, she heard Janelle's quivering voice saying she wanted her mommy. She smelled the fruity hand sanitizer Janelle used to get the marker ink off her hand after completing the math activity she'd done that morning.

"Do you have a picture?"

"Of course." Janelle's mother pressed the side of her phone. "Here."

Jenna held back tears. "She's beautiful. Tell her I said so. She was one of my favorites, though teachers aren't supposed to have favorites." How could she help but feel a strong bond to a child with whom she faced such a life-changing event? "She looks so much like you."

"God bless you. Looks like they're ready to start. Let me find my husband."

A young woman bundled in a wool coat, black

boots, and ear muffs climbed onto a small, portable podium at the entrance to the new building. She wrapped her leather-covered hand around the microphone. Jenna whispered to Max, "That has to be the new principal."

"Welcome. For those who don't know me, I'm Mrs. Wells, principal of Elmwood Charter. I know it's freezing out, so I'll be brief. This building is dedicated to the memory of the loved ones we lost during the most horrific day this school has ever experienced. The names of those we lost have been etched into the cornerstone and in the spring, a memorial garden will be planted with benches dedicated to each of those we lost but won't ever forget."

Jenna felt herself disintegrating into a puddle of tears. Max handed her a wad of tissues from his coat pocket. *Would they be honoring Giles if they knew his secret?*

"And as we honor those we lost, I'd like to read their names aloud. Principal June Kaminsky. Coach Poller. Teacher assistant Karen Silverberg. Student Rubi Goldberg. Student Jada Camois. Student Alicia Hernandez. Let's have six minutes of silence for the six we lost before we cut the ribbon to our new building dedicated to their memory."

Jenna looked at the sad faces around her, who were all glancing toward the ground. Alicia Hernandez? That was the name of Isabel's sister. She recognized all the names mentioned except hers. Wait. Alicia Hernandez. Santiago couldn't talk about how Isabel's sister died, only that it was tragic. Allie Hernandez. Allie! It hit her like a strike of lightning. Alicia Hernandez, Isabel's sister, was one of the two students killed in the band room that day. She'd only ever heard her referred to as Allie. Her pulse raced.

The principal called up the teacher who had been shot and injured that day but had ultimately survived. He approached the podium with a limp. The principal helped him up the step before resuming her speech.

"We are honored to have our beloved teacher— now retired teacher—cut the ribbon across the entrance to the building. Feel free to go inside, take a look around, and then join us in the cafeteria for refreshments."

Jenna felt as though she was on a merry-go-round. Alicia Hernandez. Allie Hernandez. Band student. Giles' student. Giles, the child molester's student. *How did I not connect this before now?*

"Jenna, you okay? We can go home if you want to. You put in your appearance."

"No. I think Allie Hernandez and Alicia Hernandez are one and the same. I want to confirm."

"Alicia Hernandez, Isabel's sister?"

"Yeah. Only I'd only heard her called Allie."

They took a brief walk through the building, then on to the cafeteria. Jenna recognized a colleague who taught in the high school.

"Jenna? Last time I saw you was at Giles' memorial service."

"Yeah. I'm doing much better than I was then. I have a question. Allie Hernandez. You taught twelfth grade. Do you remember her?"

"Of course I do. She sat right in the first row."

"Allie. Her name was Alicia, right?"

"Yes, but everyone called her Allie. Nice girl. So sad."

"She was in the band. Giles taught her, right?"

"Yes. I chaperoned at a few of the football games."

"What was she like?"

"Sweet girl. Generally upbeat, but she'd gotten a bit withdrawn the weeks before she died. I even talked to Giles about it but he didn't think so. Said she was just acting like a moody teenager." Someone called his name. "That's a parent. I'll keep in touch."

Sure you will. She found Max and said, "Do you think it's too late to pay Santiago a visit?"

"Give him a call."

Santiago told them to come right over. His apartment wasn't far from the school.

"I feel sick. Giles was a teacher, for God's sake. He was supposed to be trustworthy."

Max shook his head. "Sickening."

"How could I have not known? I feel so guilty."

"You can't blame yourself. This is all on Giles, no one else."

Max pushed the speed limit and pulled in front of Santiago's place in record time.

Santiago answered the door on the first buzz.

The small, ground-floor apartment, a one-bedroom from the looks of it, was bachelor utilitarian. White walls, beige carpet, black leather sectional. The coffee table held a stack of papers and a single paper plate with a petrified pizza crust.

"I made coffee. What's wrong? It sounded urgent."

Jenna wriggled out of her coat while she explained. "Was Isabel's sister one of the students killed in the Elmwood Charter shooting?"

His face turned pale. "Yes. So horrible. Isabel never told me. I found Alicia's obituary the other day when I went through her things."

"She was called Allie, right?"

"Never by Isabel, but that night at dinner, her boyfriend called her Allie. Why are you asking?"

"We just came from the dedication of the new building at Elmwood Charter. Alicia was one of my husband's students."

"Are you sure?"

"Positive."

"Wait. I found something else in Isabel's things—in the box from storage. Let me get it."

While he retrieved it, Max said, "Are you sure you're ready to face whatever comes to light tonight?"

"Yes. I can handle it."

Santiago returned. He opened his hand and revealed a crumpled photo shaped like a heart.

Jenna willed the vomit to stop crawling up her throat. "That's my husband. That's Giles. He must have sent the locket to Alicia. She sent it back. That means..." She needed to sit before she fell. She lowered herself onto the couch.

Santiago said, "Alicia was pregnant. She wrote about being with a teacher."

"Oh, my God." The words swirled around her head. *Was Giles the baby's father?* She hadn't thought that far. "This keeps getting worse and worse. I think the teacher Alicia wrote about in the diary was my husband."

Max said, "Even if that's true, how does it figure in with Isabel's death?"

Santiago said, "Isabel had recently gotten Alicia's things. Maybe she didn't know until just before her murder. Reading the diary, she may have put it together."

Jenna said, "Do you think that's why she wanted to talk to me? What if that's why she came to the campus? It can't be a coincidence."

Max said, "It still doesn't make sense with her being murdered."

"She wanted me to know the truth about my husband. It makes perfect sense."

Santiago added, "So she was coming to talk to Jenna, but the killer was in the woods. The co-ed killer got her first? He was in the woods that day? A coincidence?"

Max said, "Too convenient. Brooke witnessing the murder, yes. Poor timing. But Isabel? There are more pieces to this puzzle."

"Alicia is dead. Giles is dead. Who cared if Isabel found out now?" Jenna yawned. Her body was at its limit.

"You look exhausted," Max said. "We should be going."

"I'll let you know if I find anything else." Santiago walked them to the door.

During the drive home, Jenna wavered between falling asleep and rehashing the evening. When she got home, she took Bijou for a short walk, then fell into bed.

In the middle of the night, she woke up feeling someone had been standing over her. Had Bijou barked? Is that what woke her up? She thought she saw a figure exiting the bedroom, but maybe it was the side effect of the sleeping pill she'd taken.

She pulled up the quilt, her heart pounding. Just when she was about convinced she'd been dreaming, she heard the stair creak. One step, halfway up, creaked if you didn't step right in the center. Bijou barked, his ears erect.

Fumbling for her phone on the nightstand, she called 911. Then, she did something she wouldn't normally have the courage to do. She commanded Bijou to stay in place. Thank goodness for obedience training. She looked around for something to use as a weapon, settling on the metal flashlight kept in the nightstand drawer. She padded to the door and down the staircase, avoiding the creaky step. The police would be here soon, but surely the intruder would have disappeared by then. She had to get a look—get a description.

She reached the bottom of the stairs, and held her breath, listening. *He's in the kitchen.* Her plan was not to confront him but to get a glimpse and give a description. Heart pounding, she hugged the wall and inched her way to the dining room. She peeked through the broken wall, holding her breath. *He's in there. I have to get a glimpse of his face before he runs out the kitchen door.*

She tiptoed into the kitchen. Then, everything went blurry. The figure grabbed her, spun her around, pushing her to the ground. The door slammed. Catching her breath, she scrambled up and rushed to the window, but it was too late.

Her arm ached from where she'd fallen on it. She managed to find her phone. Unsure how much time had passed, eventually, flashing lights blared through the window.

Detective Russo pounded on the door. Aching, she hustled to open it. A squad car pulled into the driveway seconds behind him.

"There was an intruder? You're sure? You didn't get a look at him?" asked Detective Russo.

"I woke up and heard someone in the house. I called 9-1-1, then tried to get a look but he pushed me down and ran out before I could see."

"Is anything missing?"

Jenna looked around the living room. Her purse was right in plain sight. That's where she found her phone. She opened her wallet and counted two twenty-dollar bills. The credit cards were still in their slots. "He didn't touch my purse. I don't see anything missing."

"Did you see if he was wearing gloves? Did he touch anything?"

"I don't know. It was dark. He ran out the kitchen door. He had to have touched the handle."

"I'll have them check for prints. Is there someone you can call so you don't have to be alone tonight?"

Was there a hint of an offer? His voice had regained a bit of the warmth it had from the last time he'd spent the night. She didn't want him to feel obligated. "I'll call my friend Hayley. I'll be okay."

"Did you change the locks on your doors?"

"Not yet. I'll call the locksmith first thing in the morning."

After the police left, Jenna considered simply going back to bed but knew she'd never sleep. She looked at the clock and weighed the inconvenient time against her friendship. *If I don't call her, Hayley will kill me when she hears about this.*

"Jenna?"

"I know it's late. I had an intruder tonight. Can I stay with you?"

"An intruder? Are you okay?"

"Just shaken. I'm not hurt."

"Want me to come by and pick you up?" asked Hayley.

"No, I can drive. We'll be right over."

Jenna packed up clothes for the morning and loaded Bijou into the car. Hayley's light was on when she pulled into the driveway.

Hayley met her at the door. "Are you sure you're okay? Why are you hugging your arm? Do you need a doctor?"

"No. I fell on my arm but nothing's broken. It's not even swollen."

"I'll get you an ice pack."

"No, it's okay. I'm so sorry to wake you."

"I was up. Oliver just got home a little while ago. From one of his business trips. You could have been killed."

"Don't be so dramatic. Whoever it was had every opportunity to kill me while I was asleep in bed, but he didn't."

"That's supposed to make me feel better?"

She followed Hayley inside. Oliver had started a pot of coffee and was setting out mugs.

"What's going on? Hayley said you had an intruder in the house?"

"The police came. He didn't hurt me or steal anything. I'm fine. Definitely getting the locks changed. I don't know why I didn't do it earlier."

"That does it. You're getting a security system."

"Thanks, Oliver. I don't have the money for that. I'm barely paying my bills."

"You're getting a security system if I have to pay

for it myself." He poured her a mug of coffee and sat at the table with Jenna and Hayley.

"I can't let you do that."

"Giles would never forgive me for not taking care of you in his absence."

"Thanks." *No way will I let him pay for it, especially with all the money they're spending on fertility treatments.* "I went to the dedication for the new music building at Elmwood Charter last night. Wait, I guess it was technically tonight. Or…"

"How did it go? It must have been difficult," said Hayley. "I probably should have shown my face."

"You were long gone before it happened. No one expected you to be there. I saw Janelle's mother. Janelle's in middle school now."

"I remember you talking about her. The little girl with the cornrows, right?"

Jenna smiled. "That's her. But the big news is I think I found a connection in the murder puzzle."

"What connection?"

"Isabel Hernandez's sister was Alicia Hernandez. Allie Hernandez. I don't know how it escaped me."

"And?"

Anger boiled in her veins. "She was one of Giles' band students. I think he got her pregnant. I think Isabel had just found out when she read Alicia's diary and she wanted to tell me." Once again, she had to hold back the vomit.

"That's ridiculous," said Hayley. "Giles would never…" Hayley looked at Oliver. "He wouldn't, would he? Look me in the eye."

Oliver cleared his throat. "Sorry, honey. Jenna may be right." He turned to Jenna. " I never wanted you to know, I mean, why spoil Giles' memory."

Jenna wanted to slug him. "Are you kidding, Oliver? You knew this and never told me? Did Giles admit to getting his student pregnant?"

"No, nothing like that. It's just…"

"What?"

"He was fired from a few jobs because of his issues. He had a problem but he swore he'd changed when he met you. I thought he had."

"A problem. A few jobs? He had a history? A history of what?"

"He sometimes misinterpreted cues. He wanted what he wanted and it wasn't always what the girl wanted."

"Sexual harassment? Rape?"

"I wouldn't call it rape."

Hayley said, "That doesn't explain why someone killed Isabel. Alicia died three years ago and Giles has been gone nearly a year. What was the point in Isabel even telling you this?"

"Do you think the murder was random? There is a co-ed killer on the loose and she was at the wrong place at the wrong time?" asked Jenna. *How naïve can she be? Of course it wasn't random. Didn't I just have this conversation a few hours ago?*

Hayley said, "I just don't know."

Jenna had enough. She felt angry and exhausted but didn't want to lash out at Hayley over it. "I should let you get back to bed."

"I put an extra blanket in the guest room for you and clean towels in the bathroom."

"Thanks. For everything."

The guest room doubled as an office. Although the

bed was covered in a frilly quilt with matching pillow shams, a small desk and rolling chair were nestled in the corner. Not wanting to sleep in total darkness, Jenna turned on the desk lamp. A collage of photos was pinned haphazardly on the corkboard over the desk and a coffee mug reading *'Teachers are a work of heart'* held miscellaneous pens and pencils. *This has to be Hayley's corner.*

The pictures made her smile. One was from Hayley and Oliver's wedding. *They look so happy.* She remembered it clearly—the awful bridesmaid dress. She couldn't figure out what had gotten into Hayley. Ruffles weren't normally her thing. Thinking about the wedding made her contemplate what a sham her own was. At the moment, she wanted to shred every photo of Giles—and there were many.

A Halloween photo caught her eye. Oliver and Hayley. Hayley was dressed as Little Red Riding Hood and Oliver as a woodsman. In a red plaid jacket! *Anyone with a Lands End catalog can get a plaid jacket practically overnight.* She dismissed the thought. Or tried to.

Chapter 26

Jenna didn't sleep well. *I can't believe Oliver knew about Giles' sickness and never said a word. If he'd only spoken up, I could have gotten Giles help. I know Oliver is hiding something else.* The sun had yet to rise. She heard a car starting outside and peeked out the window. *Where is Oliver going so early in the morning? Another business trip?*

She tiptoed past Hayley's closed door, down the steps, and past Oliver's home office next to the kitchen. When they bought the house, their first major argument was whether to use the room as a den, or a home office. Hayley relented after Oliver promised to screen in the patio. They could watch TV outside in the fresh air—at least during the spring and fall when it was neither too hot nor too cold to sit outside. Jenna thought Hayley had given in too easily and told her so, but...newlyweds. What could she say?

Is he hiding something in there that Hayley doesn't know about or doesn't want to know about? Something drove her to try the door. She gently turned the knob. Unlocked. *Oliver left, and Hayley sleeps like a rock. She won't be awake for at least another hour.* She'd been duped by Giles; she wanted to make sure her friend wasn't in the same position.

All those business trips, and late nights. Who gets back from a business trip late like he did last night, and leaves for work before dawn? He hasn't changed jobs; he hasn't gotten a promotion that would require more hours. He's hiding something, just like he was hiding what he knew about Giles' past.

With Bijou in her arms, she pushed the door open, hoping it wouldn't creak. Not that Hayley would hear it upstairs with the door closed. Opposite the door, a large mahogany desk with a leather office chair was the focal point of the room. There was a closet to the left, then a three-drawer filing cabinet. A tall bookshelf, which matched the desk, took up the wall to the right.

Let's start with the papers stacked on the desk. She rifled through and found a catalog of office supplies, UPS receipts, and utility bills. She held one of the receipts close, wishing she had her reading glasses on her.

He sent a package to Nashville two days ago. She picked up another. *He sent this to Atlanta. Both cost around the same and both were expedited, meaning expensive. Why didn't he do his mailing through his office rather than paying for it out of his own pocket?*

She opened a desk drawer and found a stack of folders, each with the photo of a young woman paper clipped to the outside—at least half a dozen. *Is he looking for a mail-order bride?* If Hayley found these, she'd have come directly to her for support. *He has a criminal record.*

She froze. *Why do I hear a car pulling up?* Through the spaces in the blinds, she saw headlights. She quickly clicked off the desk lamp. While she contemplated what to do next, she heard the kitchen door open and footsteps clicked across the tile. Now what? *Bijou, please don't bark. We have to stay quiet.*

The footsteps stopped. She let herself breathe. Then they started again, coming closer and closer.

In an instant, she opened the closet door and ducked inside, clutching Bijou. She curled into a ball, grabbing her knees and ducking her head under hangers full of musty winter coats and party dresses.

She saw the light from under the closet door and heard the desk drawer open and shut. The footsteps came toward the closet. She held her breath once again. The filing cabinet squeaked like nails scratching across a chalkboard. *What's he looking for in there?* A slam, then another drawer opened…and closed. She clutched her heart when she heard Oliver's voice.

"Hello?" *Oh my God, he knows someone's in here.* Her mind raced for explanations as to why she was huddled in the closet with her dog.

"Brooklyn? Yes. I wanted to confirm our appointment. My flight arrives tonight at six p.m. Text me the address. Looking forward to our meeting."

He's just on the phone. She'd dodged the first bullet, but now what? Her legs had fallen asleep. She moved slightly and hit into one of the hanging dresses. She heard the wrap-around hanger slide into the next garment. A panic attack slammed into her like a wave approaching the shore. Bijou licked her face. She nuzzled him against her neck. *Breathe in, breathe out. Hanger, coat, dress.* She braced herself, knowing the door was about to open. But it didn't.

Oliver slammed a filing cabinet drawer closed. Next, she saw the light disappear from under the door and heard the office door close. *Please, God, let him be gone.*

She waited until she felt it was safe to crack open

the door. She heard the car pulling out of the driveway, the headlights disappearing. A few minutes lapsed before she dared to shake her legs awake, unfurl her body, and stumble out of the closet.

When her breathing returned to normal and her pulse stopped hammering against her veins, she left the office, closing the door softly behind her. She prayed Hayley was still asleep. The downstairs lights were still out, and it was quiet as the room in *Goodnight Moon*— the book she'd read to Ryan and Janelle under the tarp in the media center.

She bundled up Bijou and left. When she got home, she texted a thank you to Hayley, then tried going back to sleep but couldn't. She took a warm shower and guzzled a few Oreos for breakfast, washing them down with a cup of coffee.

Afterward, she did a search for locksmiths. She called the one that opened the earliest and arranged to take the day off from the university. Kyle agreed to cover her classes. Then, she called Max to tell him about the intruder. Should she mention the closet incident? And the photos of beautiful young women? And the phone call setting up an out-of-town rendezvous?

"Why didn't you call me? You could have been killed. Let's drop all of this right now. You found out why Isabel wanted to see you that day. Isn't that the mystery you needed solved?"

She opted against revealing the details of this morning. "Seriously? The police think I killed her. Why did she have my scarf wrapped around her neck? Detective Russo is going to pin this on me if we don't find an alternative."

"I'm doing some work for another client this morning. I'll call you afterward."

"I'll be here."

Hayley texted her. —*Glad you're okay. Take the day. Kyle and I have you covered. I'm going for an ultrasound after school. Fingers crossed.*—

Jenna hoped and prayed Hayley would get good news this time. She'd be a natural mother judging by how she treated her students when she taught at Elmwood. *If Alicia lived to have the baby, I might have been a stepmother. Sick. Surely if Alicia and Giles were still alive, Giles would be behind bars.*

The locksmith showed up shortly after breakfast.

"So you want the front door lock changed? Which others?"

"There's a back door through the kitchen, and can you put a lock on the interior doors? Like the one leading to the garage?"

"Sure I can."

"And how about a bedroom door? Right now there's a padlock on the outside of the door. God knows what the previous owners kept in there, but I'd like it removed and replaced with an interior lock if you can."

"Must have had a teenager. I've thought about it myself. I'm just kidding. Done. I won't even charge you full price."

While he worked, Jenna's thoughts turned to Oliver. Why was he spending so many nights away from Hayley? He'd been out last night, arriving home just before she got there. Hayley had a key to her house, for emergencies. *He and Giles were like brothers. He owned a plaid jacket. No way. Don't go grasping at straws so the police leave you alone.*

She jumped when the doorbell rang. *Not again.*

"Good morning," Detective Russo said. "I went by your office and they said you were home today."

"Did you figure out who was in my house last night?"

"We got a partial print from the back doorknob. Has anyone besides you used that door recently?"

"Not that I can think of. I thought he wore gloves?"

"Maybe he took them out to fumble with the lock, although there were no marks indicating the lock was tampered with."

"Meaning?"

"The intruder may have had a key. Besides you, who has a key to this place?"

"No one. I mean, Hayley has one. She and Oliver watched over the house while I was staying out of town with my parents. I told her to keep it in case of an emergency." *In case I locked myself out in my not-so-predictable mental state back then.* She kept that to herself.

"Not related, but coincidently, we recovered a gun. It washed up along the river a few days ago."

"And?"

"We're thinking it was stolen. We traced it back to your husband, Giles. Did you know he owned a gun?"

"No, I mean, yes. I recently found a gun receipt in his things. I didn't find a gun. I know he talked about getting into hunting."

"This wasn't a hunting gun. Your husband purchased it legally at a gun show several years ago. Did your husband mention being robbed or having his car or office broken into? Or that he had a gun stolen?"

"No. Never. And he wouldn't have kept it in his

office, or his car if he owned one. I'd been in his car many times and his office was in the back of the band room at school." *And if he owned a gun, why not shoot himself instead of jumping off the bridge? It would have been simpler.*

"He didn't file a stolen gun report."

"What's the difference if he had a gun and if it were stolen? Neither Isabel nor Brooke was shot. I wish you'd concentrate on the matter at hand."

"He didn't report it. Maybe he didn't realize it was missing. The other option is he resold it but the paperwork wasn't filed."

"Who cares? You found the gun, and my husband's been dead going on a year. Don't you think you should be focusing on finding out who killed Isabel and Brooke?" asked Jenna.

"The gun is tied to another crime. One we've been trying to solve for some time. It's the first break we've gotten. Anyway, we're still waiting on DNA on the scarf."

"Is there something else?"

The detective looked her in the eye, then swallowed. "Let's sit down." His tone had softened.

"What is it?" She followed him to the sofa and sat.

"We recovered remains, near where we found the gun."

"A body?"

"Bones, actually."

"Bones?"

"A human femur and a skull, to be blunt. The medical examiner says the bones are from a male and have been in the water for at least several months. We think it may be your husband, based on the river's flow pattern and the fact they were recovered near your husband's gun."

She felt sick and was glad to be sitting down. Her head felt like it had been hit with a taser. "You found my husband's body?"

"I can't say for sure until we run tests, but I think so, yes. Are you okay?"

"Yeah. I mean, it's a good thing. We'll have something tangible to bury—or cremate." She didn't feel connected to the words leaving her mouth. Without a body, she'd always hoped maybe he'd survived somehow. Maybe he'd gotten amnesia and was living a few towns over. *I watch too many soap operas for my own good.*

"Can I do anything for you? Do you want a glass of water?"

"No, thanks. I'm okay."

The detective fidgeted. He got up, then sat back down next to her, then got up again. "Looks like you're taking care of changing the locks. Stay safe."

I knew he was dead. This is closure.

After the locksmith finished, Jenna took a nap. When she woke up, she felt a little better, and not wanting to be alone with her thoughts, she took care of a few errands while she had the opportunity. She stopped at the cleaners to pick up the clothes she'd dropped off.

The man handed her the dresses she'd brought in. "Do you want to take your husband's jacket as well?"

She put the dresses back on the counter. "What did you say?"

"I've got a jacket that belongs to your husband. It's under the same account."

Took them long enough to get to it. "Sure."

He grabbed a hanger from the rack. "Here you go. It's heavy. Need help?"

"No, I can manage. How much do I owe you?"

He handed her the ticket. She looked and gasped. "Why so much?"

"Leather jackets need special care. Besides, looks like there were numerous stains."

"Stains?"

"That's what it says on the ticket."

She took out her credit card and handed it over. She recognized Giles' black leather jacket through the plastic. He'd fallen in love with that jacket on their honeymoon but it was way out of budget. She'd written down the information, put aside a bit of each paycheck, and surprised him with it for their first Christmas. It brought her as much joy watching him open it as it did him receiving it.

It meant enough to him that he took it to get cleaned. It's probably one of the last things he did before his suicide. He wanted me to have it to remind me of our first Christmas. Tears rolled down her cheeks. She was angry at herself. *He proved to be a liar and a sexual predator. Why am I feeling sad at all?* She'd bring it up at the next grief support meeting.

She got back in the car and draped the clothes across the back seat. By now, it was early afternoon. On the way home, she got a call from Santiago Salas.

"Jenna, I can't reach Max. Do you know where he is?"

"He's working on a case. That's all he told me."

"I found something very important. Can you come by the apartment?"

"I'll be right there." She turned the car around and headed to Santiago's apartment complex.

When she arrived, she rang the buzzer. Twice. *Where is he? He called not fifteen minutes ago.* She tried again, then called his phone. No answer. She was about to give up, but something inside told her there was a problem. She peeked through the window. While doing so, a car peeled out of the parking lot. A black sedan.

She went to the other window and peeked in through the partially opened curtains. *Oh my God.* She screamed and banged on the window. Santiago was lying on the floor, papers strewn all over the place. And there was blood.

She tried the window, but it was locked. She grabbed her phone from her purse, fingers shaking, and called 911. It took three tries to correctly punch in three digits.

"Hurry. A man is lying on the floor and bleeding. I don't know if he's dead or alive and I can't get into the apartment."

"Stay in your car and wait until help arrives. Don't go in alone."

Heart thumping like a jackhammer, she sat back in her car, tapping her fingers against the steering wheel. *I can't stand the waiting. I'm going to jump out of my skin if this takes much longer.*

She tried Max, but it went straight to voicemail. *Every time I really need him, he's not available.* Waiting and doing nothing when a man might be dying a few yards away was difficult. She'd been in a similar situation once before, hearing glass shatter and doing nothing but waiting for gunshots.

An ambulance screamed as it neared. A patrol car pulled up behind it. Detective Russo jumped out. The manager was waiting by the door to let them in.

"What happened?"

"Santiago called and said he had some important information to share. He wasn't able to reach Max so he called me. It took less than fifteen minutes for me to arrive and I...he didn't answer the door so I peeked in the window. There's blood and I don't know if he's dead or alive."

"The EMTs are in there now. Wait here. I need to get in there."

She followed Detective Russo. "I saw a black sedan peel out just after I arrived."

The EMTs were doing chest compressions. *At least he's still alive.* Then they loaded him onto a stretcher and wheeled him to the ambulance. The detective turned to her.

"Didn't I say to stay out? This is a crime scene."

"I...I won't touch anything. I had to see if he was alive." She looked at the mess on the floor. File folders and papers all over. She could see some names.

"Get out. Now." The detective was called away by an officer.

Jenna walked around the outskirts of the mess, squinting and bending down to read the names. *Santiago said something about a contract in Spanish Isabel had been translating into English. John...*

"Ma'am, the detective said to escort you out before he puts you under arrest."

"I'm going."

She tried Max from the car. No answer. Then she drove to the hospital to see what was happening with

Santiago. She prayed he was alive.

She flew into the emergency department. "My friend was brought in a little while ago. His name is Santiago Salas. Can you tell me how he's doing?"

"Are you family?"

"No."

"I'm sorry, I can't give out that information." She watched an officer go through the waiting room and into the door. "Can you at least tell me if he's alive?" She didn't get an answer.

A middle-aged Hispanic couple brushed by her as they ran through the door and to the counter. "Our son was brought in. Santiago Salas. Can we see him?"

"Of course. Go on back."

Jenna stepped outside to get a signal and tried Max yet again. This time he picked up.

"Finally. Santiago Salas is in the hospital. He was attacked in his apartment. Someone was looking for something. Isabel's files were all over the floor."

"I'll be right there."

She paced around the waiting room. If only she'd gotten to Santiago's place five minutes earlier, she may have been able to prevent the attack. Her head ached and her stomach growled. *I need some fresh air.* An ambulance screeched past her, lights flashing. The wind numbed her face in a matter of minutes. Her blood vessels constricted, having the opposite effect on her headache than she'd hoped for.

Jenna went back inside and plopped on the hard orange chair. Not a fan of hospitals, she wrapped her scarf around her nose and mouth as protection against the old man hacking away next to her. She flipped through an ancient magazine, finding it hard to concentrate. She poured hand sanitizer into her palms when she'd finished—a habit from her elementary school teaching days.

Once again, she paced around the room, hoping Santiago's parents would step out; knowing they'd probably not leave his side. A blast of cold air rushed in when the automatic doors opened and Max walked in.

"Any news?"

"No."

His parents came out just as she was about to retell the story to Max. She went right up to them and introduced herself.

The mother said, "You found my boy? They say if he'd been on that floor any longer he'd be dead. Thank you."

"How is he? Will he be okay?"

"They're doing some tests. He hasn't woken up. He has a gash on the back of his head."

"Will you keep us informed? Max and I have grown close to him."

Max said, "I'm a private investigator. Santiago hired me to find Isabel's killer."

"I thought the police were doing that?"

"They are, but he wanted an extra pair of eyes."

"Poor baby. He was so in love with Isabel. We loved her too. She was perfect for him." Her eyes glistened.

"I'm so sorry for your loss."

"Let us know if we can help in any way," said Max. He gently led Jenna back to the parking lot.

"Want to get dinner?"

"Yeah. Where were you today? I called and called. When I saw Santiago on the floor like that, I was so scared."

"I'm sorry. I spent the day with my daughter. Saying goodbye."

"What? Did you…"

"Pull the plug? Not yet, but I've decided to let her go. She's not winning the battle against the nasty infection from her feeding tube. I called my ex-wife. She's flying out tomorrow so we can do it together."

"That's a big step. Maybe you'll both find peace now. She can move on to a better place."

"I don't think I'll ever find peace—even if the hit-and-run driver is caught. I love Taylor more than I've ever loved anyone. I didn't know what being a father meant until the moment I held her. She was pink and soft. She fell asleep in my arms, trusting me not to drop her. I'd never held a newborn baby before."

"She knew she could trust you. I think babies have an instinct that tells them who their parents are."

"You think so?"

"I do. I was pregnant once. For a short while. But the moment I found out, I had a bond with that baby. I think he or she felt it too."

"We had our arguments—especially when she was a teenager."

"All parents do. You know that. You were a teenager once. They talk about the terrible twos, but from what I've heard, the terrible teens are far worse."

"I was so proud of her at her high school graduation. She was third in her class. And she was athletic. She ran cross country and played volleyball. We used to ride bikes together."

"I know how hard this is. If she's getting infections, she may be in pain. You don't want that."

"Part of me thinks when we turn off the machines she'll start breathing on her own and come back to us."

"I don't know what to say. Nothing's going to make it hurt any less."

He began to sob. Jenna hugged him tight, and they stayed that way for what seemed like an eternity.

He pulled back and blew his nose. "It's freezing out here, and I'm hungry. Let's share a pizza."

He put his arm around her and they walked silently to the car.

Chapter 27

The next morning, Jenna checked her phone before getting out of bed. She wasn't sure why. Even if Santiago hadn't made it through the night, it's not like his parents would have made calling her a priority. She wondered if they'd even kept the business card she put in his mother's palm.

She texted Max to say she was thinking about him. He'd be heading to the airport soon to pick up his ex and head out to his daughter's nursing home. He responded with —*Wish me luck.*

Sitting next to a dying daughter has to be awful, but sitting with your dead daughter? Even if it was the right decision, it had to be devastating. There's no coming back from death.

Her thoughts turned to Giles. She should make some sort of arrangement for him. Was there enough left to cremate? She couldn't make herself go there. She'd planned to talk to Max about it, but after hearing about his daughter, she couldn't bring it up.

"Bijou? Come on, boy. You're coming with me today."

He wagged his tail as if he knew exactly what she was saying.

At school, she knocked on Hayley's door. "Can I come in? Why's it locked? Are you okay?" She heard the door click open, and Hayley whisked her inside.

"You look awful. What's wrong? You were fine last night."

"I had bloodwork done this morning. It's not looking good. The IVF isn't going to work and I..." Her voice broke. "I'm never going to be a mother. Maybe God is punishing me for waiting so long or putting my career first."

Jenna embraced her. "Nonsense. You said you have three tries. One more, right?"

"I can't go through this again. I feel like a piece of me died. This baby I always imagined having is now dead. I know that sounds weird, it's not like I had an actual miscarriage." Her face fell. "I'm so sorry, Jenna. I didn't mean..."

"It's okay. I've made peace with losing Giles' baby. It wasn't meant to be."

"I know you love kids."

"And I'll find a way to have children in my life when the time is right. If it means waiting for my sister to make me an aunt, or taking in a foster child, or doing after-hours tutoring. You don't think it will happen, but you never know. I think you shouldn't rule out adoption."

"I told you Oliver has a record," Hayley snapped.

"I'll bet there's a way. When the time comes, you'll figure it out."

Hayley blew her nose and wiped her eyes. "I have to teach in a little while. Do I look like a disaster?"

"Brush your hair and throw on a little lipstick and you'll be good to go."

She didn't know if it was really the best time to ask, but she did. "In the guest room, I saw a photo from Halloween where you and Oliver dressed up as Red

Riding Hood and the Huntsman."

"Yeah. A few years ago we dressed up for a friend's party. That's out of left field."

"Does Oliver still own the jacket? I mean, it looks like the fabric we found in the woods."

"What are you saying? You can't be implying…"

"No. I'm sorry. I shouldn't have asked. I'm grasping at straws right now. Forget I said anything."

"I think he borrowed it from Giles. They were about the same size. I've got to get to class."

Jenna returned to her office. She'd managed to insult Hayley, suspect Max, and be insulted by Kyle all in the span of a few days. No wonder she felt alone. She needed Hayley to keep her balanced and Kyle to remind her to smile once in a while. And she needed— wanted—to be around Max. Poor Max. With the ordeal he was facing today, she needed to support him rather than the other way around.

She picked up Bijou. "I'm glad I brought you along today."

He licked her face. "I can always count on you to make me feel loved." She kissed the top of his head. "Let's get to class."

Kyle wandered into class fifteen minutes late, carrying a coffee cup, which he threw not in the recycling, but in the trash. She swore he'd smirked at her as he did it. Back to his old habits. They barely spoke during class.

Afterward, on her way back to the office, she texted Max to let him know she was thinking about him.

It would be hard for Taylor's mother, too. Although she'd been advocating to remove life support, she was sure the reality of her daughter being declared dead would hit her hard. Losing a husband was difficult, but losing a child? When she miscarried the night of the shooting, she was devastated for months and she'd only been pregnant a few weeks. She couldn't imagine letting go of a child who'd been with you for close to two decades.

Detective Russo called, jarring her from her thoughts. "Ms. Blake, can you come by the station?"

"Again? What is it this time? Do I need a lawyer?"

"No lawyer necessary. Santiago Salas regained consciousness. I want to crosscheck some information, that's all."

"Santiago's going to be okay?"

"Yes, looks that way. His parents are grateful to you for finding him. You probably saved his life."

"I'll leave now. See you in fifteen minutes."

Once at the station, she was ushered directly into Detective Russo's office.

"You wanted to see me?"

"Have a seat. Santiago Salas found out the employment contract he was translating was for a band director position at a school in Colombia."

"Band director?"

"Your husband taught band at Elmwood Charter, correct?"

"Yes, he did."

"Did he give you any indication he was contemplating leaving the country and moving to Colombia? Maybe he asked you to go along."

"What? No. Colombia? He doesn't even speak Spanish, how would he teach in Colombia?"

"It was a band position. Music is the universal

language, isn't that what they say?"

"Ridiculous. And if he was thinking about fleeing, why did he opt to kill himself instead? Anyway, what makes you think Giles was the one asking for the translation?"

"The file is missing. It seems to have been what the intruder was after when he broke into Santiago Salas's apartment. There was a passport photo attached to the contract. Salas says he's positive it's the same guy as in the locket picture he found. He said you'd know what he meant."

"Yes. He found a heart-shaped photo that matched the size of the gold locket my husband purchased—for Isabel's sister, Alicia. They're both dead now. So what if my husband contemplated fleeing the country as opposed to killing himself? He felt enormous guilt over the two girls who died in the band room that day, one being Alicia." *The sleaze ball thought about taking off to Colombia without telling me. I'm glad he opted for suicide. The coward didn't deserve to live.*

"Since the file is missing, we aren't sure of the date the translation was completed. I wondered if you could offer any insight?"

"No. Like I said, this is the first I heard about him fleeing the country. Do you know when I can get his remains? I want them cremated."

"I'll let you know when the lab is through identifying them. If you think of anything, give me a call."

"What about the DNA from the scarf? It seems to be taking a long time. And the partial on the key chain piece?"

"I'm going to call and check up on it. The report

should have been back by now. The locksmith finished the job, right? All your locks have been changed?"

"Yes. I even had a lock installed on the interior bedroom door for extra measure."

"Good. Keep your eyes open. We still have a killer out there."

She was glad he'd separated her from 'the killer.' "You don't need to remind me. Let me know when you get back the lab results."

"I will. Oh, and one more thing."

"What?"

"I received a blurry picture that seems to have captured Isabel's murder. It was sent anonymously. Do you know anything about it?"

"Blurry picture?" *That's why he stopped treating me like a suspect.* Inside, she was shaking. Could he tell she was nervous? Did he think she was the one who sent it? "No. I certainly don't. Are you sure it's authentic?"

"According to the lab, it is. No matter. If you don't know anything, you don't know anything. Simple as that."

She pulled the door shut and took a deep breath as soon as she left the police station. Had she pulled it off or did he know she'd already seen the photo? Worse, he probably thought she'd sent it. It didn't matter. It got her off the hook.

Jenna went home and flopped down on the sofa. How had she been so blind? Giles was planning on fleeing the country, and she had no clue. She'd been so naïve—so trusting. Getting a teenage student pregnant, taking photos of half-naked teens, child porn sites? In a million years, she couldn't believe that was the man she married.

She'd dozed off and was woken by her phone vibrating.

"Max? Are you okay?"

"Yeah. It's over. I'm on the way home. It was the right thing to do. She looked almost peaceful. I guess if she was suffering, she isn't anymore."

"It had to have been hard."

"Yeah. My ex fell apart when they pronounced her dead. Funny. She's the one who'd been pushing for it all this time."

"Taylor was her daughter, too. Your head can say whatever it wants, but you can't stop your heart from feeling. Are you doing a funeral?"

"No. We're going to have her cremated. I want to spread her ashes somewhere beautiful where I can go and feel close to her."

"Like your special spot?"

"Yeah. I'm surprised my ex agreed, but she did. I'll call you when I'm home."

"If you want to stop by, feel free."

"Thanks for the offer, but I think I need to be alone right now."

She couldn't help thinking about Giles planning to flee the country and normally would have talked it out with Max, had the circumstances been different. What made Giles decide to kill himself instead of running? He was lucky the shooting happened when it did. Alicia was on the verge of accusing him of rape from the looks of it. *All this time, I thought I was responsible for his death because I didn't see the signs and help him through the guilt over the shooting. Now I wonder if the guilt over what he did to Alicia also played a role.* The phone buzzed.

"Santiago, how are you feeling?"

"I've got a terrible headache, but I wanted to thank you for saving me. It's too bad the contract is gone. Something I wanted to tell you, but now I can't remember. The doctor says it's common to have a little short-term memory loss right after a trauma, and to give it time."

"You rest up. If it is important, you'll remember. I'll drop by the hospital tomorrow."

"Call first. If all is on track, I'm being released tomorrow. My parents are going to stay with me for a few days."

"Good. Get some sleep."

She wanted to be patient but was dying to know what he wanted to tell her.

Hayley called practically the moment she ended her call with Santiago.

"Jenna, I have to tell you something."

"Go ahead." She was glad Hayley didn't sound angry after she accused Oliver last night.

"I asked Oliver about the plaid jacket. I was right. It wasn't his. He borrowed it."

"From who?" asked Jenna.

"From Giles, like I thought."

"Are you sure?" Her stomach twisted into a knot.

"He swears he returned it to Giles right after the party."

"Okay. Thanks for letting me know."

"And there's something else."

"What?"

"Last summer, Oliver was cleaning out the barn. He has this fantasy about raising chickens and cows.

Like that's going to happen."

"And?"

"He found something."

"What?"

"He found black jeans he swears belonged to Giles, a black shirt, and…"

"And what?" She wanted to reach in and pull the words out of Hayley's throat.

"One of those ski masks. The kind that covers your face. They were hidden in one of the horse stalls."

"Hidden? Why would Giles hide clothes in your barn?"

"Because he didn't want them found. Because he planned to retrieve and burn them later. We haven't been inside the barn for years. Who knows how long they were there. I guess we can't ask Giles."

"Why is Oliver telling you this now? He didn't mention it when he found them?"

"I think he was protecting Giles."

"What are you talking about?"

"There's more."

"More?"

"The clothing is stained," said Hayley. "With blood."

Chapter 28

Oh, my God. The thought of Giles having a part in the Elmwood shooting hit her like a steel wrecking ball. *No, he never could have done something so horrendous. Maybe it was Oliver and he was lying to Hayley.* She felt nauseous. *Then how can the bloody clothing in Hayley's garage be explained? He tried to help the victims. He ran over and felt for pulses, applied pressure to their wounds. That would explain the bloody clothing, but not the ski mask.*

Wait. The leather jacket. The dry cleaner said it had stains. Had Oliver borrowed it? Last Halloween, he and Hayley dressed up like the couple from Grease. Did Hayley actually see the bloody clothing and ski mask, or was she taking Oliver's word for it?

With unsteady hands, she punched in the number for the dry cleaner. Her throat was so dry she could barely swallow. "I was in the other day and picked up my husband's leather jacket. The cashier mentioned it had multiple stains. Is there any way to know what kind of stains they were?"

"I can check the order. Special chemicals are used for difficult stains. Can you read me the order number?"

She fished through her purse and read him the number, then waited on hold, trying to keep her heart from beating through her chest. *What if his jacket had been stained with blood? Does that mean he wore it the day of the shooting? He wouldn't have shown up for work in a leather jacket.*

"Ma'am? It looks like they were blood stains."

"You're sure?"

"Yes. We use a specific chemical on blood stains."

She didn't remember putting away the phone. This was more than she could fathom. *Was my husband the school shooter? If so, why? Because Alicia Hernandez was about to turn him into the police. He'd raped her and she was pregnant. There was no backing out. Giles would have been arrested.*

She picked up the sledgehammer and hacked at the dining room wall. Every so often, she'd rest, then resumed the thwacking. The top half of the wall had crumbled, and she picked at it until the opening was below eye level. When she couldn't lift her arm another time, she collapsed on the sofa, never making it to her bed.

The next morning, she gulped three aspirins, hoping to make a dent in her horrendous headache. *Was it all a bad dream?* She washed down a handful of chocolate cookies with two cups of coffee and poured clean water into Bijou's bowl. *Did I really discover my dead husband was the school shooter? How stupid could I have been? Living with a rapist and a murderer and not noticing?* Her head felt like it was no longer attached to her body. She doubted her ability to drive but somehow made it to campus in one piece.

Hayley met her in the parking lot. "Are you okay after last night? Maybe there's an explanation for the clothing Oliver found."

"I know the explanation. I keep thinking back to that day at the school. The bodies of the two girls were found just outside the practice rooms. Giles said he was setting up the seating for his woodwind ensemble, which met the following period. The shooter would have come upon Giles before getting to the girls, so why did he survive? In that scenario, the shooter confronted him, walked past him, shot the girls, and left?"

"It does sound unlikely."

"Especially since Giles claimed to have tried to protect the girls. I never had the courage to picture how it all took place before. I wasn't able to let my mind visualize it all."

"But it's Giles we're talking about. Maybe he ran out to his car or chickened out and hid in his office."

"They never found the shooter. It's like he disappeared off the face of the Earth. And how do you explain the bloody clothes and bloody leather jacket he dropped off at the dry cleaners? Did Oliver ever borrow Giles' *leather* jacket? You said he borrowed the plaid one. Maybe for last Halloween?"

"No. He has his own leather jacket. Giles' jacket was at the dry cleaners? How long do they keep those things? The shooting was three years ago."

"I don't know. Maybe it got mixed up in the back or something. It was stained. With blood."

"There has to be another explanation. Maybe the blood came from the victims. Are you sure Giles dropped it off? It was his jacket? Sometimes they mix up those cleaning orders. It's happened to me."

"Wait a minute." She had a flash of something not adding up. "I have the receipt in my purse." She dug it out. Her stomach dropped to the floor.

"What's wrong? Are you going to pass out?"

"The date. His jacket was dropped off a month ago. How's that possible? Did Oliver drop it off? When did you say he found the other clothing?"

"Last summer. He never said anything about a leather jacket."

Jenna couldn't help wondering if Oliver was the guilty party after all. He'd been traveling excessively, found the clothing, and he 'borrowed' the plaid jacket. *What was his motive? What was the real reason he had a criminal record and couldn't be approved for adoption?*

"Are you okay?"

He and Giles were like brothers. What if he did the shooting to help Giles get out of the mess he'd have been in if Alicia went to the police?

"Yeah. I need to get focused on my class. I have no clue what I'm doing, and I haven't seen Kyle around, have you?"

"Come to think of it, I haven't. It's going to be okay. We'll talk later? There's my TA. I need to catch her."

"Yeah. I'll stop by after my class."

The room spun and Jenna grabbed onto the wall. Hayley was out of sight, which she was happy for. Jenna didn't want her to know she suspected Oliver was behind this. All his traveling—was he doing business on the sly and planned on running off to Colombia? Maybe Oliver was John Talbot. He and Giles could have passed for brothers—both with the same brown eyes and mousy brown hair. Oliver had a key to her house and knew the repairs that were needed. Jenna worked her way over to a bench just as her phone buzz beneath her coat.

"Santiago? Are you back home?"

"I'm waiting to be released. I remembered what I had to tell you. The date on the paperwork was recent. Whoever Isabel was working for, he wanted the contract translated because it had to be returned before next week."

"What are you saying?"

"The doctor just came in. I'll call you back."

Jenna tried to make sense of the timeline. Oliver had a job. What business was he hoping to join in Colombia? He wasn't a teacher, let alone a music teacher. Giles was. But he was dead. They'd just found his remains. Or what they assumed were his remains. The official report hadn't come in yet

She worked her way to her feet. Then, the phone buzzed again.

"Ms. Blake, it's Detective Russo. We got the lab results back. The DNA on the scarf? It belongs to Giles Blake. So does the fingerprint partial on the key chain piece."

"What? How? How do you even have his DNA and fingerprints?"

"The fingerprints are in a database. All teachers are fingerprinted. You must not remember."

"No, you're right. I do remember being fingerprinted when I started working. But the DNA?"

"We accessed one of those ancestry databases."

"Like you did for me? How am I supposed to believe you?"

"Do you remember him using such a kit?"

"I bought him a kit last Christmas. He wanted to know if he was more Irish than English." She guessed the detective was being truthful this time.

"You may be in grave danger."

"Are you saying…"

"I'm saying I think your husband is still alive. And I think he knows we're figuring it out."

"But you found his remains. And his gun."

"So far, the lab results are inconclusive as to whether those bones belong to Giles. We're waiting on further testing."

She felt herself fainting, but maintained control. "You really think he's alive?"

"Yes. Where are you now?"

"At school, outside the education building."

"Go inside and lock the door. I'll send a car to pick you up."

She heard what sounded like an explosion. "What was that noise? What just happened?"

"Hang on. I see it on the scanner. Gunshot. At your campus. They've called a code red. Get inside *now!*"

Jenna pounded at the entrance, which was locked. "Let me in. Somebody. It's Dr. Blake. I'm locked out." She pounded and screamed until her knuckles were as raw as her voice. She knew it was protocol not to open the doors during a code red. She scanned her key card knowing it probably wouldn't work. It didn't.

"Dr. Blake, are you still there? Are you inside?"

Her chest felt like it was being strangled, looking at the nearly deserted campus. "I can't. The doors are locked."

She heard another shot. Her whole body shook.

"Take cover."

"Where should I…hello? Detective Russo? Detective?"

Another shot echoed through the quad. She hugged

the building and looked across at the gunman. The way he stood—even at this distance, she knew it was her husband. Then she heard his amplified voice.

"I'm going to kill everyone in sight. You can't hide from me. I'm not going down for Elmwood Charter and I'm not going down for this. Jenna Blake, come outside and let me explain. If you don't come out. I'm shooting each window, starting with the education building. And every student left out in the open is fair game."

She felt wobbly and her body again wanted to faint. *I can't. This is all up to me. If I don't go across that open quad and meet him face to face, he'll keep shooting. Breathe in, breathe out. Building, sidewalk, bench. I thought they recovered the gun used in the shooting. Did he have his own arsenal?*

She put one foot in front of the other and steadied herself. She stood, looking across the open quad at her husband. *I can't do this.* Her agoraphobia strangled her. *If I don't go, we're all dead.*

"I see you, Jenna. I have to have the chance to explain. Come closer. I won't hurt you."

Her head spun to where if she looked across the way she was too dizzy to move. *Close your eyes. You can do this.* She took several steps with her eyes shut tight. The locket, the pictures…She held back vomit. The porn sites, the gun, the bloody clothing…*Don't pass out or we'll all be dead.*

She felt the fear that enveloped her that day crouched under the cart in the media center. Ryan's heart beating, his tears dribbling like rain onto her arm where she nuzzled him like a hen protecting her chick with her wing.

"Come to me. You're almost here."

She prayed the others would stay quiet in the closet. She whispered in Janelle's ear. *Good night comb, goodnight brush.* She was the old lady whispering hush. The glass shattered.

"Come here, Jenna."

She took a tentative step. Her thoughts swirled inside her head. *Goodnight stars, goodnight air. Goodnight, murder?*

She screamed across the quad. "Why did you have to kill all those innocent people? To cover up Alicia's death? You're a sick man. You need help."

"She was going to call the police. I had no choice."

"You were a coward. Instead of facing the consequences, you faked your death? I trusted you. You lied. Do you know how hard it was for me being alone?"

"I took care of you. I made the repairs I promised. I stood guard over you."

"You're sick. If you surrender, I'll bet you won't even go to jail. They'll put you in one of those psychiatric hospitals and you'll get the help you need."

Police sirens screamed. She looked up at the building across the quad. Was it a SWAT team? There were snipers on the roofs all around the quad. She heard an authoritative voice break through the air.

"Put your gun down. Hands over your head. You're surrounded. There's no way out."

"I have a bomb." He pulled something out of his pocket, which she couldn't clearly see. "Back away or the whole place explodes. Jenna, it's your last chance to save this campus."

She heard Detective Russo's voice over the loudspeaker. "Dr. Blake. Turn around and come back to the building."

"Turn around and we all die," said Giles. The ground was spinning under her feet. *Breathe in. Breathe out.* She was almost there. Almost in front of the man she thought was dead for almost a year. Almost in front of the monster. She willed her feet to move. One foot, then the other.

"Okay. I'm here. Put the gun down. Set the bomb gently on the ground." Drenched in sweat, she shivered from the cold. Yet, there was a strength that overcame her.

"You have to forgive me. I didn't mean to let things get so far with that girl. When she said she was pregnant and she was going to have me arrested..."

"You are sick. You should have gotten help. You still can. I should have realized and gotten you the help before it came to shooting up the school. Surrender and we can get you better. Together. I'll stick with you, I promise." *Like hell.* She wished the snipers could get a clean shot. The bastard didn't deserve to live.

Looking at the vile monster before her, she wanted to grab his gun, grab the bomb, shoot him, throw the explosive in his open mouth...

"Jenna, do you still love me?"

She gulped. "I do. In sickness and in health." She felt like throwing up. "We can make it work. I know you took care of the repairs we spoke about. And I've nearly demolished the dining room wall. We can be happy again. Just put the gun down." She took a step closer. "Set the bomb down."

"We can have a family. I'll get better, I promise."

"Then you have to surrender to the police before someone gets hurt. Put the gun down."

She saw his hand quiver. He started to lower the gun.

"That's it. Nice and steady."

He was about to put it down. Jenna felt her balance going. She toppled to the ground. Giles turned the gun on her. She rolled away, giving the sniper a clear shot. Then bang. *Goodnight noises everywhere.*

The SWAT team moved in. Detective Russo approached. "Are you hurt? There's an ambulance waiting right outside the entrance."

"I'm okay. I really am."

Max ran to her and hugged her. "You could have been killed. I don't believe this. Giles was alive all this time?"

"There's a lot to fill you in on."

"Why did you go to him? You could have been killed?"

Detective Russo said, "It was foolish."

"He said he had a bomb."

"It was foolish—and brave. You've got courage, Dr. Blake. I'll give you that."

"What about the bomb? Did they get it?"

"There wasn't a bomb. It was a bluff. Do you need medical attention?"

"No, I just want to go home."

Chapter 29

Outside, the wind howled and snow swirled. When Jenna and Max entered Hayley and Oliver's place, the warmth and coziness were in stark contrast to the outside world. Santiago drank wine in front of the fireplace. Kyle and Ross were engaged in animated conversation with Oliver, and Hayley took their coats and poured them wine.

Hayley whispered to Jenna, "I almost forgot. No wine, right?"

"Not tonight, but I'm planning to speak with my doctor about being weaned off the antidepressants. I'm feeling stronger."

Kyle jumped up. "Look at my hand. What do you see?"

Hayley didn't miss a beat. "You did your nails?"

"Funny. Notice anything different?" He waved his fingers in front of her nose.

"The shiny engagement band? Is that what you're talking about?" Jenna inspected his hand and examined the ring. "It's gorgeous. I already told you that."

"Look closer. We had them inscribed."

"I'm supposed to see through the ring. I haven't got x-ray vision."

"They're engraved on the outside."

"Leave it to you to do it your own way."

"Mine matches," said Ross. "But mine's bigger."

"Just because your fingers are fatter," said Kyle. He kissed Ross.

Max said, "Get a room." Then gave them both a fist bump. "Seriously, congratulations. I'm looking forward to the wedding. June, right?"

Kyle pulled out his phone. "Look at the venue we booked. They had a cancelation right when we were touring the place. Otherwise, they were booked a year in advance. Oh, and the baker loved my cake idea. Red velvet, German chocolate, and fun-fetti with cannoli cream between the layers. He suggested a cream cheese frosting."

Hayley said, "You can order a specialized cake topper with two grooms. I saw an ad."

"Already done. You'll all be getting *Save the Date* magnets as soon as I finish submitting my dissertation proposal." He looked at Jenna. "It'll be on your desk by Friday."

Oliver said, "Any weekend date is fine. I won't be traveling anymore."

"Hypothetically, are children invited?" asked Hayley.

Jenna gasped, "You aren't?"

"Pregnant? No. But the reason Oliver has been traveling so much was to interview potential birth mothers. He didn't want me to get my hopes up."

"Turns out the shoplifting conviction isn't an insurmountable issue like I thought it was. I've been working with a lawyer who specializes in private adoptions."

Hayley's face rivaled the glow from the fireplace. "There's a mother-to-be in Virginia who is ready to sign the paperwork."

Jenna jumped up and hugged her. "I'm so happy for you."

"Hope you're up for being a godmother."

"I'd be honored."

Max said, "Santiago, what's next for you?"

"I'm still raw from Isabel's death. I'm going to attend the support meetings and maybe try running. I heard exercise helps."

"Chamomile tea, also," added Jenna. She shared a smile with Max.

Oliver said, "It's too hard to believe Giles did these horrible things. I can't believe I didn't see it coming. I knew he had an attraction to younger girls, but he swore he'd resolved it."

"He picked the only way out he could see," Hayley said. "To his credit, he tried to look out for you, Jenna. He did the repairs around the house like he promised."

"And stalked me when he thought I was seeing another man."

"What would have happened if Isabel didn't realize he was still alive?" asked Hayley.

"She'd still be alive," said Santiago. "The detective said Giles was teaching piano lessons the next town over.

If only she hadn't put it together..."

"He'd be off in South America living free. Not that it's much consolation, but Isabel is responsible for putting an end to his evil. You know what would have happened had he disappeared to South America." Max sipped his wine.

The timer dinged. "Dinner's ready. Come on before it gets cold."

Hayley got up and started for the kitchen. "I forgot

to tell you about Delores."

"What about her?" said Jenna.

"She was offered a tenured position at a small private college in Maine. She and her hubby are moving when the semester ends."

"Good for her. Looks like we're all moving on."

"Hopefully so," said Max. He squeezed Jenna's hand. She felt a glow from inside.

Hayley cleared her throat. "Like I said, dinner's getting cold. Let's eat."

Jenna said, "Did I tell you what I'm planning with the insurance money I'll be getting now that I can prove Giles is dead and it wasn't suicide?"

"A trip to Europe?" said Hayley.

"No, I'm calling in a professional contractor to finish the renovations on the house."

Oliver said, "Are you finally going to knock down that eyesore of a wall?"

"I'm going to build over it. Use it as a foundation and turn it into an island so we can pass food through, even get a few stools so we can eat at it. Kind of like a breakfast nook."

"We?" said Max. "Has a nice ring to it."

"Didn't you say the food was getting cold?" asked Kyle.

Max put his arm around Jenna. "We're going to see where this relationship goes. "I'm expecting a future of breakfasts in the new nook when we get through with the renovations."

Jenna smiled and squeezed his hand. "Me, too."

Bijou joined the celebration, kissing her face.

A word about the author…

Diane Weiner is the award-winning author of more than 30 mysteries. An animal lover and mother of four grown children, she shares her Florida home with her husband and 3 precious cats. In her free time, she enjoys running, spending time with her family, and watching scenic British and Scandinavian mysteries under a cozy blanket with the air conditioner cranked down. To learn more about the author, visit her website (www.dianeweinerauthor.com), or follow her on Facebook (dianeweinerauthor), Amazon, Goodreads, Twitter (dianeweinerauth) and Bookbub. Contact the author at:

dianeweinerauthor@gmail.com
www.dianeweinerauthor.com